COLDNESS
of
MAREK

RACHEL O'LAUGHLIN

COLDNESS

of

MAREK

the F I R S T in the
SERENGARD SERIES

DUBLIN MIST PRESS

MAINE

Second Edition. August 2013.
Published by Dublin Mist Press.
Printed in the United States of America and the United Kingdom.

www.rachelolaughlin.com

ISBN: 978-0-9849194-1-3
e-Book ISBN: 978-0-9849194-2-0

Coldness of marek : Serengard, book one / by Rachel O'Laughlin

1. Fiction—Fantasy—Epic
Library of Congress Control Number: 2013944694

Edited by Rebecca A. Weston.
Cover and Interior Artwork Copyright © 2013 by Dan Tare. All Rights Reserved.

FOR MY BOYS.

N
Freibourge
Fourth City
Serengard
■ city ◆ fortress ● town

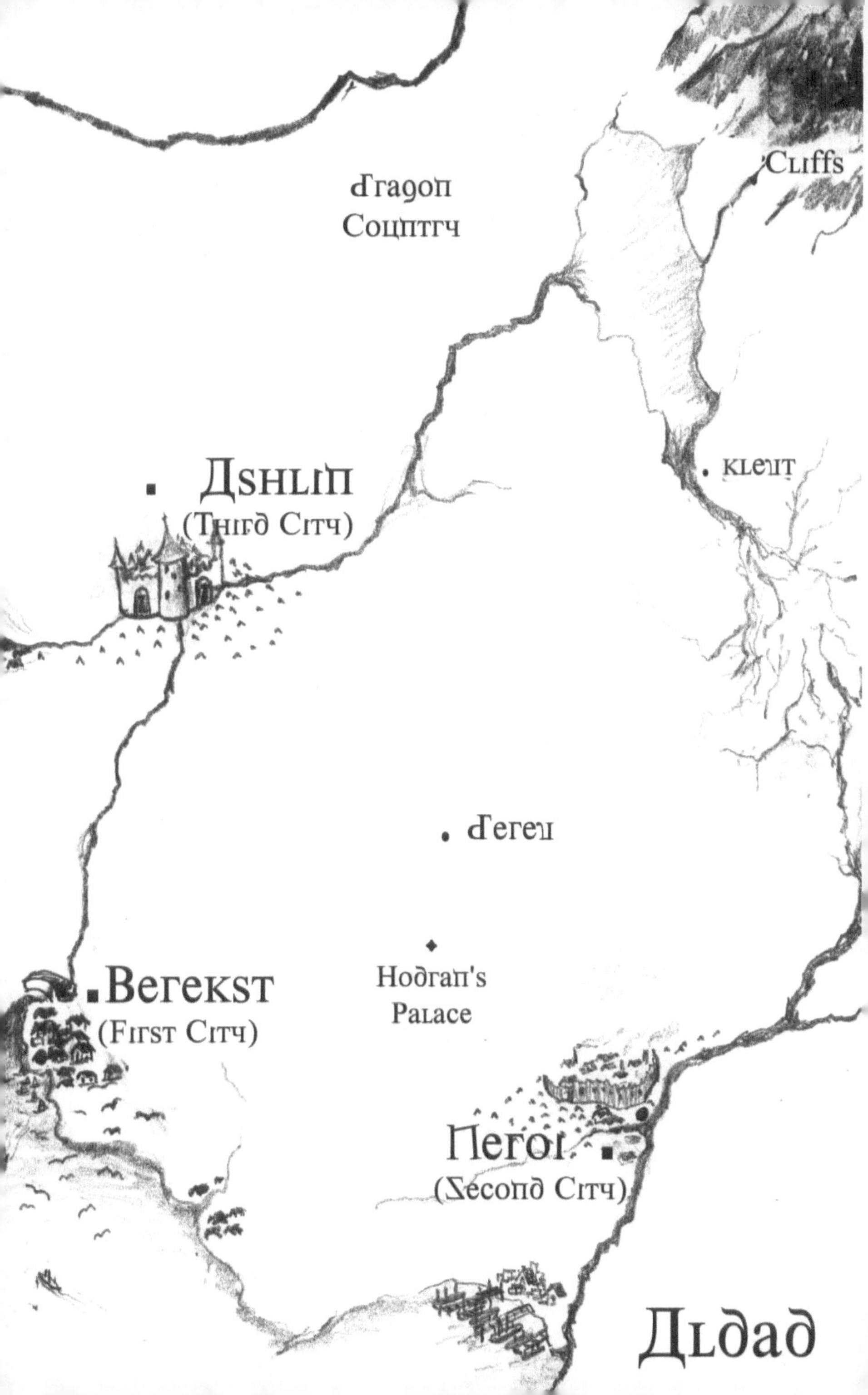
dragon
Country
Cliffs
Ashlin
(Third City)
kleit
deren
Hodran's
Palace
Berekst
(First City)
Nerol
(Second City)
Aldad

The Recent Kings

the past two hundred years as measured by the Serengard Orions

---

Ⅲαгек

Ruled for 7 years

Кагамоυ

Ruled for 21 years

♂егеυ ɪɪɪ

Ruled for 36 years

Таме

Ruled for 34 years

Сацм

Ruled for 19 years

Дιтгцп

Ruled for 42 years

Ɪzαппан

Ruled for 36 years

Реттоιαι

Ruled for 24 years

The Zai

originally known only as the Kymsai

Corsai

Appointed by Tame Orion to Organize Tributes

and Uphold Trade Within the Cities

Kymsai

Appointed by the First Derev Orion to Keep the Lands,

to Ensure a Fair Crop Every Year,

and Enforce the Law That Every Man Plant a Field

Nersai

(A Slang Term, Originated in the Years of Izannah Orion)

Any Owner of Land Who Adheres to the Tradition of the First Derev

to Plant a Field Every Year and Pay Tribute

{1}
Нощ

To the east of Dragon Country.
In the 10th year of The Four Cities.

THE HILL COUNTRY WAS SUPPOSED to be safer. Trzl would have put boards over her doors and windows like the rest of the settlers, but she did not believe in signs like the stirred fog and other nonsense.

"The fog is not lying still," her neighbor told her, shaking his head. "Something is churning it, far away, up in the mountains."

Rem was ancient and believed in the old sayings. Sayings that had kept people enslaved, kept them bound to nature. And it was too late in the year for cold dragons or fanged cats. Even Trzl knew that, and she was from the city.

But Malcom—Malcom looked worried, too. The last time Trzl had seen him afraid was two years ago, when a snake came into their pantry in broad daylight. Even then, he had been brave enough to kill the reptile. Her son was no weakling. His very name meant simply, in the Seren tongue, *ground.* A certain type of ground. Firm, high, far from the storms of the sea or the quicksand of the desert or the lowlands that flooded. His soul was older than most boys of his years, and she knew it.

Now he stared out the window, shivering.

Then again, her house was cold. It always was on mornings like this.

They all heard the hoofbeats at the same time. More than one horse. At least a dozen, moving at a smooth canter.

They swooped into the village common, the mist parting to reveal their bulky figures. Their heads and shoulders were covered with animal furs, broadswords heavy and well-fired. Nothing like any raiders she'd seen. These were more like the legends Rem spoke of around the village campfires as the children listened, wild-eyed and dreaming—Swamp people? Cliffmen? Tribes from the plateaus? She hoped not.

Malcom let out one little screech, then stood stock-still, huddled against the windowsill, watching. Trzl fingered the small, insignificant dagger she kept on the inside of her waistband. She caught her son by his arms and tried to drag him to the cellar. "Come. We must hide. Malcom, listen to me. We must!"

But there wasn't time. The door was broken in and five of the raiders fit their large shoulders through it. They caught at Malcom's hand, yanking and dragging him clear across the room. Trzl screamed. One of the men glanced at her as he threw the boy over his shoulder. Another walked toward her and she did not back away. Malcom was out there, and she wanted to go to him. The man grasped her roughly, tossing her onto his shoulder. She was a slight woman and felt like a child in this huge man's arms.

Then they were outside in the heavy morning mist. She heard the calls of the renegades as they stamped their horses about in a circle. Someone was yelling at them from across the common.

"This is no slave raid," one of the renegades bellowed back. His accent was strange. "We come for these two." —He gestured to Trzl and her son.

If he said more, she didn't hear. She kept her eyes locked with Malcom's. His dark brown hair was rumpled, his face already scratched by the rough material the renegades wore. Trzl wanted to tell him not to fear, but that was probably a lie. *Just keep your eyes on me, little man.*

These men were probably going to kill her. Hang her in the nearest town, wherever they could find an audience, find a way to put a face to their hatred of the Empire. She closed her eyes, whispering a prayer to Allel. She doubted He would do anything for her—if indeed He did exist—but perhaps he could be persuaded to do something for her son.

Trzl and Malcom were thrown onto separate horses, ordered to remain quiet. Men mounted in front of them, clutched the reins and urged their strong mounts out of the village and into the fog.

Now it did scare her. The stirred fog. There was something horrible and surreal about it, as if this should all be a nightmare. She tried to see Malcom, a few horses away and quiet as a bat. She hoped he could not sense how afraid she was.

They rode north, far up into the hills, and beyond them. Soon there were rocks, as large as chariots or draft carts, slowing their climb, forcing the horses to work up a lather. Trzl could hear Malcom's teeth chattering, whether from cold or from fear—it worried her. They both knew what lived in this land. Huge cats, mammoth beasts. Most villagers had never seen them, and Trzl always pretended that she thought their stories were just legends. But when she felt this chill in her bones and heard those horrible, echoing coos and caws from the caverns of these rugged, strange rocks—

Malcom's horse tripped and he screamed. The man who held the reins almost slid off and took Malcom with him. After he righted himself, he laughed at Malcom. Trzl shot the man a dark look, rejoicing when he swallowed and looked away. She had some power over him, and thus there was a chance for escape, albeit slim. Maybe tonight while they slept.

But night came, and no camp was made. She grew more and more suspicious that they were being led in a circle. To confuse them? Were they to be slaves after all? She knew the way of the cliff folk. They took people from the valleys whenever they pleased.

There was a slim canyon with a smooth floor, likely a dry riverbed, that they took by the bright moonlight. The air was bitter and cold up here. Trzl found herself leaning against her rider, trying to draw warmth from his heavy coat of...well, whatever animal skin this was. She did not recognize the texture of it. After a moment, he removed his coat and wrapped it around her. It was huge, enough to fit back around the rider after enveloping Trzl.

"Malcom," she whispered, then regretted it. If they had any doubts, which it seemed they did not, they were now assured of her son's identity.

"You want something for the boy?" her rider asked gruffly.

Might as well ask. "A drink of water and something warm around him."

Her rider must have been their leader, because he grunted toward Malcom's captor and the man did her bidding. She let some air out through her teeth. She would not thank him. He could not expect that surely.

Trzl must have slept because she woke a few times, her eyes snapping open at horrible sounds in the night. She made an effort to stay awake, to stay alert. Wherever they were going, it could not be for a public execution. Perhaps Malcom's father had finally decided to get rid of her quietly? He had always hated Malcom. He would not wish to use his own guard for such a thing, and he *would* hire renegades to keep it from being traced to him. But she didn't think he cared a whit about her anymore.

Wide awake now, the possibilities circled wildly. Escape plans that all failed in the first few steps of theory. Would the sun never rise? This riverbed was far too long.

Then it ended and she wished it had not. Above them were the sheer cliffs of ghost stories. A shrill cry woke Malcom, startling Trzl into looking around her. It cried again, an inhuman shriek, and she saw it. A huge, dark bird. It swooped about in the air above them. What kind of bird soared at night like that?

They rode forward again, straight toward the cliff. There was an opening, much like a hallway, much like stairs, a little of both. The horses climbed it, tired, soaked, but jumping with an energy made possible only by the best of feeds and exercise. Trzl pressed her legs against their mount and tried to feel his muscles through her frozen limbs, distracting herself from the pitch blackness of the cave.

Malcom had either fallen asleep again or he was silent with fear. She wanted to call back to him, to tell him not to be afraid. Mem was here. She would think of something. Only she knew there was nothing that could get them out of a fortress such as this in terrible country. Nothing.

The climb was not as long as anticipated—or perhaps Trzl lost track of time—because they broke out into a large cavern lit by torches. The horses stopped without being told. Her head started to thrum as her captor swung her down from the horse and tossed her toward two waiting men. They caught her arms and pulled on her roughly. She whined Malcom's name—then saw he was right behind her, wide awake and staring.

"Malcom, it will be all right..."

Malcom did not pay her any mind. He looked around the room at the tall walls; the torches; the women running in to take the horses' bridles, lead them about in circles, cool them down.

"Mal—"

They were shoved down on their knees, and Trzl stared at a hard floor made of some kind of marble. A strange, pigmented color she had seen once before but could not remember where. Then came a voice she *did* remember. It was not husky and accented like the men who had taken her. It was clear, almost cultured. Disguised behind a deepness that was not its own.

"You are certain these are the two requested by Anaqi?"

"That's them. The house was marked and they are the right age, aren't they? Truthsome, they speak as if they were from the city."

"Do they?"

He knelt down, using the handle of a knife to shove her face upward. Trzl knew she should not do it, but her eyes shot up from the floor and into his. Just as quickly, a glove came down from one of the guards and slapped her across the face.

"How dare you look Lord Marek in the eyes?"

It stung madly, and she dropped her gaze. *Lord Marek. The Lord of the Cliffs. Are we that far north?*

Lord Marek said nothing. He turned her face from side to side, examining her features as one did with a new falcon.

"Strange sort of fair, isn't she, my lord?" a voice said from the dark, somewhere behind him.

Still Lord Marek kept his peace. Trzl wanted him to speak again, wanted to hear his voice. But perhaps not. Perhaps hearing it appraise her so coldly would make her fear worse.

Finally he said, "It isn't beauty I'm concerned with, Tev." It *was* him. And then he spoke directly to her. "You are from the Third City, or from another?"

Trzl searched her brain for a suitable answer, frozen by confusion. *You are supposed to be dead.*

Again the slap of the glove against her face. "Answer your lord."

"I...am from many places. I've not lived in a city for many years."

"That is not an answer."

Oh now she wanted him to stop talking. To never speak again. *I have not thought of you since a lifetime ago. It was supposed to stay that way.*

She did not look up, but she could hear his insincere smile. "Put them in separate dungeons. I will question the boy after you have fed him."

Lord Marek turned to leave, heavy leather shoes with steel soles clacking on the marble. Then—a turn, an afterthought.

"Feed the woman nothing."

part one

Ashlin

Inferiors revolt in order that they may be equal,

and equals that they may be superior.

Such is the state of mind which creates revolutions.

— Aristotle

{2}
THEN

The village of Derev, in the heart of Serengard.
Ten years ago, in the 24th year of the reign of Petrolai.

TRZL SUCKED IN HER BREATH as the village woman tried once more to heighten her breasts. "We have to do something with these."

"You'll have no luck," said Trzl. "Those have never been my strongest feature."

"Oh, and what is? Your hips? Which cannot be seen through these miles of fabric. The men are always listening to you. You just have to make them look." The woman tugged hard at the cords of Trzl's waist. "Your grandfather knows nothing about rearing a girl or he'd have bought you dresses like this long ago. Here, let me raise this up a few notches. Give your prospectives something to look at."

Trzl let her do as she pleased. The idea that a man—any man—might look at her chest was rather dizzying.

Her dark hair was arranged in eight braids, a style that emerged in the spring. This velvet dress was a peg or two above her station, to be sure, and had never been worn before tonight, but Grandfather had splurged. He would be proud of her ability to show it off…if he found the time to notice. Tonight was special. The first time all of their leaders would be gathered together in one place, at the halfway point between Ashlin and Neroi. The first time their numbers would be evident to the world.

Evident they were. Trzl could hear the sound of thousands of chattering voices on the wind the instant she opened the door to the house, could sense the excitement before she topped the hill and beheld the common. It swarmed as a wasp's nest. People spilled from carriages on either side of the road. She had to press her way in, begging pardon of the many bookish young men who peered at her through their spectacles and nudged each other when she walked by.

"Have you seen Trzl?"

"I always thought of her as one of our rank."

"A little errand boy."

"Not this Trzl."

"Save me a dance, my pretty."

She climbed the steps alone. None of those she brushed by would have guessed that she fell asleep in a friend's haymow last night or that she had been dressed by the farmer's wife.

Grandfather had already been here for hours in the backstage rooms, meeting the new blood from the countryside. On every balcony and in every box usually reserved for nobles and royalty, crowded flocks of unorganized but passionate citizens of the country of Serengard stood, those who felt that their only route to rise above the level of a serf was to dissolve the Orion monarchy in any manner possible. To break their hold on this land forever.

Secrecy had always been a must. Formerly, they had acknowledged each other only by a nod or by showing a blue ribbon tied or sewn onto their right cuff. They'd memorized each other's faces but never learned each other's names. Tonight, they showed their boldness. Let the king arrest them if he wished, if he dared. And in their places would rise up a hundred thousand more. This land and her cities belonged to the people.

The heightened cinch did its wonders immediately. Trzl felt her hand being grasped, a warm thumb pressing on it.

"You are with the group from Neroi, are you not?"

She knew the voice. She met his eyes, feeling confident. Hodran, the Corsai of Neroi. The most powerful man in her home city. A rebel on the fence—not sure he wanted to sink his family fortune into a ship that might not float.

"I am."

"I must say you are brilliant tonight. A dazzling figure. My god, I cannot look away."

Why don't you get me something to eat instead of complimenting me? It was an excellent choice of words, though, for him to call her brilliant. She could have easily called him beautiful. He was the perfect height, his brown hair combed back from his forehead in a smooth wave. Every bone in his face was perfectly placed.

Yes. No wonder the girls fawned over him.

"I know we have met before," he spoke again, a voice as smooth as his hair, "but I have forgotten your name."

We have only been introduced half a dozen times. "Trzl."

"Trzl. I will remember now." He bowed over her hand and kissed it. "You will save a dance for me? After the first show?"

As much as she tried to be immune to it, she felt a little ripple of excitement run through her. "I will."

Most of the girls her age were a part of the rebellion in the interest of meeting the fiery, scrawny young men among their ranks, the ones who talked with their hands and used big words. Trzl had never cared. She was here to exercise her rebel brain more than anything.

But then, those were boys. Not men with more money than they knew what to do with.

Slipping away from the Corsai's aura, she stole a cherry cordial from one of the scrawny boys and inserted herself authoritatively into the middle of a debate.

"You see why we must disband the ownership of land," she told a young man who shrank beneath her tone. She wrung her hand. It still felt as if the Corsai were holding it. "If any single person is allowed to own land, he will make himself rich and give himself means to buy more and more, eventually acquiring power over his fellow man, until he has made himself a king."

Her statement was met by a half dozen nods and a number of knowing looks.

"But surely someone must be allowed to own something."

Trzl looked up at the cultured voice that broke into her arena. He was tall, healthy, well-built. Skin darkened by the sun, hair strikingly blonde, which meant he was from the north. She could not see his eyes in the dim light, but she almost dropped her drink due to his self-posession. He was terribly out of place.

"The people should share their belongings, not hoard them," she offered as a first defense.

"Of course, if you wish to dictate morality. But mustn't they do so willingly? Else it is not sharing. It is man stealing from his own equals."

Trzl blinked at him. She had never been met with anything but agreement and acclamation in this circle. Who *was* this person?

Her deep wine dress set off her black hair tonight, and she knew it. She let the magic of the moment go to her head. "Would you be a proponent of the mercenary system of the monarchs? The tributes on the land, their ways of making all of us pay for purchasing goods that the crown need know nothing of?"

"I will always hold that taxation is an unnecessary evil." He seemed cautious now, perhaps defensive, a sign in her favor. "A tribute tax is only warranted when the people expect money from their monarchy; money to settle debts, to give them loans, to build roads. If they did not demand such, it would be much simpler to eliminate this evil tax of yours."

"I don't think the people demand these things. The monarch imposes them."

"An opinion likely brought on by being painstakingly educated and yet completely unexposed to life as it truly exists and persists."

Trzl wanted to slap the man. She thought about it for a second, and then she did. The boys around her guffawed and jeered, but her victim only smiled.

"Pleased to have met you." He bowed to take his leave, turned his back.

"Wait. You have not waited for my response," Trzl insisted. She meant to gather herself and win this argument.

"You can always come find me."

Desperate to expel the frustration that flooded her at being misunderstood, Trzl exited her group of admirers and followed him, down from the balcony, through the dancers, to the second staircase.

Wait. He was going still further down. To the basement? To the rooms that were only for the leaders of the underground? A sudden respect bounded in her chest. She quickened her step as fast as her silk slippers would let her, brought herself up on his heels.

"Where are you going?"

"Why are you following me?"

He grinned at her again, and she saw his eyes in the light from the staircase candelabra. They were green—dancing green. He took a step back up the stairs, toward her, bowed slightly to introduce himself.

"Mikel." A very common name. Why, she knew four of them. No, five. "I hope you will forgive me for not sharing a city of birth, the names of my parents, where I break bread…"

She laughed. "Trzl. I hope you will forgive me for the same."

Then he offered his arm for the stairs, and she felt nervous and strange. She shook her head and rested her hand on the railing. She could tell he was charmed by her independence, but annoyed also, since he kept looking at her hand as if he meant to seize it.

"Are you one of the leaders?" she asked him in a low voice.

"No. More of an idle observer."

"And you are allowed down here?"

"Isn't everybody?"

"Well…" Yes, in a manner of speaking. But there was an unwritten code of conduct. "I have never seen you before, is all."

"You must consort with these people often."

Had he just tricked her into revealing that, or had she been so clumsy? "Oh, no," Trzl laughed. "I merely enjoy the dancing. The theatre."

"You do not lie well. Any toad can see you care nothing for the dancing and everything for the rebellion."

She turned to face him in the hall at the foot of the staircase. "Do you intend to argue with me all evening?"

"I did not think we were arguing. Are we?"

She changed the subject abruptly. "You are not from here. You are from the capital? From Ashlin?"

"I am from Ashlin, yes. I only work in the farmland during certain seasons, hence my stepping into your friendly little meeting at the theatre tonight. I came to have a good time, to watch you rebel people as I would a show, not to discuss the woes of society."

"You find it dull?"

"Very."

"Is the rebellion as strong in Ashlin?"

"Stronger. The city is far more monetarily stable than Neroi or Berekst. Tradesman are able to riot on a higher coin. This kind of thing," he gestured to indicate the grandiose theatre, the food, the music, "happens every night."

That was why Grandfather would not let her go to Ashlin until he thought she was ready. She felt cheated. "Does King Petrolai realize what is going on in his own city?"

He was openly amused by this. "It would not be as strong if he were not there. People are far more stirred to passion when they can see someone to blame. There have always been factions who hate the Orion monarchy, whether it be Altrun or Petrolai on the throne. It is human nature to dislike authority."

"That is because it is an insult to a man's humanity to be made to obey someone who knows nothing of them or their circumstances."

"That is why the role of a king is not to force obedience to his own will, but to enforce justice."

"Justice does not exist under such a system. In fact, I am not sure justice exists at all." She frowned at him. "Are you simply toying with me? I think you are arguing from such a stance to make me angry."

"On the contrary, I am doing my best to end this conversation."

"So you claim."

A sudden swoop of people broke into the hallway from the underground rooms. Voices were wild with heat and excitement, and the push of them shoved Trzl away from Mikel. He waited on the other side of the crowd, a secretive smile on his lips that made her curious. They had almost dispersed when the last two men broke from the room, fairly flying down the hall, voices raised to a frenzy—Grandfather and Kovim, one of the king's counselors.

Trzl wanted to panic for a moment. She had no knowledge of who this Mikel was, and here he was observing two giants of the rebellion engaged in heavy conspiracy. She looked up at Mikel as they passed, trying to hide her worry. He showed no sign of recognition. Good.

Grandfather appeared too engrossed to notice her, but after a moment, he came bounding back. "Trzl, Hodran of Neroi spoke to me about you. He has been quite struck. Consider your influence over him, my dear. It could prove very valuable…very valuable indeed." Then he seemed to remember something important and ran off. Grandfather always moved quickly, especially on a night such as this. He was like a giddy little girl.

Mikel finally reached for the hand he'd been eying, catching it with a dastardly look of triumph.

"Come," he whispered. "No more treason talk. I will show you the finer traits of this building."

Trzl glanced behind her, knowing she should not allow him to escort her. There was the Corsai of Neroi to dance with.

He tugged gently on her gloved fingers.

What harm could there be? She roamed the streets of Neroi alone. And she carried a dagger.

{3}

dreams

TRZL KEPT HER EYES DOWN at first. She'd never seen anything quite like him. The confidence was all his own and rightfully so. There was something cunning as well—as if he possessed great skill and knew it.

Look away. Do not let him see that you are impressed.

"You've never been to Ashlin, have you?"

"No." Trzl did not really want to admit it. It would be nicer to pretend she was as worldly as he. She could do it with all the other men here. Why did she feel vulnerable all of a sudden?

He flashed a smile, and the feeling was gone. He dashed ahead of her, led her up staircases, higher into the theatre boxes than anyone else would dare to go tonight, into cubicles rich with velvet and black satin cord on every corner. There were gilded walls that must be worth a fortune, fine murals and carvings, statues made of Ashlin stone. He told her of the artists who created them. He knew the life story of each one— the times they lived in, the wars, the struggles.

It made Trzl fidget. She hadn't read these things in the libraries, as she'd ignored all bits of intrigue that she assumed were useless knowledge. But when Mikel spoke of these people he wove an intricate story that told the tale of Serengard in a glowing, living web—gorgeous to behold. All at once, she wanted to know everything about them. Had she really ignored this much history?

It did not last long. (Or perhaps it had been hours?) Hodran of Neroi must have a gift of sorts for he located her all the way on the seventh floor, where the crowd was scarce, and asked her for his dance. Trzl reached for Mikel, but found she was standing in front of the Corsai alone. Mikel had released her hand and was disappearing behind her.

"Wait!" This time it was she who reached for his fingers.

Hodran did not act annoyed. He turned politely to another guest and made a comment about draperies. Mikel kept his face hidden, away from the lantern light even as she spoke to him.

"Where can I find you? I will be here another day. I should like to finish our conversation."

He hesitated. She watched an argument on his face and wondered if she was just tonight's dark-haired flavor. If tomorrow there would be someone else.

Then he said, "The largest farm in this valley. Take a left at the crossroads."

She smiled to herself as Hodran led her down several staircases, a vision of Mikel completing itself in her mind. He spent his days tossing hay on one of these farms where the men worked from first light to sundown, hefting and pulling and gaining that dark, rich skin from the full days of summer sun. Why, his shoulders were probably thicker than she imagined under that shirt. No wonder he was too busy to shout for liberty with her friends.

Hodran did not seem upset to have competition. Or he was too dense to perceive Mikel as such.

"Imagine my surprise at finding you here among us tonight, Trzl."

His touch warmed her through her clothes.

"I don't know why you're surprised."

"I know your grandfather as one who cares for these things, but I did not know you shared it. I'm sure you must enjoy a good party?"

"Enjoy?" Well, she was enjoying it, yes. She led him out on the dance floor so that he would stop looking her straight in the face. "I have my finger on the pulse of the rebellion as much as my grandfather. You could have seen me sitting in on many a meeting had you any wish."

"Ah, I am sad that I missed seeing you." Hodran danced smoothly. His arms were strong, the strength of the Corsai and Kymsai who possessed time to train with swords and lances for fun, to play at games of skill with horses. He leaned in and whispered, "I would have been interested."

How could he make a political meeting or two sound seductive? "I was a child."

His perfect mouth turned up at the corners. "Trzl, you've not been a child for quite some time now."

GRANDFATHER COULDN'T HAVE BEEN HAPPIER.

"The Corsai is interested in funding our handbill printings, food for the rally in Ashlin, and supplying excellent horses of breeding for the couriers. *And* he implied that, if I were to ask for more, he would not hesitate to offer."

Trzl sat on the edge of Grandfather's bed. It was nearly dawn, but neither of them were tired. The farmhouse they were packed into was mostly quiet, except for the whispers of two or three of her rebel clan clustered about the fire.

"We've a definite ally in him at last, my girl. What kind of magic did you work on him? One horse in particular is to be yours, a gift for the lovely lady who dances so fine."

Trzl found she did not care. She thought him laughable. A rich man in his thirties with two previous wives, enough property to make any noblewoman fall in love with him, and he might be bothered to notice a printer's daughter? Only because he thought it might be fun.

But perhaps, when Serengard was overturned, being related to her grandfather—Otreya, the Pitching Boar—was as desirable as being related to Hodran, Corsai of Neroi.

Grandfather and the others finally slept. Trzl didn't—not one bit. She slipped out of the house just after the sun rose and went on foot to the Derev crossroads.

She was not usually out this early, especially in strange country. Here there were carts, horses and drivers loaded down with grain and straw and hay. The smells were foreign to her. Her native Neroi was a city of tradesmen—smiths and wheel makers, potters and jewelers. The air there was full of compounds and woodsmoke, not pollen and dust.

When Mikel said the largest farm, he did not indicate what would come to mean the largest. How many barns? How many horses? Some were occupied by more cattle than she could count—others, more stables. One had at least eighteen plows out turning over stubble at once.

Trzl felt a little foolish. What was she thinking, trying to hunt down the face of a stranger she had taken a fancy to last night? Perhaps she'd drank a bit too much cherry cordial. Perhaps she was—

She jumped out of the way as she was nearly run over by a pair of draft horses. The driver tipped his wool hat in apology but said nothing to her. She bit a fingernail, uncomfortable, and tried to decide where to go next. She watched a herd of shiny, broad chested horses crest the far hill and spill over it. There must be hundreds of them, most without riders. Those that were bore tall, built men with varying shades of tan. The men were almost as beautiful as the horses, and she recognized Mikel even with a hat on.

Whips cracked in the air, coiling and coming back on themselves. Trzl raised her hand to protect her eyes against the rising sun. She wanted to call to him, but she was too awed to speak.

He already saw her. He rode down the hill at a swift canter, coming up to her with a grin.

"I did not expect to see you."

"No?" Trzl looked down, noticed she was standing in manure of some kind. Not horse. "I needed a walk this morning."

He reached down for her hand. "I doubt that."

Trzl swung her arm through his meekly and swung onto the horse, feeling as if she had stepped outside of herself. As if he could see through her little façade. Did she wear a façade?

His back was warm. She leaned against it and clutched his waist immodestly. Even in the sunshine, her clothing was not warm enough for the north, and he did not offer any of his many layers to her.

"I usually take a carriage in Neroi. Or walk."

"There is nothing like a brisk ride. There are sights much finer than those you'll find on the road."

"Except that I'm cold, and you are warm."

He smiled and untied his cloak. She pulled it from his shoulders and wrapped it around her own. It was heavy and soft.

"Do you not have work to do?"

"My men can do without me for a few hours."

Trzl felt the dream tower she had built of him begin to disintegrate. "You are a noble. A Kymsai?"

"Not a Kymsai. But I do own this land…and these horses."

"The fields and the cattle I saw on the way here?"

He was frowning as if he hadn't meant to tell her this. "Yes."

Of course he would turn out to be as dull as all that. "Then you are a Nersai yourself. You believe in the old laws. That anyone who owns land must tend it, that only those who have proven they will grow and produce with their soil be allowed to obtain it. How far beyond the reaches of your mind it is to imagine that men who feel differently should own it with you."

"You would put me in a potter's mold so soon, my lady. I have reasons, beyond selfish ones, for disagreeing with your utopian ideals."

Trzl giggled, trying to make it light and careless, but she was actually a little hurt.

"Ashlin and all of Serengard is in a state of glory," he went on. "The past several reigns have brought only prosperity for her people—even for the Desert People and the Drei. It is the only way your kind can afford to have time to rebel. Your wild progressives forsake the keeping of the land, and they will sacrifice all knowledge of how it is done. They will have nothing to inherit, unlike the generations who were required to sweat to raise one stick of wood and place it atop another."

This time she really did laugh. "Required to by the Kymsai and enforced by a wretched king. And how would you know anything about it, being from this generation of lazy folk?"

"I understand it because my parents were not born with infinite riches, as I'm sure you assume. Being Nersai is a title of responsibility, not inheritance."

She was growing anxious to move, afraid he might prove her some kind of simpleton before they had any fun. "Are you taking me for a ride, or not?"

Mikel urged his horse suddenly enough that she jerked backward and had to clutch at his waist again.

The countryside of Derev was much like Neroi, only colder, the leaves already a dark brown in preparation for the crisp winters in the heart of Serengard. Trzl was happy to be from a southern city. Their land was peaceful and speckled with cottages and townhouses. Here, closer to Ashlin, everything was happening fast. As if a man were pulling the millstone with twice as many mules as necessary, making wind that no one needed. Everywhere she looked, she saw people scurry, working desperately to get supplies under cover and into cellars.

It did have an excitement to it—something Trzl was addicted to. Something she always drew from Grandfather and his treason. She leaned against her rider and breathed in. He smelled of fresh worn leather and heavy earth. She liked him. Liked his boldness. Men did not usually dare to boss her, let alone lay claim to her with the same angst that she employed. It was nice to be with an equal for once.

Yet she was surprised when he swung her off the horse and onto her feet, landing her smoothly on the embankment of a stream. It was strange for him to be this familiar. As if he owned her.

"Where are we?" she asked.

She needed to adjust the laces on the back of her dress and knew he was watching her. But he was not some poor farm hand. He could probably have any woman he chose. He could just be amusing himself with her.

"Not far from the next village. You've never been to crop country, have you?"

"No."

"Horse and cattle farms are the only landmarks. Everything else is food."

Does he ride all day in this manner? All cavalier—like a gypsy. "Did you come to the theatre last night to meet a milkmaid? Were you that bored?"

He looked about him. "I know you find it hard to believe, but as I told you, I came because I was interested in the meeting. Not the politics, true. I wondered more about the strength of it."

"If you want to know about the rebellion, I can tell you anything." She checked herself. That had not been prudent. But if he were a spy he would probably have tried to pry her for information, and he was doing anything but that.

"I heard quite enough last night," Mikel admitted, looking her up and down. "Your father was a printer, a poor man. But your grandfather is a scholar, maybe a man who tutors for a living. You don't have to work for your food, but you work hard enough, I imagine, seeing to his whims. And to his pet project, the one he is the mastermind of. You are related to the man they call the Pitching Boar? With your passion for the cause, you are easily Otreya's blood."

Trzl frowned, frightened for a moment at his knowledge. "You cannot have guessed all this."

"There is enough gossip spoken in fifteen minutes to tell your life's story."

"Have I that many admirers?"

"I wouldn't call them admirers. They like to talk about you, but they are all rather scared of you."

The pounding of hooves interrupted their conversation. A group of riders were headed straight for them. Most of them were dark of skin and rode warm-blooded mounts of aquiline face. *Desert People? This far inland?*

Trzl fought the urge to step behind Mikel, even when he raised an arm in greeting. He was tense, as she was.

The leader of the group drew his horse up and let out a stream of Seren, heavy with an accent that was hard for her to understand. "The Corsai of Ashlin has ordered the tally a week early to account for possible rearrangement of the king's council, but we will not have concluded our harvest until the—"

Mikel interrupted in a language that was entirely foreign. He must be speaking Aldadi. Trzl wished she had at least a basic understanding of the language, but most of the rebels wanted to sever ties with Aldad once the monarchy was dissolved. They thought the Desert People unpredictable and violent. For true, the men before her had frowning mouths. Their hair was smooth and black—as hers was—and for a moment she indulged the thought that she could have Aldadi fire in her veins.

Mikel must have noticed her shivering. He tossed her his cloak without looking at her. His voice had grown frustrated, and the desert man was not helping matters. At last, he and his men turned their horses around and returned the way they had come.

"What was that?" Trzl asked immediately.

"I must return by noon. My overseer wanted me back sooner, and he doesn't take rejections with much grace."

"That man works for you?"

"Yes."

"Then why does he get to insist you return by noon?"

He gave her a bemused smile. "I told you Nersai are not what you think they are. We work as hard as anyone."

"Next you'll be saying the Corsai work. I know what you are. Rich and spoiled, but you have to obey the king, just as anybody else. And I don't like your men. They are rude."

Mikel brought his horse to her. "Then we should go where they cannot find us." His hand gripped her leg firmly as he helped her up and she thought, *My hips are my most beautiful feature. I wish he felt them.*

Then she wanted to smack herself for being an idiot.

{4}
POSSIBILITIES

"AND WHAT WAS SHE DOING with this serf?"

"Not a serf, sir. A Nersai."

Hodran waved his hand. "Nersai, then. What do I care if he is a man of consequence? He has no power unless he has a reputation."

Hodran rented the most expensive house in the area, a veritable palace built of rugged stone from the Caps, kept clean by an old locksmith and the man's two daughters. This morning he took breakfast on the highest cupola, but the cream was sour. It would put a bad taste in his mouth for the day. He already had enough cause to be angry.

"Well?"

His trusted man was somewhat embarrassed to speak. "She was seen touching him, er—intimately."

Now Hodran was not annoyed but amused. He chuckled to himself and popped a lone berry into his mouth. At least it was firm.

There was an upside to this opponent being a Nersai. It presented vulnerability. Where there was property, there was potential for blackmail. Trzl and her motivations became more fascinating at once.

"Was she?" He looked his man up and down. His people followed him from place to place—as did the staff of any Corsai—but his were unfailingly loyal. "How intimate?"

"Her arms around his waist, astride a horse, sir."

"Ech." Hodran returned half-heartedly to his breakfast. He had hoped for wilder goods. "You ought to know me by now. Tell me something with some skin next time."

"She's a virgin, my lord Corsai."

"And how would you know that? How long have you been following her? A month? That is nothing. She could have been tossing hay with farm boys for years already. She could have four whelps of her own."

"I know my facts. You need to question my sources?"

"Well, enough for this morning, but there may come a time I want to know more about possible offspring. Is Kovim here yet?"

"Was he supposed to come?"

"He was *supposed* to come while it was still night. Now that the whole world can see, I wouldn't count on seeing him. The man is unreliable."

Hodran gave up on his meal. He would wait until midday and hope for something better. It annoyed him there was no one he could spill his plans to. No lovely little redhead or skinny servant girl. Not even an old ally from the King's Council, as he could not be seen with any of his new cohorts too often lest he endanger them. He was eager to get back to Neroi, the city that understood him.

"What does one do for entertainment here?"

"There is the theatre—"

"Besides that?"

"There are some dueling pits, but there are no duels planned."

"Find me someone to challenge who will put up a good fight. I need a laugh."

The servant placed a scroll on the table and backed away. "With your permission, a rider brought this message at daybreak."

"To the Derm with you," Hodran swore. "Why did you not bring this to me immediately?"

"It was carried by a rider of the King's own Guard. He said it was not urgent and could wait. He wants to escort you—"

Hodran had already read the message. "Yes, I'll depart immediately."

MIKEL SLIPPED DOWN FROM THE horse after a few miles and led her by the halter. Trzl missed him right away.

"What is it?"

He rubbed his horse's neck. "She is tired."

"Too tired to carry me?"

"No."

Trzl pulled his cloak tighter about her, watching him closely. Something had turned him sober all at once. There were firm lines on his brow and a definite bite to his jaw. Had it been the Desert Men? The change in plans? That seemed unlikely, but she did not know him.

It was too awkward, this not speaking. "You have lived here long?"

He glanced up, surprised. "Long enough."

"You hire some of them? Desert People? I thought they did not work land."

"There aren't so many of them in Serengard. A few, here and there."

Two answers that were not much of answers at all. She was not accustomed to that. People typically answered her questions, no matter who they were or how she asked them. "They—"

"They aren't dangerous, like you southern people think. Desert People who come north are in search of work, not trouble."

She would have liked to argue about whether anyone ever wanted to work, but he seemed to know more about these people than she did. "Let's stop."

"Tired of my lady already?"

Trzl smiled distantly, a little puzzled, before she realized he had just called his horse a lady. She slid to the ground without help, though it would have been an excellent excuse to touch him again. "I am not good at sitting a horse, but she is a sweet one."

"I raise only the best, and she is one of my favorites." He ran a hand along her hindquarters with a sort of worship. "Some of them haven't the nicest temperaments, but that is expected with any animal of spirit."

They stood facing each other, the air tense between them. He broke away from her gaze and sat down on the cool earth. They were on a hill, with a little patch of hardwood behind them. The valley below was swathed in tall grasses with tiny blue flowers on the tips. Trzl didn't know what crop they were. She settled herself next to him, not too close.

"Do you sell your crops for a profit?"

"Yes. A considerable one."

She giggled at him. "Your face is covered with enough clay for you to be a cart horse yourself."

"Your own face is etched with dust."

"It is? Get it off. Please!"

Mikel reached for her face with his bare hand. She stiffened, surprised at the roughness of the fingers she felt against her skin. "I did not think you would…use your hand."

"I did not think you would let me." He lingered on her chin, cupping it. The hold was possessive, yet it did not disquiet her.

"Your hands are rough. I would think a man as rich as you should have soft hands."

He gave a snort of disbelief. "What kind of farmers have you been consorting with?"

Trzl just shrugged, a tiny smile tugging at her mouth. She was annoyed by the way he talked, all sophisticated, but his voice was deep and vibrant. She wanted to hear it all day. Wanted his hand to stay on her chin all day.

"You believe in the monarchy. In the Books of Derev, the rules of the land."

"I believe in them, yes. As everyone once did."

She laid back and rested her head in the grass, wrapped his cloak about her and tried not to shiver. The sky above her was a clean blue, the kind of clear one never saw in Neroi.

"You believe your fellow men should be forced into a way of living for the sake of your own class?"

"No one has ever forced them. It is tradition. Keeping the ways of the books is for all of our sakes. If the land is not cultivated and the law of the books kept, ruin will come."

"The Orions invented the lie to ensure they always get their tributes."

"You say that, but the land has always reflected the care with which it has been treated. My parents and their parents before them can attest."

"You know your parents?"

"Yes. Did you know yours?"

"No."

"I'm sorry."

"Did they give you your money?"

"I earned it."

"I would hope." She felt an inexplicable anger toward him. Why did he have to be deathly committed to something so wrong? She knew she could never put up with his beliefs. Not for more than an hour or two. And she wanted desperately to put up with *him*.

He put a finger to her lips. "I've never taken a woman riding with me before now."

She caught the nervousness in his voice and gathered that it was some great secret, though she could not guess why. Maybe because he was grown? He must have passed twenty. Maybe he was lying to her.

"Even I have been riding with a boy," she said, "which is saying a lot. Most of them think me a strange-ling."

"You *are* different."

His finger was still on her mouth and it made her tremble. She shifted away from him—not because she wanted to but because she felt weak and it was frightful. "And why am I different? Is there something specific you do with women you take riding? The boys I ran with were dedicated to the cause and would not dream of harming me. You...I do not know."

"Why do you not know?"

Because I could always make them do what I wanted. But that sounded horrid. "Because you are stronger than me, and that is a rare thing."

He looked puzzled for a long moment, and then he stood, disgust stamped across his face. "I would have borne you off by now if I were that kind of man."

His admission made her smile slowly at his confusion. That wasn't the strength she meant. "I have been told never to trust a Nersai."

"That is good advice for one your age, but you could probably trust any Nersai more than the vagabonds you drink fruity liquor with every night." He reached for her hand and drew her gently to her feet. "We have stayed long enough, I think. Should I leave you at the crossroads?"

Trzl nodded, but as they rode back, dissatisfaction chafed her. If this was what made a Nersai noble, this stiff adherence to rules, she understood why their whole class was going the way of the monarchy...to extinction.

It was nearly noon by the time Mikel jumped off at the crossroads and reached for her. Her feet hit the soupy muck of the road, and she felt as sullen as ever. Then he took her hand without her permission and kissed it. She looked up at him, not sure what that was for.

He leaned in and touched her lips with his, just barely. His voice was gravelly when he said, "Let me hope I may someday earn your trust."

She stared at him, eyes wide, but not willing to walk away. Not yet. "I am going back to Neroi tonight. I will not see you again."

She hoped he would contradict her. He did not. But he also did not take his cloak.

BUT THEY DID NOT LEAVE for Neroi in the morning. They left for Ashlin.

Trzl found herself shaking in her shoes the entire three-day carriage ride. There would be a whole new group of people to meet, most of them rebels of her kind. She would run with them, do the footwork that kept the cogs turning in their precious clock. And, hopefully, she would be there to see it all explode. Watch Serengard take the shape of a new world.

Grandfather sat next to her, talking, almost to himself. "Kovim declared all effort fruitless last night. It is time to overthrow Petrolai. This winter."

Trzl frowned. "Who is Kovim to decide? He hasn't done anything."

"He is our last advocate and voice to the King. His writings may sound moderate to you, but you must bear in mind that he has many people to please."

Trzl would have spit if they hadn't been inside of a carriage. "If I were on the King's council, I wouldn't waste time writing plaintive sonnets as he does. Petrolai has blood as cold as the Northern Caps. Do you think he hears any of it? No."

"I am sure he hears it, and I am sure he twists it to mean what he wishes. But the longer we can forestall action on the part of the crown and the more foolish rules he insists upon enforcing, the greater—"

"—our numbers grow. Yes. It doesn't make me like Kovim. We are going to kill them, aren't we, Grandfather?"

Grandfather pretended to look shocked, his long white beard nodding up and down. "The royal family and the Castle Guard?"

"If they do not step down gracefully."

Grandfather shrugged innocently. "Why, I don't know. I'm sure I won't have anything to do with it."

"Who will, then? Kovim?" She let air out through her teeth to say that Kovim was incompetent.

"I am sure your questions will be answered when we reach Ashlin. There are many of spirit there, the same as in Neroi, and I am sure they are arranging things."

Trzl stopped demanding answers then, but she was anxious. She wanted to know all of it now. Was there to be a coup from the inside? A riot and demands made? An armed force rallying on the moors across the river? Maybe they could occupy the old Fortress of Orion on the southern bank.

They were heading toward it now at breakneck speed: the culmination of everything she dreamed of since childhood. She looked up at Grandfather, breathless. He caught her excitement. His bright blue eyes snapped with unearthly dreaminess.

Yes. She was very much his flesh and blood.

{5}

Plans

DREMIR WAS USED TO THESE new recruits staggering in, their hopes for a rebuilt Serengard not quite as high as their hopes for a breath of action. But this one was different. She had a wildfire in her that was as honest as it came. She was a true believer, and so few were.

"Do I know you from somewhere?" he had to ask.

Their table—a large one in a dark corner of *The Broken Spade*—was always busy on a night like this. She was drinking white brandy with the rest of them, and she shrugged at him.

"You might. I am Trzl, granddaughter of the Pitching Boar."

"I knew it." He had heard her reputation. That she would do anything for the cause…and that anyone would do anything for her. "You know our rules of secrecy?"

"I did this in Neroi. I was involved in every meeting the city over."

"Your Corsai is sympathetic in Neroi. Our militia has been fighting here for nearly a year, and we've been meeting together for over a decade."

Trzl rolled her eyes. "I had thought it far longer than that. What have you planned for tonight? Throwing rocks at the castle wall?"

Dremir glared at her. "Tonight is not an armed attack. Tonight we are scouting." He tossed her a jar full of a slightly explosive concoction, wrapped in a thin piece of muslin. She caught it in midair, frowning with confusion. No doubt she had heard he was reckless. Not really. He'd known she would catch it.

"If we are scouting, why are you giving me a weapon?"

"To see if you recognize it."

"I do. What do you want me to do with it?"

"Toss it back."

She did without blinking. Good. He liked her, in spite of her sarcasm.

"All right. You can join us. But you're not coming tonight as you don't know the city."

"I can take orders."

"I doubt that."

"I want to come."

Dremir locked eyes with her, thinking he would stare her down. Instead, he could not break her gaze. He cleared his throat, troubled by the compelling need to give her what she asked. "As you wish. You may come."

The night had a chill, but the city was brightly lit. Dremir did little more than watch her the entire time, relying on the others of his troupe to assess the entrance to the Gate of the Guard. It was unlike him not to be at the front, and it frustrated him. When they returned to the tavern, Trzl's eyes were glowing brightly with excitement, but she did not thank him. He thought she owed him some kind of apology for disrupting his evening. He didn't have to trust her, and he had chosen to.

At least, he thought he had chosen to. Something about her made him feel as if he had not, even as she settled across the table from him and asked bluntly, "Do you have a man on the inside?"

"Maybe," he evaded. "But we don't need one. Do you know how many are in the militia alone? Our numbers, not counting those outside the walls of Ashlin, are in the thousands." He needed to impress her. After all, she was Otreya's granddaughter, and Otreya was the heart of the underground in Neroi.

"Well, of what significance is a plan if it hasn't some part that will impress me?"

Now she was just teasing. There were coos and mumbles of approval at her wit. His Ashlin folk liked her, did they? But pitting oneself against him was never considered wise.

Dremir took her attempt at banter as a challenge. He grinned slowly, a patronizing smile. "Do you read, Trzl?"

"Naturally."

"Have you memorized Kovim's works?"

She shook her head. "No. There are many. And he writes dreadful dull."

A snicker or two met her claim, but Dremir was disgusted. "I have memorized every word, and I do not generally read as a rule. I've devoured them with a passion because I am a man who is never given enough for the hours and hours that I toil. You—you are the granddaughter of a scholar, you have time to be well-read, and yet you have not memorized the works of Kovim."

Trzl swallowed, shifting uncomfortably. "I consider it important to understand the whole of society, and that requires reading other works," she shot back.

"The whole of society does not know what they are about or what the King is about just behind their backs. You will find very little satisfaction in that school of thought when the new Serengard is formed and you are left far behind in the dust because you had not the stomach for it."

"Are you picking on me because I am young? Because I am from Neroi? Because I am a girl, and you're intimidated by me?"

Those eyes snapped again. He was starting to want her out of his pub. Then again, maybe someone with such bewitching power could be very helpful…if he could figure out how to use her.

"There are many young ones involved in our cause whom I admire and respect," he started.

"Stable girls and factory boys with few shekels to their names?"

"Oh, I do think you are pampered if that is what you're asking."

Trzl's face turned dark, but her breath remained even. "None of us are pampered. We are all forced to adhere to the whims of the monarchy. You are saying I must be oppressed to get on your good side, yes?"

"Nothing of the sort." But he was not really sure what he was saying, and he was never one to lack clarity. "Are you even aware of what our 'oppressed' militia has accomplished here in Ashlin? Last year, we blew up the bridge to the Gate of the Guard, killing near thirty of their number. In response, King Petrolai placed portions of the city under heavy guard until after the riots ceased. And why did we not manage to bring the riots into full fruition? Because Neroi hadn't brought in the 300,000 pieces of gold needed to arm our people. We were waiting on *your* city."

"I don't know anything about your arms, except that you could have raided the castle armory if your leader had any guts."

"You should go now. Some of us have important work to do."

Trzl lifted her chin and slid off the bench, tossing a glance at him over her shoulder. But she didn't leave. She stood by the door and struck up a conversation with another girl her age. They were talking loud enough for him to hear, no doubt by design.

"Dremir is a foreman? At a factory?" Trzl said. "He claims to desire equality, but the greener grass for him would take him down a few notches."

Dremir turned to the person next to him, a young woman whose name he hadn't learned. "How do you like that? Trzl from Neroi, the legendary. She reminds me of the crown princess—all sure of herself and elevated to a popularity she hasn't earned. Oh, and terribly ugly, with features like a man."

TRZL DIDN'T INTEND TO PROVOKE the leader of the Ashlin militia. Maybe her time in Derev had shaken her more than she thought. She felt like she was returning to a confined space after having been freed. Was it Mikel that did that to her? Had she been a purer version of herself when she was with him?

That was a barrel of rotten squash. She was herself, always.

She caught a glimpse of a Guard every time she rounded a street corner. Their armor glinted in the streetlights and reminded her that she was not home, but other than that, they did not bother her. She thought the city would be cold and dark. Instead, it was vibrant and colorful, with banners and lamps hanging from almost every structure. She was used to meeting in shops or houses. Here, they met in taverns mere steps from the gates of the castle courtyard, a literal stone's throw. Their boldness was frightful—especially with the Castle Guard lurking about.

Grandfather was preoccupied when she returned, busy with his cohorts. She didn't recognize any of the faces here tonight. Maybe if she had stayed home, she would have made more friends. She was slightly angry at him for being busy, for not having time to listen to her yell about how she hated Dremir. She thought of how Mikel would make Dremir look like a fool if he were lucky enough to engage him, and it made her giggle.

When Grandfather concluded, he had other things on his mind. "Hodran, the Corsai, is a decent man and you like him, yes?"

Decent? Maybe. Decent didn't matter. If the man had influence, she was interested. And he wasn't terrible to look at either.

Grandfather did not wait for a reply, he just sat quietly, thinking. His mind jumped around all the time. It was a miracle he managed to stay focused enough to inspire any of them. "Kovim and I are putting together a group of leaders for the new formation of territories and cities. I will be among them, and we hope Hodran will as well. We will need his money. I know this will make you dislike him, but he is much richer than we originally thought him to be."

She tried not to sound bored. "How rich?"

Grandfather leaned forward and lowered his voice. "As much as is held in the castle coffers is within his personal possession. And not just coin. In trade, he is rich also. He owns several slave vessels in the ports, properties from border to border, even some of the old keeps that used to belong to the Guard before the time of Altrun."

That much? Why, perhaps they could overturn the monarchy by buying out the Kymsai, claiming Hodran owned half of Serengard and was the rightful ruler. Just long enough to set up a proper council that would involve her and Grandfather, of course. He could certainly be worth marrying.

"He owns slave vessels? Grandfather, our cause does not believe in slavery any more than Orion does."

"He does not import the slaves, only owns the vessels. Money without the responsibility. I tell you, I like the man. Now, help me make copies of this map of the lower side of Ashlin. I'm sure you'll need one of your own. Oh, and Trzl, I received word scarce an hour ago that you were fighting with the militia leader here. We haven't the time for that, my dear. Both of you are leaders in your own right. You are superior of mind, but all the more reason to be patient with him."

"He incites my ire. I wish I could melt his mind."

"Could you not find yourself a loyalist to hate?"

That made her snicker, but it wasn't really funny. It gave her an ache, just slightly, in the back of her throat. She had forgotten to ask

Mikel how often he came to Ashlin. If only she could find him—if only he *would* step into their rebel troupe and argue with Dremir and save her the trouble of playing the Treacher's side.

THE PASSAGES OF THE OUTER court were dark this time of night. Hodran frowned to himself when he observed it. Was the monarchy afraid of an attack? Already? It would not suit his plans if the rebels moved now. What was more, it would mean Kovim and his cohorts were lying to him, which would never do. How many times must he tell them that *he* was the one taking the most risks?

As his feet echoed down the long halls, memories of years spent here picked their way into his thoughts like a tradesman's chisel—some of them pleasant, some of them not so much. His favorites were of the things he did in corners; eavesdropping, of course, but especially the moments he shared with the most powerful woman in the kingdom. Touching her face, kissing her hands—

"Ahem." An aide stood at a door ahead of him, looking uncomfortable, and Hodran realized he had stopped walking and placed his hand against the wall, sobered by the fact that he would never come back here.

Damn that Kierstaz Orion. She got inside him like a poison. Not many women could.

The man was a youth of nineteen or twenty, a member of the King's Guard of such a stature and feature that he could have been of Orion blood himself. As he started to walk again, Hodran was sorely tempted to snicker at the lad, at the Guard and their pompous belief in their royal family. He'd learned to ignore the gravity the Orions imposed, to rise above it with his own savory attitude of superiority—though it could never rival the superiority *she* exuded.

The youth brought him to a council room, one of the large ones near the Tower of Tame, and told him to wait. There was a lone candelabra on the long, polished table in the middle of the room, but it cast little light into the corners.

Hodran smiled again. Lovely corners.

King Petrolai, by contrast, did not smile when he came out of the shadows. He bowed shallowly. Hodran looked closely to be certain there was not a dagger in his hand. It would be just like an Orion to stab him to death at a friendly meeting.

"Corsai."

"My king." Hodran went to one knee on the floor as was the custom. Regardless of the neutrality Hodran attempted to imply, King Petrolai knew who was among his friends...and who was not. His strong-boned face was cold and aloof.

"I have a request to make of you."

"You have but to name it."

Petrolai paced around the other side of the table, staring at the wall. No doubt he kept his own memories—probably far less interesting. "I need you to look after my daughter."

Well. This was awkward. "Why, my king—"

"You know my days as king of Serengard are numbered. Whether I escape with my life remains to be seen. In such a case...Kierstaz must be protected by someone who knows how."

"The Guard?"

Petrolai waved his hand. "Not physically, Hodran. Politically. You have always been a favorite of the people. You know how to present her so that she will not be feared."

Hodran could not believe his luck. What he could learn today would trump anything Kovim knew, that was certain. "Why would you ask this of me, my king?"

"You are an ambitious man." Petrolai turned at last and faced him. The look in his eyes made Hodran's blood run cold. It was a look so detached and unfeeling that he wondered if the man were completely sane. *I, at least, have a heart.*

"I will look after her. On my honor, as the Corsai of your third largest city, a knight trained in your service, and a loyal member of your council."

Petrolai raised a hand. "Do not mock me tonight of all nights."

What, Hodran wondered, *is happening tonight?* Damn the rebellion for keeping him, literally, in the dark.

"I have told you I will protect the political interests of your daughter."

Petrolai turned away as if he could not stand the sight of him. "That is all I ask. You may go."

Hodran took his leave and was able to pass unaccompanied through the council chambers.

Petrolai did, indeed, have cause to worry. If there was a war, it would be a short one. Serengard had never acquired a very substantial army beyond the Castle Guard and the fifteen thousand stationed at forts along the western and southern borders. There was no army to the north or the east. It was unnecessary, since the climate was cold, the land was expansive, the people were hardy. Not only did the farmers defend themselves, raiders were few and invaders still fewer. Only the renegades from the swamps and the plains—and sometimes ghosts from the cold Cliffs of Marek—ever ventured down into the settled areas.

And now, when at last the king needed an army in the heart of Serengard to protect his very own throat and those of his wife and children, there were few volunteers. The men who did not consider it unfashionable now considered it suicide.

On the first staircase, Hodran nearly ran into a knight in the full battle dress of the Border Guard, black hair plastered against his forehead and a sweaty helmet under his arm. They nodded to each other and passed on. Curious. Had Petrolai called back the Border Guard? But this man's face looked familiar. He could not place him. Many years ago, they had been contemporaries, of that he was sure.

Ah, well. Perhaps the lucky knight was going to be asked to look after Petrolai's wife. An amusing thought, to be sure.

DREMIR HAD A DISTINCTIVE KNOCK that he used on the door of every rebel leader, and tonight was no different. But he felt as if he wanted to run back the way he had come.

"Are you here to see Grandfather?" Trzl asked him, clipped, rude.

He knew he looked like a misplaced kitten on her doorstep. His mop of curly hair was wet from the mist of the river, and his pant legs were streaked with grease. He had been in and out of more than a few back alleys.

"I will have to talk to him, but I am here because I need a favor from you."

"From me?"

"What's all this?" Otreya came to the door, his cap askew. "Dremir. What can you mean coming here?" He pulled him inside. "Someone may see you. I am certain my house is watched at all times."

"I have to ask a favor of Trzl." He shifted, hoping he could say this with dignity. "We have a message of Kovim's that we must get to the whole city tonight. All of our usual couriers are behind the lines in the Third Quarter."

Trzl hugged her arms across her chest, frowning. "The Third Quarter?"

"There were riots there today. The Castle Guard has sealed off the whole quarter—no one out and no one in."

"I know that. But *all* of them are in the Third Quarter?"

"Every girl we have," Dremir said. It was a lie, but a white one. He knew she could talk her way out of anything with the Guard, and he needed that in full strength tonight. Her mesmerizing quality worked on others besides him. He'd seen it more than once in the past month.

Otreya was surprisingly unconvinced. "Why should you send Trzl? She is not one of the usual couriers—would they trust her?"

Dremir shrugged. "Many of our leaders will know her face. She is your granddaughter, and she is the right age and pretty."

That admission hurt a little. Well, he had lied when he called her ugly. It wasn't that she was all that beautiful, but she didn't look a thing like the crown princess.

"Let me go, Grandfather. I can do this."

Otreya was still frowning in the dim light, but he gave a grudging nod to Dremir.

Dremir let out a breath of relief. "The rebellion will be grateful."

"I am as much the rebellion as you are," Trzl said. "Where do I have to go?"

"Into the high side of town. I've a map to show you, but we need light."

Trzl pulled on his arm in the dark, drawing him into the study at the back of the house. He waited while she lit a candle. She had a smirk on her face, and Dremir had to work hard to hide his own.

He handed her a brown leather bag. "This is your pretense. Try to hold onto it as long as you can. If the Guard takes it from you, your story will be far less believable."

"And my story is?"

"That you are selling valuable herbs for your master, but you are late, you must finish by tomorrow...so forth and so on." He could not help a bit of sarcasm. "Try to act poor and wretched, if you think you can manage."

"And *are* these valuable herbs?"

Dremir's eyelashes snapped down and then up again. "Yes. They are very valuable. None of this is simple nor is it a game."

"I don't think of it as a game. What is the message?"

"It is in the lining of this cap. Take it off at each stop, recite it, and put the cap back on. Do not let them copy it down. It must be memorized. You mustn't mark your stops either." Dremir held the map up to the light. "You have twelve stops—here, here, here…"

His finger moved fast. Trzl blinked hard, and he could tell she was struggling to concentrate. She could do this, though. He was sure that a mind like hers was as sharp as her eyes.

"You've learned it?"

"Yes."

"You have a horse, I assume. But you must pretend it is your master's, not yours."

"I'm no simpleton, Dremir. Nor am I as pompous as you."

"Here." He tossed her some working girl's clothing, clean and plain. "Change into this with all speed. I'm leaving by the back door."

{6}
Fortune

IT WAS HARD TO SEE, even with the lamps on each side of the street. Trzl could have sworn they were dimmed after a certain hour. Some kind of subtle message to the citizens of Ashlin? *Go home and go to bed?* Yet many of the taverns and public houses were still open and making a fine ruckus. It would have been comforting to go in and down a drink before she set out, but she didn't dare. She'd never seen Dremir's face that pallor. Did he know things she did not? He said he owned men inside the Castle Guard. Was their cause truly gaining strength? Or was this crack down by the Guard a move that would quench their fervor?

She hoped not. Hoped the message she delivered was strong and bold and would incite the people to action.

Hoped Kovim had the guts.

If only Grandfather would not trust him so. If only they could choose one of their own friends to lead them, someone they knew was loyal and capable. Maybe Dremir, though it pained her to admit that he would be a good choice.

And then there was Hodran. A marriage between them may be what Grandfather wanted but it was also what *she* wanted. Gaining his ear and thus his undying loyalty to her would be a feat, and one rich with reward. She had confidence that she could do it, too.

A guard stopped her in the Merchant Quarter and asked her what she was about and why she was out this late. His dialect was complex and smooth, something she did not hear in the ale houses of Ashlin. Having him near made it hard to breathe, and he could not remove his hands from her horse's bridle fast enough to suit her.

Thankfully, he believed her story.

The next guard that stopped her was very young and believed it just as readily. He let her continue into the higher part of Ashlin, near the river.

Each doorstep was dark, and hands pulled her in off the street, memorized their message by the light of a lone candle and slipped her back out. There was a fear that suddenly took hold of the rebels—something that was not there when she first arrived. It made her wonder just how brutal the Castle Guard could be.

Panic hit her for a moment when, after her eighth stop, she suddenly could not remember the ninth. Her heart beat faster as she searched her memory, trying to see Dremir's finger in her head.

Then she heard the sound of hooves in one of the side alleys—one she just covered. Heavy metal horse shoes hit the stone streets. The echo broke through the night and made it sound louder than it was.

Was someone following her?

She urged her own horse—Hodran's gift—into a trot, trying to make the wider road ahead, the one with lamp posts. She did not know this side of Ashlin and many of the streets were dark, but she knew her tenth stop by the map in her head. Information on paper seemed simple. In the dark and at eye-level—

Trzl did not even jump when the scruffy man seized her horse's bridle. She was expecting something imminently; it was almost a relief.

"Unhand my horse." She used her most commanding voice, but inside she was not so still. She had served the rebellion many a time and never been caught, not in Neroi nor in the outskirts. She didn't know if her punishment would be imprisonment, a beating, or perhaps—in the King's city, it could even be a hanging.

"Look, pretty lady. I only want a moment of your precious time. You don't belong 'round here, do you? You must be one of us. One of the underground."

She relaxed a little. "What do you need?"

"I am lost." He spread his hands. "Do you have a map of the city?"

The question sounded innocent enough, but she still felt uneasy. *Do not get off of your horse. Do not get off of your horse.* But she had to get off to reach the map hidden beneath her saddle.

"I...do not know the city myself. I am sorry—I cannot help you."

"Please? You can offer me no information?"

What could be the harm? He was a rebel as she was, in need of direction. She swung down, turned to her saddlebags. "Perhaps I can. Give me a moment."

He caught her instantly from behind, gripping her neck. "D'not scream," he whispered in her ear. "Scream, and you're dead."

She wasn't planning to scream, but she was confused as to what he wanted. No one in Neroi tried to seize her, no matter how late she stayed out. But then, she was usually with friends.

He dragged her toward the shadows. And then she saw there were two more, hastily snatching at her things, her horse, her cloak. She was being robbed, in this part of town? There was supposed to be a heavy Guard presence. Nice to know the Guard cared to stop her if she was a rebel but felt no obligation to protect her from thieves.

"Shh! Hold that animal still!" one of the men said. They were distracted, trying to keep their booty away from the dim light of the street.

Trzl heard the echoing clip-clop of the horse from the alley—still coming—heavily shod and calm. As soon as she could see the silhouette of the approaching animal, she slid her fingers down inside her garments, brought out her seven-inch dagger, flung herself free of hands and held the blade in front of her.

"Do not take a step closer to me," she shouted. "Or I run you through."

One of them laughed. "Oh, she fights."

She backed away from them as fast as her split skirt would allow. Not fast enough. They ran at her, into the street. She kicked one of them away, nicking another with the tip of her blade, but then they were all nearly trampled by the dark, ghostly horse. The rider drew a long, straight blade that shone, even in the dark. In a swift slicing motion, he felled each of the men. All three of them.

Trzl stood shakily, staring at their writhing bodies. They were not dead. They each had been slashed through a right arm. Her stomach wanted to retch, looking at the useless, dead arms dangling in their sleeves, hearing them scream and grasp at the cuts, their fingers turning dark with their own blood.

Without a word, the rider extended his hand to her.

Quite certain it was Dremir, she shook her head and stepped away. "I have...a horse."

"Best get him, then."

It was not Dremir. It was Mikel, and he was not happy. What cause did *he* have to be angry with her? She quickly caught the reins of her horse and swung up into the saddle.

He turned his head enough for her to hear him and said, "You shouldn't ride alone, Trzl. I ride this street often, but not at this time of night. You must call this pure fortune."

"I was doing well for myself before you came. I would've had them subdued given a little more time." She was still in awe of the swiftness of his blade, still a little afraid she would throw up. "How did you find me? And why were you following me?"

He did not answer her question. "As I said, pure fortune."

Suspicion flooded her mind. Pure fortune? Why had she not seen him around Ashlin until this night, the night she could be implicated in treason against the King? Not only that, she could implicate others. Dremir and Kovim, for a start. "You followed me on purpose. Admit it."

He shrugged. "I do know where you and your grandfather are staying. That is no secret."

"It is supposed to be. How would you know such a thing?"

"I have friends."

"Are you among us now?" That *would* be a lovely turn of fate.

Mikel laughed. "Must I be a rebel to rescue a girl from some thieves? Surely chivalry exists outside of your little world of treachery."

Trzl shifted, thinking of the three severed arms. He said nothing about her poor woman's garb. Perhaps he hadn't noticed in the dark. "I am not sure I approve of you."

"Your approval is hardly required."

"Perhaps it should be."

"Perhaps you should listen to me and not ride alone."

"You ride alone."

He put a hand on the hilt of his sword. "I know how to use this."

She did not want to bicker. Not now. What she would really like to do is pull Mikel from his horse and kiss his face. She hadn't thought she would see him again—ever—and she'd been resigned to it. But now that he was here...

There were three more stops that she could not make because of his presence, and she still needed to find Dremir, ask him about the one she had missed. She had to get rid of Mikel, yet all she wanted was to keep him close. With him came a cloud of warm calm that settled over her. Made her wish she had accepted the arm he offered and left the expensive horse from the Corsai to wander home...or wander to the sea. Either would be fine.

What was she thinking? Hodran was her key to power, and she cared about the rebellion far more than she cared about Mikel. He was muddling her head already.

"Do I owe you a debt, Nersai?" She bartered as a shopper would, hoping to make him leave, even as she thought, *Don't go. Don't go.*

"A slight debt, and you needn't call me a nobleman. My property makes no difference between us."

Oh, but it does. "Well, will you name it?"

Their horses moved at a slow pace toward the square, slow enough that she could watch the shadows on his face. His stern frown slowly disintegrated, but he still looked overly grown-up under the street lights. "Let me take you to a lovely little music tavern, buy you some arabica, some fine Ashlin-style pastries and cream. Show you some true culture."

Trzl's stomach did a flop. Was that the Ashlin way? She hadn't heard. "That would be adding to my debt, not canceling it."

"I am generally bored with local women as company. You fascinate me, and that is worth a good deal. Or would your grandfather be offended by such a thing?"

"Grandfather does not care what I do, so long as I eventually succumb to my fate and marry the Corsai of Neroi."

Mikel shifted, just slightly, at the mention of the Corsai. "On the morning of the Sabbath—do you have plans?"

"I don't think so."

"Meet me on the steps of the Red Horse Tavern at one hour to noon."

At one hour to noon she should be sleeping off the past night's treason. "I'll be there."

"Meanwhile, teach your horse that you are his lady. He should have fought for you back there."

"You like to tell people what to do, don't you?"

"It becomes a habit when one must do it all day."

"Do you like telling me what to do?" She knew that *she* liked it. But it could get old.

"I'm not sure how you mean that. I like that you've a sharp mind, and you answer me." He appeared to be genuinely puzzled. For true? He did not realize he was bossing her? "I have to go. Somewhere I must be."

"I'll be fine," she told him.

He reached across, gripped her hand in his own and nodded.

She waited until he was long gone before she turned her horse around for her final three stops. And as she stared at the map, she suddenly remembered the ninth from earlier. Dremir would have no chance to crow over her after all.

THE CITYWIDE RIOTS COMMENCED ON the first day of snow, immediately following the King's refusal to lower the tributes on grain. The request was made by Kovim, and the response could not have come at a more pivotal moment. The harvest had just concluded, the weather was coming, and city people especially were never optimistic about the winter.

"It is a glorious day," Grandfather said each morning as he woke to the sound of yelling in the square, the breaking of windows. This morning he was in especially good spirits. "I am glad we are deftly close to the fulfillment of our dreams, Trzl, my girl. Have you been out this morning? There must be news."

Trzl smiled to herself. Grandfather was living his dream. He was not a practical man. To him, the noise making, the telling of words from street to street were all that was required. Trzl felt she knew better. She had been to the meetings every night, listening to Dremir, talking with the foot soldiers and metal smiths and alley rats. They needed weapons.

They needed strategy. Their entire cause could be lost in an instant if the monarchy made a move that allowed the people to doubt its inherent evil. That inherent evil was tantamount.

The King could resign. He could pass rule to his daughter prematurely. He could hand control of Serengard to the council, which would certainly be more amenable than Orion rule but would destroy their momentum.

One wrong move on the part of the rebellion...two or three traitors among them...and they could all be caught behind bars.

Grandfather broke into her thoughts, "Trzl, if you are not going out, I must speak to you about something."

"After I clean up this dastardly mess you left in the kitchen. Did you try to cook last night? You should leave that to me." She laughed—a forced laugh—then reentered his study and shrugged. "What is it?"

"It is Hodran. He has asked to court you. I confess it was not the question I expected."

Trzl breathed. No, it was not the question she expected either, but it was a relief. Weddings happened quickly among Serens. If a man fancied a woman or a woman fancied a man, they spoke of it, pricked their fingers, and mingled their blood with the thorns of roses. She knew this was not always the way among the Corsai and Kymsai. They would often court for months, wooing and lying to each other, making a simple thing far too complicated. She had forgotten that Hodran was one of them— that he would want to flirt with her first.

Thank Allel.

"Well, my dear? Will you court the man? There is a chance he will not ask you to be his wife. I do not want your hopes to be hurt."

Trzl hoped she could pull a significant mask over her face. She didn't want him to see her laugh or to see that laugh turn sober. "I do not think I will get hurt, Grandfather."

His face brightened at once. "Excellent! I will tell him that you will court him?"

"You may tell him."

"Or you may tell him yourself. We are to dine with him this Sabbath afternoon where he expects your answer."

Trzl frowned. "Grandfather, I have somewhere else I promised to be on the Sabbath."

Grandfather frowned. "You are not going to one of those strange temples of the Desert People, are you, my child? I have heard that many of the Ashlin crowd believe in Allel. Some even read aloud the books of Elohai."

Trzl laughed. "No, Grandfather, I am not going to a temple."

"Well, I am sure you can disappoint someone else today and not someone desperately vital to our cause."

She stared down at her feet, feeling suddenly like a hypocrite. "Tell me what time I must be here to leave with you."

{7}
Loyalists

TRZL TRIED TO PUT ON all the face paint and jewelry that the Corsai might think attractive—or that Mikel might think attractive. She was not used to this ritual. To anyone caring what she looked like. She could wear green on her feet one day and green on her face the next; they still looked at her sharp nose and dark eyebrows and called her Trzl.

Part of her wanted to rebel—tell Hodran and all he promised to go to the Treacher. The other part was nervous to the point of shaking. She did many a frightful thing under cover of darkness, but going for pastry with a loyalist in broad daylight? On penalty of death maybe. But not willingly.

Yet she was going...more than willingly.

Mikel's cloak lay on her bed. She picked it up and studied it. This fabric...it was expensive. A mix between soft canvas and some kind of foreign muslin? It was hard to tell. For all she knew, Mikel could have as much money as Hodran. If only she could convince him to use it for an appropriate cause. She glanced in the mirror again. She had always been vivacious and wild, long before she was grown. Mikel seemed to like her even with her hair all mussed up and her figure not so revealed. It was a nice feeling.

That's when she knew—her face paint and jewelry were for Hodran; the rest of her was for Mikel. The realization made her tremble with excitement as she threw the cloak over her shoulders and slipped out the front door.

The air was cold, but the sun peeked through the clouds every few minutes, warming the dark fabric on her back. She listened to the click clack of her fine wooden soles on the cobblestones. Listened to it compare with hundreds of others.

The occasional metal sole.

Each one made her look up, try to find the soldier in the midst of the commoners. The armor they wore was dark, molded leather, the breastplates compact and thin. Not always easy to spot. When she succeeded in locking eyes with one, she got a horrid shiver up her back bone.

The Castle Guard.

Trained with all of the secrets of generations of warriors. Secrets kept from the average Seren. How were her people to win a war against such a force?

She passed a number of small carts and horses, other people walking, dressed for peddling or for socializing among the city's many taverns. Between the patches of sun, snow drifted down, taking its time in the absence of a breeze. For an instant, it made Trzl deeply sad to behold its beauty. They were going to destroy this city, she and her comrades. And Mikel was right about one thing: it was unlikely that it would ever be returned to its former glory. Not without nobility to profit from its rise. All the same, it would be worth the sacrifice. Freedom and equality was far more important than beauty and tradition. Mikel would see that too in time. He would come to understand that loyalty to the monarchy was equal to a chain about the ankle.

He simply didn't know what it was to be free.

The square opened before her—public houses, land offices, shops and cafes…and behind them, the cold, stark towers of the Castle of Orion. The ugliest architecture and the ugliest symbol to those of the rebellion, yet it was picturesque in the gentle snowfall, probably for the last time.

And there was Mikel, waiting for her on the steps of the Red Horse Tavern. He tapped a riding crop against his leg, his horse lazily nudging him. She hadn't set foot inside the place. It was one of the largest public houses, with six stories of rooms and dancing halls, the favorite living place of traveling musicians. Unfortunately, it was also known to be favored by the Guard.

"You are not so punctual in the morning," Mikel laughed.

"What—I am late?"

"Very. It is almost noon. But I have been told to expect as much from scholarly folk who have nothing to do but sit at books all day."

"Have you never taken a girl out for pastry before either?" She asked it somewhat selfishly. She liked the idea of being the first.

"Only a few."

"Well, how is it done? You must enlighten me to this Ashlin tradition. It is not done in Neroi."

"Or not done in your circle," he revised.

"You are a snob, do you know?"

"I, a snob? Well, tell me this. In your circle—or in Neroi, whichever it is—does a lady not offer her hand to the man who escorts her? Because I am constantly trying to reach for yours, and you are determined to avoid it. Among people of my kind that means you are refusing the man who offers it, saying you will not go with him or accept him as company."

Trzl stopped walking and fairly gaped at him. "What stupid formality. We have no such thing where I am from. It must be something that only you rich folk do."

"You'll not be as eager to rub my money in my face after you have tasted some of these." He dropped his horse at a hitching post, snatched her hand without permission and brought her down a staircase that led underground. A heavy door stood closed at the bottom of the steps. Mikel pushed it open.

Her ears were bombarded with music that was loud but friendly, a mixture of instruments and sounds that reminded her of a summer storm—sweet and intimidating at once. Her eyes tried to adjust to the light, to determine where the sound came from.

There. A corner full of five or six musicians, crammed together and looking more like they were having an intimate reading of olden books than playing at music. The air was thick with smells of delicious food, smells that reminded her of desert spices and rare types of grain. The clientele was decked out in laces and jewelry, the men wearing velvet coats tailored to fit their chests.

"What is this place?"

Mikel leaned toward her to indicate he could not hear her. She waved her hand. No matter.

He led her to a secluded table, one with half walls on three sides and a collection of lamps scattered around it. He guided her arm until she was seated across from him, then smiled as she slid herself into the corner. Closer.

"What was it you said?"

"I asked what is this place?" He let go of her arm, but she held onto his hand under the table, the skin of it making her go hot and cold inside.

"It is a forte house—actually a stolen tradition of the Dreis. There are dozens in Ashlin. They only open once every seven days, will often bring in different food each week, and it is a hobby of some to hop from one to another, trying them all. And then do it again next time they have new food."

"It is marvelous."

"You must have them in Neroi. Even some of the villages do, and they are not as expensive as this one."

"Why is this one expensive?"

"Because this one is the best." He grinned at her, and she caught a wild excitement in his voice. Was it because of the setting or because of her?

A girl set plates of crumbling pastry, each smothered in fresh berries, on the beaten wood of their table. She claimed the dish contained citrus from the port of Sherp and returned a moment later with steaming cups of arabica that she said was a new variety, from the desert.

Trzl let go of Mikel's hand, feeling suddenly shy, realizing that he was treating her to something unusual. "You do not do this every week, do you?"

"No." Mikel tipped his head to the side to look at her and then touched her face with his thumb. "And you do not usually do this. What is it?"

Oh. Her face paint. "I am sure you've seen it before."

"Only on those who wish to lure me into something sinister."

Trzl frowned at him. He was terribly old-fashioned. She should be laughing, but instead he was worrying her. Was he really this conscientious? All the time or just in public? "I thought there was cause to dress up."

"For me?"

"I have a dinner engagement after this. Grandfather's friends." She avoided mentioning Hodran by name.

He gave a quick little laugh. "I should have been prepared for you to be very busy, shouldn't I. Selfish of me to want you for the whole day."

"The whole day?" Her face might have fallen, but her stomach seemed to fall much harder. The food did not look so good anymore. This dinner was important, though. There was so much to be done, and Mikel didn't fit into her plans at all.

"Only if you are not tired of my company by then. There are places to walk, to see. I dare say your rebel friends have not shown you the banks of the river or the old fortresses alongside it." Trzl thought she heard bitterness in his voice.

"I did not...but this is a special engagement. I was not aware of it when I said I would come with you. Grandfather only just told me."

"You could have sent me a more cordial message, I think. If my attentions are unwanted—"

She caught at the words. "Your attentions?"

"A man takes a woman riding with him alone, I think he is making himself obvious."

She could not breathe, let alone take another bite of this wild-tasting pastry. "You...want me."

His face turned a strange shade and he sat back as if she had struck him. "I told you I was not that kind of man."

"I don't see why you shouldn't want me. All of me." She brought her dress-encased legs onto the bench, around the table until she could lay herself in his arms.

He recoiled and pulled away with her whole body upon him. "Trzl, I didn't mean—"

She put a finger to his lips and reached behind his neck with her other hand. "Especially when I want you."

"Is this a game to you?" he countered, his voice hoarse but starting to grow stern.

"No," she insisted, not even sure if maybe it was. It was all turning to a painful muddle in her head. The Corsai. The King. Ashlin. And Mikel, a counterpoint to everything she was.

He slid his fingers into her hair and pulled her face gently back, forcing her to look him in the eyes. "I have tried to be honest with you. Please be honest with me."

She didn't know how to be honest, not when it came to men. Men were stepping stones to achieving status and power. Mikel had nothing for her. She cradled her head against his neck so she would not have to look in his eyes. "I…don't know what you want me to say."

Mikel lifted her shoulders off of his chest and slid her away from him, giving her space to fix her hair or whatever else she might have unraveled. That annoyed her, and then he started to talk.

"Please, tell me now if you have other plans. If your only thought as to whom you flirt with is how much influence they have, whether it is a waste of your time as the granddaughter of Otreya, than I am sure I am not in your class. How can you think you are worth so little?" He ran a finger through the air to indicate the deep plunge of her neckline in a gesture surely meant to disgust her.

"You complain because I am not wearing my bosom straps tight for you or because I might be wearing them for you *and* for another?"

"You have some idealists you may consider more worthy of you than I. But if you start playing pawns with men such as your grandfather's friends, you will find yourself ill-treated at best. You are young and innocent. Most would not be considerate of that."

"Who are you to claim I am innocent? I am not a fool."

"No." He leaned close to her and touched her face, intentionally smearing her make-up, ruining it for Hodran. "No, you are not."

Trzl smacked his hand away. She had figured this day all wrong. He thought he knew everything about the world, but it didn't matter if he worked day and night and grew tan and strong. They were all the same. Pompous, self-righteous loyalist bastards.

She stood up, rapidly reined in her thoughts, amending her plans. There was dinner with Hodran waiting. She must be there. She couldn't be here with Mikel. She'd been stupid to come.

"I am going home. You are as bad as the rest of them. I wanted to believe you were different."

She left as quickly as she could, afraid he might try to convince her to stay...knew it might work. As she made the street, she could feel him behind her, his eyes watching her, his footsteps cautious but swift. By the time he caught her and spun her around, she couldn't stop the sobs that wanted to come.

"Forgive me," he said quickly, his grip neither tight nor loose on her arm. "I cannot claim to know you well enough to be so familiar. It wasn't my place."

"You told me you wanted me."

"I didn't mean...I didn't mean it that way." He paused for a moment, and Trzl glanced up at him. "Walk with me. The river is only a few streets over. I'll bring you home this afternoon, and you won't have to see me again."

"I *want* to see you again."

He laughed a little bitterly, a muscle working in his jaw. "Don't lie."

"It is no lie."

He caught her hand—much as he had the night they met—and swung it gently. "Come."

{8}

Strangers

THE TIME GRANDFATHER WOULD LEAVE for Hodran's passed. Trzl felt the moment come and go, ignored it, choosing instead to listen to Mikel's footfalls on the chipped stones of the river walk. They found little to say. Clouds stormed in from the north, covering the sun with a heavy gray blanket, and sometimes it looked like it would hail. It was too cold along the river for most of Ashlin's residents, and they met few others.

"I have made a horrible mess of your pretty face paint," he said, his horse's reins dangling in his fingers.

"I don't mind."

"I thought you did."

She didn't want to talk. She just wanted to watch him, to soak up a few moments with him. She knew she would go to the Corsai's dinner party later. She had to be there. Didn't want to miss anything.

Sorry, Mikel.

He stopped under a gate that must have led somewhere—once— leaning against the posts. His fingers slipped away from hers.

"I don't mean to anger you so. I told you when I met you that I was curious about the rebellion. If you were to take me only at my word, it would—"

"I saw beyond your words, Mikel."

"I don't want to make this more or less than it is. I'm not the most skilled at conversing with a—"

"A what?" She thought he was going to say rebel.

"A woman such as you." He looked at the ground, glancing up into her eyes every now and then.

He knew how to argue politics with her. He knew how to lecture on riding in the dark or trusting the Desert People. What else did one converse about? "I'm like any other woman, I'm sure."

"You're not like any other woman. Not at all."

Trzl could not stand this distance just now. She felt that her body belonged close to him; it was wrong to be this far away. She reached for his hand, and he closed his fingers around hers, but that was too docile for her. Too friendly. She caught at his heavy coat and pulled herself up to him, unable to reach his mouth, kissing his chin.

"Do not," was all he said. His hands came up to her shoulders, and he pushed her away. There was something terribly final about the gesture— a finality that conflicted with the pain on his brow.

She frowned. He shouldn't deprive her like this. Not when he admitted he wanted the same thing. "I am not a poison."

"I don't want to be your amusing Nersai fling, Trzl. You may find me a savage competitor when I know I can best a man, but there is no one for me to best but you. You've said as much."

Was he feeling the same dark twinge in his gut that she had felt in the forte house? The impulse to run away, to believe this would end badly? "How?"

"Hodran. You said you would marry him with a good enough reason. If that's true, you are a danger to me." He sounded as if he very much liked her danger. "I never meant to say all of these things today. I invited you because I wanted to listen. I wanted to know you."

That wasn't what she wanted. "Come now, Mikel, there is no one here. Your horse won't mind. And we've plenty of cloaks to keep us warm."

His green eyes narrowed. A wind from the river picked up his hair and tossed it into them, making his eyelashes dip momentarily.

Trzl's voice was low but certain. "Don't deny that you want to be near me. I haven't married Hodran yet. I will give you whatever you want."

He swallowed, standing there staring at her, yet he looked at home. Comfortable. "I am sorry if I...confused you. I am not one of your wild, progressive friends who tells you he cares for you only to induce you to give him favors. I've more respect for you than that."

"Respect?" She laughed with a bitterness equal to his. "I'm only a wild girl you met at a political meeting. You convince me that you care for me, and you're too full of yourself to even—"

He burst out heavily, angrily. "I wouldn't take you. Nothing you could do would induce me. Not unless you were mine alone. Not this once but forever, with our fingertips mingled in the thorns of a rose—you belonging to me and I to you. It isn't a game...to me."

His indignation prompted her to respond in kind, to give vent to what lay buried in her mind all along. "You loyalists! You leave no space for passion—just like your King. All of you Corsai and Kymsai and Nersai and your endless traditions."

"Don't give those traditions to the Corsai. Call them mine as I'll gladly claim them. You—Trzl, you must grow up. You aren't thinking where this would lead, how it would destroy us both. Let me take you home. You must be eager to see your guests."

"I'll go home myself, and you can go the way of the Treacher." She turned and ran. She could not think when she was near him. He confused her. Thoroughly and completely.

Mikel followed her again, raising his voice a little. "You've accused me of having a plan when I met you—of chasing you down. Tell me, did *you* have a plan? Was I for information or just for fun? I should have taken note of having met you in a theatre. Oh, I was an easy target."

That wasn't true at all. She hadn't meant to woo him. She slowed to a brisk walk and spoke over her shoulder. "And you now claim to have had intentions? That makes you better than I? Of course you can plan so far. You can afford to, Nersai."

She pulled up the rich, thick cloak as her evidence, then flung herself away from him, down the street, toward home. The night was her friend, and day was obviously her enemy. She should not rise before noon. It was unhealthy.

Mikel mounted his horse and followed in the wake of her cloak—the cloak that used to be his. "This is your impression of the wealthy? Any Nersai, any man with any station above that of a commoner? Surely the only reason any of our kind would want a girl such as yourself is to use her body and toss it back into the gutter. Believe me, girlish bodies— plenty as beautiful as yours—are cheap enough."

Trzl blinked tears out of her eyes, turned to face him again. "Why else should I believe you brought me down here?"

"Because I have proven to you since the night we met that I meant to do far better by you."

"Better. You think you can do something for me?"

"No. I can't do anything for you." He brought his horse around her and gestured with his chin. "You may consider yourself conducted safely home."

Trzl turned to look behind her, confused. They were standing in front of the largest house in Ashlin, even larger than the hill mansions in Neroi. She recognized the signage of a Corsai over the door, felt her blood boil a little more, and knew he was right about one thing today: She could handle Hodran's slipperiness much easier than Mikel's stringed judgment. She slid his cloak from her shoulders and handed it back to him.

"This is yours. I was going to keep it, but you did not offer it to me—"

"You may keep it. Goodbye, Trzl."

A lone hailstone hit her nose as he stormed away into the wind. It stuck there, melting slowly, making a drop of water that ran down her face. She had just lost something. Something important. But she wasn't sure what it was.

{9}
PLOTS

HODRAN HATED THE HAIL. THERE was sure to be snow mixed in by midnight, and he was not looking forward to the heavy banks slowing down his carriage wheels. He also was not looking forward to this evening lasting any later. Dinner had already been a bore, with guests only Kovim would invite. Hodran was mostly stuck talking to Otreya, the grandfather of the rebellion. Also the grandfather to the little piece of skirt he fancied.

Most of the important folk had gone home, leaving small clusters of supporters to meander about his mansion. Hodran wondered if he would find things missing in the morning.

"Do you see the lights on the hilltops?" Kovim asked quietly. He gazed out one of the large windows of Hodran's Ashlin manor, his eyes glazed to protect his thoughts from Otreya's searching orbs. Hodran knew the feeling.

"You've been watching those lights most of the night," Otreya answered softly. His face was narrow, like Trzl's, reminding Hodran that

80

the girl had not come today.

"Well. Have you seen them?" Kovim persisted.

"I ordered them, Kovim."

Ah, of course, Hodran thought. Otreya ordered a lot of things without consulting the rest of them. Hodran kept quiet, thinking mostly of going downstairs for another chalice of wine.

"And will they rally?"

"Thousands upon thousands. I am certain of it."

Kovim sighed quietly. "You know these people, Otreya. You have confidence in them. I...I have never made a decision on my own. I have only sat on a council. I have to admit, as eager as I am to serve our people, I am not confident in their belief in me."

Otreya only smiled. "You are the one who inspires them, not I—your writings, your words, your constant challenging of the King to his face. Is there anyone who has done more for them than you? I think not."

"I thought there would be more of an outcry when I was dismissed this week past."

Please, someone rescue me from Kovim's endless sensitivity. Hodran was tired of entertaining serious political heads. He wanted a party with some life.

"There will be an outcry," Hodran spoke up at last. He knew how these things were done. His money was not the only reason the rebellion wanted him.

Otreya looked over, his eyes shining. It was hard to tell what the man thought, and his gaze was unnerving.

An interruption presented itself, nearly on cue. A boy Hodran kept for messages came to the door, short of breath. "Three of your men have just returned, Corsai."

"Yes, yes." The three he had sent to the militia meetings to keep an eye on things, to keep him in the know. Hodran shifted, hoping neither of the men in the room guessed the purpose of them.

"Two of them have been injured. Some kind of—"

Hodran held up a hand. "Enough."

Kovim leapt forward. "Where did this happen? What was it?"

The boy looked to Hodran for permission. Well, nothing to be done now. He would look like an instigator either way. Hodran waved him on, and the boy said, "A skirmish with the Castle Guard. On the bridge."

Kovim gasped. "Toward the castle?"

Hodran wanted to laugh. *Do not lose your buttons over it, council friend.* "If it was a skirmish, who else was there? Why were they trying to get over the bridge?"

The boy looked confused. "Do you want to talk to them yourself, Corsai?"

"No need," Hodran insisted, touching his temple. Otreya narrowed his eyes, so he must have caught the gesture.

"All I was told was that many were hurt, some of them children."

Now Hodran and Otreya shared a smile. At last. What they had been waiting for.

"You may go," Hodran told the boy.

Otreya followed, his steps light like a young man's. "I'll go as well. Perhaps I can offer help and comfort." He left a pungent fragrance behind him, something like fennel and erinweed with a touch of alcohol. Not a bit like Trzl.

Well. By the Derm, Hodran would not be left alone in the room with Kovim. Not when he was in one of his depressing moods. He strode out behind Otreya, telling himself he had meant to go from the first. His shoes made a lovely clacking sound on the steps of his broad staircase, and Hodran frowned to himself. He loved this house. It would be a shame to give it up to the mob they were building.

The wounds were deep and already caked with a significant amount of blood. One of the men neared unconsciousness, but the other whined for pity like a hurt dog. Both of the wounds were on extremities. If treated properly, and Hodran would see to it that they were. They would heal.

Seren steel—the kind that was sharpened daily—made these clean cuts. Hodran felt the injustice of it. He owned a sword, generations old, forged from the same steel, but the common folk did not know the recipe. Only those who served the King had the right to a weapon of this material.

It *was* the Castle Guard, and it could be proved.

"Everyone must hear of this by tomorrow. Everyone. Have it in the streets, in the—" He turned, growing quiet as his eyes focused on a wet figure in the doorway. Wet and tall and dripping with more than melted hail. By the fairies, she was furious and flushed and bewitching.

Otreya jumped up to go to her, but Hodran got there first. He slid the hood from her head and let it fall behind her, heavy with ice.

"Trzl," he said slowly, allowing a grin to spread across his face. He picked up her hand and led her quickly back into the hall. He could see tracks of melting snow where she'd let herself in. It gave him momentary pause. She was distracted this evening. She should have been here earlier. He had been, in some way, jilted.

"Won't you take a tour of the house? I've a great wish for your advice on matters these men needn't hear."

Trzl stiffened briefly in his grip. "My advice?"

Hodran lowered his voice. "Matters of council. I do not trust Kovim as much as your grandfather does." He knew the girl far better than he let on. He watched her face light up slowly, watched the confidence and self-command return.

"I would be honored if you would show me the house. After you take this wretched cloak from me."

He caught the dullness in her tone. Her cloak inspired great ire, but his house bored her. That could be remedied. A girl like her must have a yearning for weaponry. She must. "The armory, perhaps?

Trzl shrugged and followed him.

"You are a very beautiful woman," he started out, hardly meaning it. She was intriguing, but not beautiful.

"Some would say so," was her reply. She was a little pompous, a little cold. He liked that.

"I'm not the kind to bestow a compliment easily," he flat-out lied. "With all of my duties as a Corsai, I am granted little chance to see a lovely face at all these days. Especially on one this committed to our cause."

Trzl just shrugged again. He led her down passageways and stone steps, deep below the manor.

"What happened to those men?"

"There was a skirmish today, at the Castle Bridge—"

She turned suddenly, pulling for him to release her hand. "I have to go to them. Some of my friends may be hurt."

Hodran kept a gentle hold of her arm. "Everything that can be done for them is being done. It would be best if your face was not seen there."

She frowned and then swallowed. "You are right."

"Glad you think so." He reached for her arm again, and she let him hold it. They were at the door to the armory, an oaken gate three boards thick, with large iron fittings that made it heavy as sin. He unlocked it with a key from his pocket and swung it open impressively.

His armory boasted the newest design in lighting—half-moon cutouts in the walls, with dark desert fuel feeding into the flame one brick at a time. Even the King could not afford it.

A pity Hodran would not be coming back to Ashlin.

Trzl sucked in her breath, her eyes going wide as the firelight fell on the gleaming steel. She was visibly impressed. She walked about the square room, putting her long fingertips out to touch the hilts of traditional blades, of broadswords, or slim fencing weapons. The only thing his collection lacked was the blue steel of Dreibourge. But that would change, once the King could no longer enforce the Orion treaty with the Drei.

"You must find life in Ashlin very dull," Hodran said.

Now she looked surprised. "What do you mean? I think it is exciting."

"Did you never go places in Neroi? To the theatre and the arena and the races?"

"No. Grandfather was always too busy. *I* was too busy."

She was perfect. Hodran put an arm around her shoulder, one she did not shake off. "I will have to take you to all of those places when we return. After Ashlin has done her part in starting the wave of revolution and our militia makes their move...if the leader of our militia can ever get over himself."

"You know Dremir?"

"Everyone knows him, do they not?"

"I find him to be a constant plague, like a frostbite."

Hodran smiled, and he knew his soft blue eyes crinkled nicely. "We have something in common, then. You have no idea how impossible it is to coordinate a rebellion when the militia leader is secretive of his plans. There is no way to spread the word, to get everyone in their place at the proper time."

She held her hand out to the edge of one of the swords. "I did not know you were involved this deeply."

"I have been closely involved for many months. But you understand, I must keep my public exposure to a whisper. If the King catches wind of my disloyalty, I could be imprisoned or worse. Those of us who are Kymsai or Corsai would be held in far deeper contempt than commoners. It is a personal act of treason to the crown."

Trzl drew her hand away from his weapons with a sudden suspicion in her eyes. "Why do you keep all of these?"

"What—all of these arms?"

"Why haven't you given them to the militia? They belong to the militia."

Hodran felt as if she caught him stealing onions. "Ahh," he chuckled softly. "But I will give them to the militia. Soon. A skirmish instigated by the Castle Guard is what we were waiting for. An excuse to arm ourselves."

She breathed a sigh of relief, the suspicion turning to a calm admiration.

Oh, this was getting good.

"Of course. It has finally come to blows." Her eyes turned deep blue, and it reminded him of Otreya at an inspired moment, making him frown again. He did not like the idea that she could see through him, and it seemed that maybe she could.

She actually smiled at him. "Now, we can start the war."

"Yes. We're gathering our supporters from every corner of Serengard, even as far as the hills of Dragon Country and the border villages. There will be an uprising that will start in Ashlin and span the entire continent. A leveling."

"You sound like my grandfather."

He wished that were a compliment, but he laughed, shaking it off. "Oh, I am not so excited about the leveling as Otreya. I am more excited about the benefits to myself. With the Kymsai and Nersai gone—"

"What do you mean gone?"

"Only disbanded. There will be no more nobility in any form."

She frowned. "Oh. Yes, I know."

"Well, those who do not join with us will be..."

"Killed?"

"Of course. They will be the first to die, a means of causing the royal family to buckle. If all of their supporters are being hung... But here I am talking violence and blood. What a bore."

"I've never minded hearing of it. And I'd like to be given one of these swords when you arm the people."

Hodran took that as an invitation to move into the space in front of her. "Choose one."

"Now?" She flicked her eyes over to the smaller weapons in one quick glance. He could not help noticing how her lashes flashed up and down. Very fine. She chose a dagger set with rubies in the hilt. Her look said *thank you*, but her voice was distant. "What if I had a friend who was among the Nersai? How could I—keep this person alive?"

"Convince them to join us."

She gulped and looked away. Aha. The person could not be convinced.

"Trzl." Hodran took one of her hands in his. "You know you can come to me if you ever need anything, don't you?"

"Yes."

"Even if it means you need something your grandfather would not approve of. You have a friend you want kept alive, I can keep her alive."

She fidgeted, looking uncomfortable.

Oh. It was a he. That was not so good. But he could work with that.

"You are uneasy with me." He tipped her head up to bring her eyes level with him, using the moment to also slide a hand down her back, his thumb loose on her hip. "Tell me what I can do to put your misgivings away."

"I...am not uneasy."

"You are. Please, let me make you happy."

He took her silence to mean she was waiting for something. From him. He leaned toward her gently, brought his face close to hers. Trzl turned away. Not terribly disgusted, but an obvious refusal. Then she said, "Haven't you a wife, Corsai?"

He felt anger rise in him and fought it back down. "Not for long."

She just kept looking at him, as if to say, *well?*

Hodran found her aloofness enticing. He moved toward her a little more. "You are quite the girl. I wish I had met you years ago." That did not quite come out right. Her expression turned to smugness, and he realized she was almost laughing at him.

"I don't need to remind you that I understand the ins and outs of this rebellion far more thoroughly than you do. I am Otreya's granddaughter. You...you are new to our cause. The least you can do is treat me as an equal. Offering to help me with my friends? I know how to take care of them."

"Oh, uh...yes." He was happy to agree to anything she suggested, but the girl was confusing. For true, he might do well to tell her what he wanted of her and let her squirm over it for a few days before she eventually succumbed. This was an especially nice moment, with his finger touching her waist. "I wish desperately to be near you, Trzl. You should know it by now."

She lifted her dagger and held it between them for one long pause, her eyes locked with his. That didn't scare him. Not at all. He just smiled at her, liking this game, thinking he might start undressing her if she said no words.

He raised his eyebrows. "Trzl?"

She ran a finger along the dagger's edge. "If I say yes?"

"There is no end to the—" He was going to say requests, but that would not be tactful, would it. "—to the orders you may give me."

Trzl smiled. A slow, girlish smile. She leaned into him, letting him press her hip with his whole hand, pull her to him for a moment.

"Thank you for the dagger," she whispered. And then she ran from his armory.

{10}
distance

THE EVENING HELD MORE PLOTTING, with Trzl as much an anchor of the discussion as any. Excited leaders from Berekst and the Drei border wanted her take because she was now in the inner circle. Her opinion was valuable, even if the question was where to put all of the village dwellers from the country who were converging on Ashlin this night. And what she said to Hodran was true: She *did* know the ins and outs of this far more thoroughly than he.

She was flushed with her day's winnings and losings when she and Grandfather returned to their flat.

Or perhaps she was flushed with wine. Or a little of both.

Grandfather went to bed, saying he would need strength tomorrow, which was unlike him. She had been staying up nights with him and his wild comrades for the past four years.

There was no way she could sleep tonight, but the wine was making her neck throb a little. She cracked open some cacao beans and sucked on them. It helped.

The rest of the underground would still be somewhere in the town square, at the corner tables and the ends of alleys, planning the next move, the next way to incite the Castle Guard to do something stupid. She longed for her own crowd.

Trzl's feet hardly made a sound on the cobblestones. The horses were around the corner, but she ignored the stable. Better to walk, as it was not far.

She regretted that decision almost immediately. It was different at home in Neroi, where the houses were her friends. Ashlin daunted her in the dark. There were no street lights, and the night was deathly quiet. She realized she had always been with a group or with Grandfather when she left the house at night, except for that one time for Dremir.

She thought of Mikel's ghostly horse following her by the sound of her hoof-beats, and she shivered. She wouldn't mind if he were behind her right now. It would be good to have company, even if he was a loyalist snob who liked to lecture her. She could dimly see the cupolas of the castle above the square—lit by torches, held in the hands of guards all night long—and she used the location of the lights to find the right tavern. There was a veritable crowd in the back, their voices raised to a fever pitch.

Someone clapped her on the back and yelled, "Trzl! Just the girl."

She smiled at them, slipping her cloak from her shoulders.

"You know Kovim has been evicted from the council? The king will not be seeing him anymore. Not for anything."

"I know." *I saw him tonight.* "This is the last straw we need."

"For true, twelve of our people were hurt down at the Castle Bridge. A dozen more were innocent bystanders. We can use that straw, too."

"Light it on fire."

"Burn the city down."

Trzl interrupted loudly, but her voice was tired. "A war will not happen without work. If all we do is skirmish, our efforts will vanish into nothingness."

One of the young women of the militia answered her. "You saw the fires tonight? We have put out the word to all of Serengard. In the next few days, there should be an exodus of serfs and scholars alike, all converging on Ashlin. We will defeat the Castle Guard swiftly and take on the Border Guard. It will not be long."

"It *will* be long if we are not prepared. Loyalists are stubborn." She knew that firsthand.

"They're fools, Trzl, and it has been so long since there was a war. They are not well-trained—not anymore. They have grown lazy. It will be fair fighting."

Not if the Guard can swing a sword like Mikel.

Another said, "Kovim is already forming his own council. They will not make the laws, only make sure everything is fair and equal for all of us."

Trzl wasn't so sure. She looked in the face of the militia man-boy, short with spectacles and golden curls. "Do you really think it will be that simple? How is Kovim supposed to calm the rioters once the Castle Guard has been killed? How is he going to tame the chaos?"

The boy frowned. "Us. The militia."

"The militia is as disorganized as they come. Kovim needs an army to take Serengard."

His mouth dropped open, and his whole face brightened. "You are right. He does need an army. One trained and outfitted well. We must build one." He pounded his fist on the table. "We must! Where are you going? Trzl, we need your help."

"I am sorry. I do not feel well."

A girl caught her arm and dragged her back. "You have to help."

She wanted to. She was just tired. So very tired. "I don't know how to build an army."

"You must know someone who does."

Yes, Hodran knew how. She narrowed her eyes. She could think like his kind—she could imagine what the Border Guard would do, whom they should strike first, how many they would need stationed where— even now, an hour before dawn, without sleep, throat hoarse from hours of talking. She was some kind of invincible.

Mikel would regret turning her down. He would.

"I AM WALKING TO THE square."

Trzl paused in the doorway of the book room, giving Grandfather a chance to reply. He said nothing, his head bowed over papers that he'd been staring at for at least an hour. She was worried about him. Ever since that night at the Corsai's he hadn't spoken to her, and she could not determine why.

She threw Mikel's heavy cloak over her and opened the door, almost running into him. "What—are you doing here?"

Mikel stood in the snow, head and shoulders uncovered. His green eyes looked gray today. Sad. "I came to apologize."

A lump leapt into her throat and she couldn't swallow. "It has been more than a week."

"I told you I would stay away."

"Then why are you here now?"

"Trzl, have we company?" Now Grandfather decided to show an interest. *But it is not who you think it is.* "Show them in. I could use some good conversation."

"Please, come in," Trzl said stiffly.

Mikel took one step toward her, just close enough to speak. "You must understand, Trzl, I am not accustomed to your beliefs or your prejudices. We are more different than I supposed."

"Please, it isn't... You must forgive me for quarreling with you. I accused you of a malice you did not exhibit." She wished she could explain the nights she'd stared at the ceiling, wishing she knew how to reach him, to tell him she didn't hate him. She opened the door wider and stepped aside. "Will you come in?"

"I will." His confidence came, too, commanding, owning the little building. "But I cannot stay long."

Trzl nodded, leading him into the book room. "This is Mikel. He's one of the rebels I met at the Derev Theatre."

Mikel raised an eyebrow at her falsehood, but Grandfather was impressed. "Ah, it is good to see all of the young blood. You are the ones who will inherit our beautiful Atlantis." He chuckled to himself. "Unlucky you are to be stuck with the name of her soon-to-be-former Prince of the Realm, though."

Mikel smiled, but it was thin with a hint of bitterness. "My parents were great admirers of the prince."

"Grandfather, don't insult his family. He cannot help that he was born a Nersai."

"A Nersai? I should have guessed by your fine clothes. Please, take no offense. I am always oblivious of a man's station. As it should be."

"I won't under the circumstances."

Trzl was eager to get Mikel out of the room. "Have you any news from the square today? I was about to walk that way."

"Nothing since yesterday, no. But there are rumors of trouble with the commoners from other parts of the country coming to Ashlin, stealing food from the farms. Some of the Border Guard are being called in to deal with them, among other things." He shifted uncomfortably. "You should get out of the city."

Trzl started. "But why? Grandfather is needed in all of this."

"He will also be the first man the soldiers come for if it turns into anything worse."

"Worse? How can it get worse?" Grandfather was warming up. "It will only get better. If there is war, let it come. It is what we desire."

"War may be what you desire, but I cannot say as much for myself. You would change your mind if your granddaughter were brought to your doorstep wrapped in a muslin shroud." He paused, and the air in the room was heavy with words neither of them would say. "I must be going. I have an important engagement."

"I will show you out," Trzl said. She followed him, watched his back rise and fall with each step.

He turned in the doorway, and she saw that his eyes were lit with a touch of fury. "Even if that man is fool enough to stay, you must get out of Ashlin."

Trzl shook her head slowly, thinking of what Hodran had said. "You are the one who should run."

His eyes narrowed, and she could tell he was struggling not to press her for details. She shuddered, knowing she should not share this information, but something made her think he would respect her confidence. "You are in far more danger than I, Mikel. If you get between the militia and the Guard—"

"You needn't worry about me."

"Please tell me what you know," she whispered. "Please."

"I don't know anything for sure, but I've heard rumors. That's the only reason I came—to warn you." He pulled a thick, rich piece of parchment from his boot, slid it into her fingers. "I am at this address if you are in need of anything...or for any reason. I will not be coming back here."

"Wait, Mikel!" She clutched his arm, a childish, demanding grip. "Is my grandfather in such danger? If you heard things, you must have heard...names."

He shook his arm free and caught the reins of his horse. "You are all in danger."

"Won't you at least walk me to the square?"

His mouth twisted in indecision. He stepped back down from the stirrup, offered her his arm. "I will give you a ride."

Better. She swung up behind him. This horse was different than the last. He was at least eighteen hands, if not more, broad-footed and well-groomed. Instant envy arose, making her cringe. Rich, stubborn Nersai that he was, Mikel would be one of the first to land himself in prison.

"You said we are more different than you supposed." She spoke into his ear, something that was almost a murmur. "I don't think that we are."

Mikel shifted slightly at the feeling of her breath. "We are. In too many ways to count."

That was very cold, Mikel. Trzl bit her lip. "When do you find time to train? You are very adept with your sword."

"I trained when I was younger. I practice from time to time. There is always someone better."

She gathered that there was more than he was saying. Had he killed someone? "I have never been to see a fight. The duels that happen in Ashlin, are they very bloody?"

"They can be. If two equals meet, they can maim each other greatly."

"Do many die?"

"Sometimes the tradesmen do. They are never well-trained."

The square was close. Only one more block.

"How did we get into this mess, Mikel?" She couldn't keep herself from asking. The ache in her throat insisted on it.

"What mess?"

"You, stuck in your own world—a world that is going to the Derm, for certain—and me, with everything I believe, unable to love you in mine."

He stopped his horse, turned his head sideways, and she could see his profile against the gray backdrop of the street. She could almost hear his smile in the crisp morning. The shouts of the square sounded miles away, the snow floating about them forming a blanket of sweet stillness.

"Is that to say that you *would* love me? If it weren't for..."

Trzl nodded, not sure what she was promising, knowing she was on the brink of betraying everything she lived for. The decision felt huge, like a weight on her chest. "But you cannot stay here. And I must."

Mikel swung down and slid her off into his arms. "You pick a hellish time to tell me this." His face was close, his breath warm and gentle in her ear. "I would have asked you to run away with me. I only restrained myself because I want this to be right. We can't say this—*I* can't say that I love you—and then never speak again. And our loyalties force us to oppose each other."

She laid her head on his shoulder. "*You* pick a hellish time to want to love me."

"I haven't chosen this madness."

She stared at the ground for a moment. "If you're with me, the militia will not harm you. We'll figure this out together."

He balled a fist, clenched it and unclenched it, letting go of her. "Given another few weeks, all of Ashlin may be a smoking heap of rubble. Everything I own will be pillaged." He came to her again, put a hand to her cheek. "It is all or nothing for me. I cannot be what you are."

Trzl would have pounded his face if she thought it would make him understand. "*Why?* Once this reckoning has passed, Serengard will be beautiful beyond belief. Mikel, after this one fight—this one war, this one purge—nothing is going to change except for the better." She smiled, put a hand on his chest, where she imagined his heart might be. "I am certain of this."

He reached for her shoulders—something desperate in his eyes—but didn't touch her. "I know you believe this, but you are wrong. It will be mayhem and murder, destruction you cannot imagine. You have not seen the things you speak of. You don't know what turmoil is to come. We will have nothing when this is over. Many will die, and I do not want you among them. By the Treacher, Trzl." He paced, frustrated, his hand in his hair. "All I ask is that you go. Stay alive. Promise me that you will."

"I cannot leave yet." Trzl felt trapped between Mikel's logic and her own, angry that she found herself beginning to doubt. "My grandfather needs me in Ashlin. Everyone needs me in Ashlin, just a little while longer. I must stay until the fate of the city is decided."

"If you need anything—"

Trzl wiped a tear from the corner of her eye. "Can't we pretend that…none of this matters?"

"I'm sorry." He said no more. He mounted his horse and left her standing there.

{11}
Promise

DREMIR WAS SEATED IN A tiny tavern behind a heavy guard of his own, next to Kovim himself. Tonight was the night.

Whoever could not fit in the city was massing outside the gates. They did not have leaders or ranks of any sort, not yet. That wasn't going to happen in the next few hours. Tomorrow, if all went well, the Castle Guard would be annihilated, and then he would see about creating an army to deal with the Kymsai and Nersai...and the Border Guard.

The one thing that plagued him was the three hundred knights that had not reported to the king for years. No one knew how to find them or what their political thoughts could be—whether they would rush to reclaim Ashlin for the Orion family or not.

"Dremir, horses for storming the gates?"

"No, horses will get in the way."

"Most of the villagers have only axes and shovels. Have you run out of weapons?"

"Yes." All of the weapons provided by sympathizing Guard and Corsai had been distributed days ago. "Try to get the better armed near the front, right at the bridge."

Even Hodran stepped in briefly to ask if there were any more favors needed. Then he returned to the neutral ground of the Red Horse Tavern. As if the King had the time or resources to round up any more rebels for his dungeons. He was probably barricaded behind a dozen doors and praying to the Desert God at this very moment. The Guard was holed up in the Castle, waiting. They knew. Only this time, it wasn't going to help them.

"Have you seen Grandfather?"

Oh. There was Trzl. Did she plan to storm the gates tonight? Excellent plan. "Not since before midnight," Dremir told her.

"Where did he go?"

"He said he was going home for some books." That was just like him, too. At all moments, he wanted his books with him.

Trzl put both of her palms on the table. In her eyes was genuine worry. "Please, Dremir, don't you know anything else?"

"If I did know, I would tell you."

She turned to go, then stopped and asked him, "Have you heard anything about skirmishes outside of the city? Between the Guard and the new folk coming in?"

"There have been some minor engagements, but the Guard is in retreat. Not many casualties. Nothing out of our hands. Your grandfather would not have left the city."

"I know. But there are rumors that some knights are nearby. Not just the Castle Guard."

Where did she hear *that* rumor? Dremir wasn't sure he wanted to know.

"We can handle any of them. There are far more of us. And we have fire on our side." He smiled at her then, a real smile. They were so close to freedom, and he had plenty of right to be happy. He probably could not be cross with anyone today if he tried. Not even her.

"He is not at home. Can you not do something to find him?"

"A manhunt would be fruitless, I assure you. We are on the brink of our vindication, Trzl. He will turn up."

"Something is not right..."

"I am sure he is at home now."

Trzl looked lost and detached, a strange state for her. Dremir didn't question it. He had more important things to do tonight.

"Then I'll go...back," she said.

He watched her for only a moment, and then promptly forgot all about her.

TRZL SAW THEM BEFORE SHE started down the street. Castle Guard, at least half a dozen, dismounting in front of the house.

"Search the building," one of them called. "Find the girl."

She stifled a scream in the back of her throat, ran back down the cobblestones as fast as her tired legs would carry her. She felt for the parchment Mikel gave her. It was there, tucked inside her cinch.

The map was complete and detailed. It took her back to the high part of town, the Marble Quarter, the side where there were breezes and fresh air, though it was far too cold tonight to enjoy it. The street he indicated was closer to the Castle of Orion than she had ever dared venture, the area where the houses backed up against the castle wall for protection and easy access to the quarters of the Castle Guard.

It made her shudder. *Mikel cannot be one of the Guard, can he? Why would he send me here?*

Tonight, every window of every house was dark. How many were vacant, and how many pretended to be? Trzl wished she had gone back for her horse before the Guard came. Fears started to creep into her, possibilities that never quite seemed real. What would happen to her if Grandfather was dead? And if they knew that a girl lived there and she could be useful, then they had reason to want her as a prisoner as well. Was this what Mikel tried to warn her about? Did they have a list of the leaders? How would he know? Could *he* have turned her in?

There, at last, was the house. It was tall white stone with marble steps, much like the rest of the houses on the street. She stood before it, her thoughts swirling with suspicion. She had no choice but to trust him. She needed someone to help her find Grandfather. Someone who knew the city. Who knew the loyalists.

She bounded up the steps and banged on the door. A man with huge shoulders answered after her fourth knock. His hair was disheveled, his eyes bleary. He held a short, jagged weapon in his hand that glittered with a rich, copper tone. Seren steel. *One of the Guard.*

"What do you want?"

She felt foolish, blinking in the doorway with nothing to say. She held up the bit of parchment with Mikel's handwriting on it. "Mikel—told me to come here—if—"

The man caught her shoulder and pulled her inside. "Are you all right?"

"Yes. I need some help. I have to talk to Mikel."

"You cannot tell me what you need?"

"No, I have to see him."

The big man sighed, running a hand across his face. "I will send someone after him. Be seated. Get warm."

Trzl was not cold. She shivered because she was worried and because this house was strange. Growing up, she always assumed Grandfather was wealthy because their house had eight rooms. But this? Where would one even begin?

It felt like an hour before Mikel came through the door. He was much too aware to have been sleeping, his brow furrowed with concerns she could not have planted there.

"What is it?" he said.

All at once, it seemed a very sad thing to her that he was the only friend she could rely upon. And she had not even known where he lived or if he had siblings.

"Trzl, we do not have all night."

"Is there somewhere else we can go? The stable maybe?" She glanced around her at the fine house, raising her eyebrows. She didn't like to speak secrets in fine houses.

Mikel closed the door to the room. He drew her by the elbow over to the fire. It crackled and popped, causing cover that he must have deemed sufficient. "Tell me."

"Grandfather did not come home today. And when I went there, there was some of the Castle Guard there, and they were looking for me. I don't know why, unless they are... I'm scared."

"As well you should be. I told the man to leave. Serengard is about to be overturned. Once the lawlessness you so desire gains its foothold, it will be difficult to protect anyone at all. Especially those who paint targets on their foreheads."

Trzl recoiled passionately. "My grandfather is one of the leaders of our new utopia. If he is not dead, if he is in prison—"

"Trzl." His look was intense, focused. "I will do what I can. But I cannot promise anything, do you understand? And not until dawn. None of the gates will be open until then. Most certainly not the Castle Gate."

"Not until dawn?"

She succeeded in checking her tears, but the trembling of her body finally took over. She fell against him and he held her—awkward and rigid—guided her head to his shoulder and gently smoothed her hair. She didn't remember anyone having done that since she was a little girl. She had relied on her own strength for a long time now. Grandfather was too busy using his brain for other things.

Trzl let him hold her, until her head started to swim with other matters, and then she pulled away, groped for a chair. "Perhaps I should also go to the Corsai. He might know what to do."

Mikel became more alert than he'd been all night. The frown on his forehead deepened. "Hodran?"

"He wants to marry me. I am sure he—"

"You cannot marry him."

She had hoped he would say that. With that finality, that confidence. "He has not asked yet. I am not going to marry him if I can help it, but he is very powerful in the south as well as Ashlin. It would be an alliance—"

Mikel knelt in front of her chair, reached up and gripped the polished wooden arms of it. "You must not give yourself to him. I tell you this for your own sake, not out of any selfishness of mine."

"What do you know of him?" She wanted to plead with him for some reason why she should be with him instead of staying with Hodran. There must be a reason.

"More than you would like to know." He stood up, turned away from her, walked back. "Please, you must simply believe me. I cannot recount his sins as they're not my secrets to tell."

"Are you speaking of my safety? Because he could be a ruler of Serengard if the rebels succeed? Or be hung if they lose?"

"The ruler? I hadn't heard. That makes your goal of dethroning a sane king even more rotten. And no, I am not speaking of that kind of danger. You have proven you can survive that, even revel in the midst of it." He ran a hand across a forehead that was beginning to sweat.

"What then?"

"You might see no sin in it, being a progressive, but a man like him uses women as playthings. A means to an end. A quick drink and then—" Mikel leaned a hand on the mantle and looked toward her under his arm, then away again. "Marry me. I will treat you far better. And do not make me beg for you."

She stared at him, stared at the floor, at the deep teal curtains in the corner. Fine velvet and silk. Something she always despised with the greatest vehemence, and now the lot fell to her to choose between two rich men. She put her fingers to her tired eyelids and tried to think. Tried to bring on the dawn. Tried to keep it away a few moments longer.

Mikel must have crossed some threshold in his mind—something that made all of his caution invalid—because he ran to her, pulled her hands away from her face. "Come away with me. I know you love me. Say that you do."

"I do. But I cannot... I cannot..." *I promised Grandfather. I promised Serengard.*

Then she could not speak anymore because he was pulling her from the chair, pressing her against the wall, against the fine teal curtains, kissing her with an abandon she didn't fully understand. Something white as a fresh fire, not yet burned down.

"I wanted to marry you since I first saw you," he murmured against her cheek, then he nudged her mouth open again, making it impossible to breathe, impossible to move, until his lips trailed from her chin to her neck and she fell against him, the air bursting from her lungs.

"You could have said."

"I didn't want to scare you." He kept kissing the back of her neck, the touch of his mouth far from seductive. It was worshipful. A worship she wanted to return, but wasn't sure she knew how. She just basked in it.

"I would if only—"

"Hang Hodran, love. I can claim you for my own if you wish it." His voice was raw, breaking for a moment. He brushed the velvet wrap from her shoulder and ran his face across the bare skin.

"What...?" But yes, that was exactly what she wanted. He would change once they were married. He would have to stay with her, and she could protect him. "How will you do that?"

"If Hodran formally asked for you—"

"He asked to court me."

Mikel kept his lips to her shoulder, but she could hear the warmth in his voice. "He may challenge me for your hand."

"He is an excellent swordsman."

"I am far better." He looked in her eyes and a faint smile played across his face. "And he is already afraid of me."

The door opened, and the stocky man beckoned Mikel. He spoke low to him, words she could not hear. Trzl watched Mikel's jaw tighten, darkness fall back on his brow. He said quickly, in a clipped voice, "I am needed. And it is almost dawn. Stay here and you will be safe."

Trzl nodded, and he was gone.

{12}
Ветгачаl

BUT SHE DID NOT STAY.

A few minutes of thought, and then the soft tentacles of dawn crept into the room. It was dead silent in the street outside the window, but a dull humming sound came from the direction of the square. She must go. Must see if the soldiers left her home. If maybe, just maybe, Grandfather had come back.

It took several minutes longer, following the southern road through the Merchant Quarter, coming around behind their flat. She didn't see anyone, but the back door was barred from the outside. She heard a shout from one of the side streets, hunkered down behind a barrel, waited for them to pass, but their steps moved north. Keeping her breath in as much as she could, she moved toward the back door.

A soldier caught her by the arms before she set foot on the steps. She fought him, but he was quite tall and muscular, and a second man came to help. Had they followed her from the Marble Quarter?

"Where is my grandfather?" she demanded as her hands were caught and bound.

There were eight soldiers in the detachment. They were jumpy, on edge. The one who grabbed her tossed her up to an older man. Quickly, as if she were a pox he meant to stay clear of. The rest of them mounted and formed double ranks behind him.

"This way," the leader of their troop said.

"Where are you taking me?" Trzl demanded.

"Say no more words, and you might live through this day."

There was shouting and screaming in the square. She smelled smoke—not the kind a wood fire makes. Something akin to heavy pitch was burning and a lot of it. They moved urgently, the horses at twice the pace of a carriage.

The square opened before them, teeming with people she did not recognize. It had finally happened, as Grandfather said it would. People from every corner of Serengard were pressing into Ashlin, hoards of them still outside the gate of the city, streaming down from the hills in wide, dark bands. There were thousands. Tens of thousands.

God was on their side. Fire was on their side, as Dremir said.

Trzl felt a rush of exhilaration. Here it was—now, today! She wanted to raise her arms to the sky, to yell with the rest of them, but she was under guard. Might get swatted on the head. Or knocked out. And the square was not yet full enough nor armed enough to take on the impressive bunch that guarded her, that was pushing her through the crowd with their powerful horses.

Suddenly she realized that she and Grandfather might never see the utopia they had struggled to begin. They might be sacrificed on this altar—the taking of their lives the last guilty deed of a doomed king.

The smoke came from a dark stack of brush several stories high that was piled against the wall of the castle courtyard. It billowed black smoke and did not seem to do any damage, but how it got there, across the bridge and through the guards, was a feat. Trzl smiled to herself. Dremir had his ways. And it would inflict a good deal of damage once the fire burned long and hot enough. She was about to try her luck at swinging about to see more when a knight decked out in full battle costume rode heavily toward them from the castle.

When he was within shouting distance, he yelled, "All Castle Guard and Border Guard in the city are ordered to the castle."

"We are to escort this prisoner—" their lead rider began.

"To the castle," the knight said again.

They went, through the mob—a mob that pulled at the armored Guard, at the feet and their horses, but still lacked the strength to stop their stampede to the temporary safety of the thick stone walls.

Please. Please be stronger. Please rescue me. Storm these walls and save Grandfather, too.

The heavy gate crashed tightly shut behind them. A man pulled her roughly from her horse and dragged her to the central courtyard. He was stopped by yet another man in battle garb, all ranks she did not recognize.

"Stop. Where are you taking this prisoner? And why do we have another one at this late hour?"

"She was supposed to be escorted from the city. We were ordered back here before—"

"Who gave the order to remove her from the city?"

"The Prince did, sir."

The knight grumbled. "Take her to the Prince, then. I was not informed of this affair."

"As you say, sir."

Her escort caught her by her bound wrists and dragged her back to the front of the castle, toward the door they just came through.

Trzl was confused. Was there something happening outside the city she didn't know about? She shuddered. Maybe the Guard was evacuating. Maybe they were holding rebel hostages outside the gates. Maybe they were executing them, even as she meant to execute the Kymsai.

"Where are you taking me?"she asked.

"I'll thank you not to ask questions. As you can see we are a bit under siege, in a manner of speaking." He chuckled, maybe a bit nervously. "Crazy rioting commoners. You never know what they are thinking."

"Do you know what might have happened to the old man they call the Pitching Boar?"

He laughed. "Good thing we didn't hang him. Would have made these people crazier."

"So he is alive?"

"Best not to push your luck, little girl. I am not about to risk my own neck telling stories to you, understand?"

They reached a set of long, winding stairs. There was an open balcony at the top and a handful of men up there, all of them muscular and broad shouldered. Or perhaps their armor made them look so. She was finally scared through and through. There was no escaping this place, was there? No one to bribe or distract.

The guard gripped her again by her hands. "Come on."

"All the way up there?"

He did not answer, simply started to drag her. She tried to keep up, tried to keep from tripping. Her cloak was heavy, the stairs were steep, and she was tired from running all over the city.

"Wait," she gasped. "I will walk. You mustn't drag me!"

"We haven't time to waste. Have to ask the Prince what he wants done with you before the last gates of the city are closed. Unless you would rather die today, maybe be fed to the mob?"

She glared at him silently, tried to climb faster. Her shins were bruised and her pride more so by the time he flung her across the landing. Knights turned to look at her—a few of them—but the rest continued to plot, to discuss as if she were not even here. She looked at the fine armor, the cold light of the winter sun just coming over the horizon, teal flags chopping madly against the azure of the barely lit sky.

Her accompanying guard stepped forward and bowed in front of one of the men in heavy armor. All she could see was the man's back. It was covered with the banner of Orion—indicative of his royal blood—and his cuffs and insignia showed he was the Captain of the Guard. The Prince. She wished for a weapon so she could slit his throat.

"Captain," the guard said, "we were unable to escort this prisoner from the city, due to your orders to the contrary."

The Prince of Serengard turned brusquely, annoyed at the interruption. "Which prisoner?"

Trzl screamed when she saw his face, a scream that was stifled quickly by her own hands. "You lied to me," she growled.

The faces of the knights were bemused, surprised at the revelation. The Prince walked to her and untied her hands himself.

"I did not lie to you," Mikel Orion whispered through clenched teeth. She tried to hit him, but he caught her hands in midair. He raised his voice to the others. "If you will excuse us for a moment."

They took their leave. Alone and facing him, Trzl pulled away while attempting to free her hands. "You made me think you were only a landowner."

He took a step toward her for each she took away from him. "Did it truly matter? I didn't change who I was, Trzl. I meant every word."

"You were playing with me. Amusing yourself with a charade."

"Playing a charade to you would not amuse me." He lost his cool, his demeanor becoming resolute and uncompromising—someone she knew he was underneath. "If I wanted a woman who would use my position to her own ends, I could have found plenty who knew I was the King's son. I wanted you to know me as a man, not a prince. I am no heir to the throne. You've nothing to fear from any regime of mine."

"But you are everything I despise. You make this country rich on the backs of us, you make yourself lord over people who are no lesser than yourself, you pass judgment and punish according—"

His hand clamped over her mouth and he swallowed hard, his eyes blinking oddly. "Spare me your memorized denouncement. I do not believe a word of it is the workings of your own mind, as you know me far better than that. You're only repeating your grandfather and your friends."

She stood there, the rage breaking through her skin, unable to fathom how low he must truly be to thus insult her mind. "You are the Captain of the Guard." She spat her breath onto his face. "Your sword will slice the skin of my friends in a few short hours."

"If they storm that wall, yes. But only because they are trying to kill my family. And I will kill as many of them as I can. They have made their choice."

Trzl kept her chin in the air, her eyes locked with his, her arms trying to twist away from him. "What do you plan to do to me?"

Mikel said nothing. His head tipped to the side as if to say he had no plan. But she was still here, awaiting his judgment, a commoner caught in misconduct. His grip loosened.

She finally succeeded in getting one hand free, and she pulled it up to defend herself. "You can keep me here in your horrid prison. Do what you will to me. Tie me up and beat me, if that is what you do to rebel women you seduce in the countryside. Or treat me nicely, if you wish, but I will never marry you now. Our blood is on your hands. All of our blood. Blood you should respect and love because it is the only reason you have breathed this long."

His laugh was far too hollow—not really a laugh at all. "If freedom is what you want, I will see that you escape the city." He looked out over the charging, smoking din of Ashlin.

"I do not want to leave. Not without Grandfather."

He ignored that. "If I die here, Trzl, remember that I loved you. That I would have—that you held me in your palm with your fire. Will you do that much for me?"

She did not answer. *You pursued me*, her mind yelled at him. *You made me want you, body and soul. And you are a man of violence. Of cold, bloody dictatorship without fairness.*

"Trzl?"

"I should have known." It came out a raspy whisper. "When you lopped off the arms of those three thieves—as if you had the right to punish them—I should have known who you were."

"I was merciful. If I were a man of more passion and less mind, I would have killed them."

Trzl shivered at the honesty in his voice. "I will do my utmost to forget I ever knew you. Because I have not known you."

His jaw tightened, but he walked away from her to one of his men. All she heard was, "See that she leaves the city."

part two
Cliffs

Pride and humiliation hand in hand

Walked with them through the world where'er they went;

Trampled and beaten were they as the sand,

And yet unshaken as the continent.

— H.W. Longfellow

{13}
Revenge

The outer reaches of the new Seren Empire, called The Four Cities.
Ten years later.

THERE WERE THREE ANIMAL SKINS in the corner. No matter how Trzl wrapped herself she could not keep warm. She sobbed, off and on, but not for herself. If Malcom's cell was like this—if he was alone and cold, if there were rats running about—and all these tales, these ghost stories were true—

Malcom could be dead already. They could have sold him into slavery. He could be sick. They might not be feeding him well, taking care of him properly.

Only a day and a night had passed, but it seemed an immeasurable amount of time before her cell door opened. The light of a lone candle blinded her for a moment, but she managed to get up and meet the figure who entered. It was hard to move. Her muscles ached from the hard ride and another night without sleep.

"Malcom?" she called. Her voice cracked.

"The Master said we could feed you now."

It wasn't Mikel, and he didn't have Malcom. She put a hand to the side of her head, told herself to breathe, to stay calm, while everything inside of her threatened to erupt into a mad mess of screams for her child. The man who entered was slim and lithe with a reddish tint to his hair and cool blue eyes. Even in the dim light, she could see he was middle-aged, perhaps thirty.

"Thank you." Trzl stammered it out, not bothering to reach for the platter he set a few paces from her.

He picked it up again and placed it in front of her on the cold stone. "Do you have a name?"

There was steam coming from the bowl. It was hot. Trzl pulled it toward her.

"Trzl," she told him.

He nodded sagely. He already knew. "I am Pier."

She brought the spoon to her lips and savored the hot liquid in her mouth. "You are not a Seren."

"Those of us who live in the cliffs are simply renegades, m'lady."

"The soup is good."

"More where that came from. My wife made it."

"Is my son... Did you feed him? Is he well?"

"I'm afraid I cannot tell you."

Trzl dug her fingernails against the cold stone. "Why do you have us here?"

"I cannot tell you that either, miss. Lord Marek has ordered it."

"You know who he is? I mean, who he really is."

Pier looked at her as if puzzled, but his voice was stern. "I'm sure you don't mean to imply anything evil about the Lord of the Cliffs. And if you do, I'm sure you will forget it before it gets you killed."

The man she had seen in that momentary glimpse had been nothing like the Mikel she remembered. Was it really him? Or had she only imagined...the voice, the eyes...

She gripped Pier's wrist—a slim, artisan wrist. "You must tell me my son is alive."

"He is not dead, m'lady. And neither are you." Pier smiled and stood to leave, light falling across his face to accentuate a sharp, freckled nose. "Best eat all of that. Lord Marek may change his mind about your food."

MALCOM HAD NEVER BEEN IN a castle before. He'd never been anywhere beyond the village of Klevt unless you counted the trips to the meadow to cut hay and chase frogs or going fishing with the boys from the corner.

He didn't mind the fact that it was dark, or that there was no music. He minded that he couldn't see his mem. But for the most part, it was not all that bad. There were other boys to play with, and they taught him a new game with glass marbles, even gave him one. He didn't own any marbles.

The tall man with the short beard came every once in a while, looked at him, and left. Malcom didn't think it was strange until the time he came and told him plainly, "Come."

He was used to being bossed by the parents of his friends, but none of them were cliffmen. They didn't carry swords and wear strange symbols on their chests and weird dangles in their ears. They weren't ghosts, as these ruffians were supposed to be. Apparently he didn't obey fast enough because another cliff man—a short, puny one—seized Malcom by the arm and lifted him to his feet.

"Lord Marek tells you to come, you must come."

Malcom nodded like a good boy, but he kept his fist clenched just in case he had to fight. The little cliffman would be easier to take, for sure. And he had a small knife in his belt that was just level with Malcom's shoulder.

The cliffman held tightly to his arm all the way down four sets of steps through a long tunnel that dripped and squeaked with mice. The sound reminded him of home. He liked mice. When they stopped, he could see nothing but iron bars. He heard the sound of a key turning in a lock. The taller man, the one called Marek, held a hand up to the shorter one, telling him to wait. Then he stepped in, leaving them outside. Malcom could not see into the room for the glare of the torch, but he heard voices. Mem ran at the dark figure of Marek and clawed at him, her fingers making a scraping sound on the leather that encased his chest.

Malcom grew frantic all at once. He'd not seen Mem all day. He was afraid for her, at first, but then he thought she was probably busy talking to grown-ups in some other room. But she was down here? In the dark?

"Mem!" He tried to run to her. Hands held him back, but he was a strong boy. He reached for the bars and gripped them.

"Wait," the short cliffman whispered. "Your mother cannot see you now."

Malcom could hear the voices, echoing clearly out of the room, so he kept quiet. He needed to hear this. It might tell him how to get Mem out.

Mem was saying, "You must let me have him." He heard her crying, saw her beating Marek's chest, thought she started to say something like, "If you ever... Mik—"

Then Marek put a hand to her mouth and whispered, but the whisper was loud. "Marek. Or so help me, Trzl, you won't last a day here. I haven't many reasons to keep you alive. You are a liability in every form."

Malcom wasn't sure what that was supposed to mean, but she grew silent for a moment. Marek was tall and heavy and frightful. Malcom didn't like him being that close to his mother. Especially when he flung her away from him and walked about her, circling slowly as a wild cat might.

"You can see that he is well."

"Damn you, let me hold him!"

"You may. After you give me what I require."

The flickering of the torch outside was only enough light to see the shine of tears on Mem's cheeks, the glint of Marek's hard leather armor, and the length of the sword he wore.

"I will give you anything for Malcom."

Malcom wanted to yell to Mem *not* to give him anything. He was fine. She was the one who needed rescuing. And he planned to find a way to do that.

"Oh, you misunderstand me. I will not let you keep him. You may see him, for a time, if you tell me what I want to hear."

Mem stared at Marek, her eyes smoldering. She was angry. Good. Mem got smart and strong when she was angry. But then she looked down and mumbled submissively, "What do you want?"

"I was told you know the sequences to the gates of the Four Cities."

"The sequences?"

"Don't play innocent. You were involved in all of it. I know."

"They have been changed by now."

Marek smiled. "Do you take me for a fool? I know the design. I know they cannot be changed. I know there are only a handful who learned the sequences, and you are one of them."

Malcom wasn't sure what they were talking about. It sounded like a game, but the Four Cities was not a phrase Mem liked to hear. Even glimpsing the flag was enough to make her purse her lips and walk away quickly.

"No, I did not...learn them. And they can be changed."

"You're lying." He opened the door to leave. "Maybe you'll be ready to talk tomorrow."

"No, Mi—Marek. Let me see Malcom just for a moment. Please."

She reached her long arms toward Marek and grasped at his legs. Malcom felt rage bubble up in him. Mem should never have to grovel at the feet of a man that way. He wished he knew the sequences—whatever they were—so that he could fix this and they could go home.

"Mem! Tell him," he yelled.

Marek slammed the door and turned the key in the lock. Mem stood up and ran for the bars, but Malcom was caught around the waist and dragged away, back down the corridor and up the steps. As soon as the hold loosened, he snatched Marek's arm, the one holding the torch. He pulled it to his mouth and took a gouge out with his teeth before the hand was yanked away.

Marek stopped walking and knelt down, looked Malcom in the eyes. "What was that for?"

"You hurt my mem."

"I didn't hurt her, Malcom."

"Don't say my name."

Marek actually smiled—a sad, empty smile. "How old are you?"

"Nine. I'm almost ten, though."

The smile disappeared. "Dermed blackguard," was all he said.

THE DARKNESS WAS TOO THICK for Trzl to decide whether another day had passed, but she assumed it had, as she was fed twice before they came for her.

It wasn't Mikel this time. She could not help but think that did not bode well for her survival. But if he really wanted the gate sequences, then surely he would not kill her immediately.

There were two men, both of them ruggedly built. They had long, tangled hair that fell a full foot past the shoulders, adorned with metal rings to weigh it down. Their clothing consisted of heavy coats made of animal skins, belts laden with jagged weapons crossing their chests. They led her up several staircases, through corridors that curved and turned over each other. Eventually they were lit with natural light and she realized this was not a cave, nor a dungeon; it was a fortress. Perhaps the

Castle of Marek? She was always told it was here, among the cliffs, and the cliff folk lived here, subsisting on the blood and bones of whatever carcasses the cold dragons left.

Whatever it was, they had clean, well-kept chambers on the higher levels. Trzl glanced into every room they passed, telling herself it was important to know her surroundings when in truth she was cultivating an idle hope that she would glimpse Malcom. Of a surety, Mikel would keep him far away from her, but the desire was still there, dominating her thoughts.

She was tossed into a room with four girls and a crackling fire. The men slammed the door behind her, and she stood quickly. She hadn't looked closely at the men's faces, but the women did not resemble the hill folk at all. Their skin was like the soft side of a tanned goat hide—creamy gray and thick. Their brows were dark, but their hair and eyes were mixed. They all wore bright red, their collars clustered with adornments.

A girl with black hair and white freckles spoke first. "You must be bathed before you see Lord Marek."

Then Trzl noticed the copper tub, the steaming water. The other three came forward, removed her clothes and plunked her in without ceremony. It was an odd, strange feeling to be waited on. Had royalty been treated this way? If so, Mikel was even more spoiled than she thought.

"Are you paid to do this?"

The girls laughed in unison. "This, we don't do much," one of them said. "Not for anyone besides our filthy brothers." They all laughed again.

"Are you slaves then? Am I now a slave?" *Not to him. Please, not to him.*

The plain girl spoke again, shrugging her thin shoulders. "*You* may be a slave. They told us nothing. They never tell us." This, apparently, was also a joke. "We are none of us slaves. We keep the castle for Lord Marek. His warriors protect us from other raiders."

His men protect you? Trzl wanted to laugh but did not think it polite. *These men keep you around because you are useful. Nothing more.*

Her bath was conducted with a sad lack of salts or oils of any kind, and the rough version of soap made her skin hurt. In the hill country villages, modern conveniences were available from the peddlers who came through, and she had a stash of coin tucked away for procuring all those things. It could still be in her house. The marauders did not waste time searching for anything. Maybe she could pay Mikel to let them go.

Not likely. He seemed to be doing fine here.

"When will I see my boy?"

"You have a boy?" one of them asked, handing her a clean change of clothes and a soft-haired brush. The clothing was an odd, woven wool tapestry, dyed bright red as theirs was. Trzl hated the shape of it. Large and billowy. She wanted her old dress back.

"Marek took him captive, too." Trzl took the clothing and stepped into it without comment.

"*Lord* Marek," one of them corrected. "You want to attract the goblins by making them think there is no lord at the Castle of Marek?"

Clever, Mikel. Fine way to satisfy your need to be worshiped.

"How old is your boy?"

"Is he handsome?"

"I would like to meet him."

"I am sure he is locked up, as you were."

"What is his name?"

"Malcom," Trzl broke in, then became annoyed that she told them anything about him. No one here wanted to help her.

"You are all clean. Do not move while I pin your hair."

"Pin it?"

"It must be up under your headdress so that no one will see it."

Trzl stuck her chin out. "I don't want it hidden. Leave it as it is."

"Down? That would be improper."

"It is proper in my country."

"Lord Marek may not understand—"

"He will understand."

The girls shrugged and, thankfully, did not bother her further. They banged on the door. The two men who brought her reentered and seized her arms.

Up more steps. Down some steps. Into a long, wide hall that must have spanned several stories in height. A long shaft of sunlight shone through a window at the very top, silhouetting a falcon that was perched on its sill. Or *was* it a falcon? It looked just like the terrible, shrieking bird that frightened Malcom on their way here.

Rich carpet started about two-thirds into the hall and ran to the far end, leading up some long, shallow steps to a large wooden chair. Trzl gulped just looking at it.

The men escorting her pulled her into a room off the side. It was not half as huge as the hall and had no windows, lit instead by sentinels of torches set into the wall and several dozen candles arranged on a table. There were six men in the room, most with beards and far too many weapons on their belts to set her at ease. She stood there, looking at them, trying to determine which was Mikel, but no one turned to look at her.

He wasn't Mikel anymore, she reminded herself. He was Lord Marek in every way possible. She heard his voice, somewhere over at the table, low.

One of her guards made a gruff announcement. "The prisoner you requested, my lord."

It was reminiscent in wording—though utterly unlike the accent of the Castle Guard—of the phrase spoken of her in Ashlin ten years ago. Thrown at his mercy and surrounded by his men. The memory gave her a shiver.

"Leave her there," Lord Marek said, not bothering to look up.

He was standing at the table, a map spread before him, his bearded, warlike men gathered loosely about him. They were casting a glance now and then, talking in their hushed voices.

At last, he raised his head and frowned at her. "Why is she not kneeling?"

That was just like him. Trzl felt herself fuming, but she knelt as he suggested. He finally turned all the way around, letting the light fall on his face so she could see the carefully controlled blankness in his eyes. Then he strode toward her, his hand on the hilt of his sword as if he thought she might assault him. An aide trailed behind him a few paces.

"What is your name?"

She blinked at his ruse. "You should know my name."

"Please tell us."

"Trzl. Daughter of Sakar of Neroi."

"Is the boy your own?"

"Yes."

"By whom did you have him?"

He *would* ask, wouldn't he. Trzl spoke as quietly as she could. "He is Hodran's son."

"Speak louder if you would." He *had* heard her. She saw the ripple of anger course through him, saw his gloved fingers curl against his palm.

"By Hodran of Neroi, the Chamberlain of the Second City."

"We know who the man is," the aide behind him fairly spewed.

"Enough, Tev," Marek said.

Trzl stared at the stones, trying not to look up at him. Not to get slapped by the aide's glove. The next question came as a half-laugh, quietly, low in his throat.

"Were you never his wife?"

"No. I was never his wife."

"You are certain the child is his?"

"Yes."

There was a stirring in the room, an obvious expression of discontent. Marek spoke from where he stood, keeping his eyes on her.

"Skommek, I stand humbled by your intuition. We have certainly been fed a falsehood."

{14}
Understandings

TRZL LET HER EYES DART up and take in the other faces. It occurred to her of a sudden that long ago, in Ashlin, Mikel may have had other spies planted inside their group of rebel friends. How else would he now find himself alive, surrounded by loyal supporters? But not only were the rest of their jaws covered with beards, they were different in feature than any Seren. Many of them were dark of brow with grayish skin, while others had sharp angular faces that could be from the west.

The man Marek had just spoken to, Skommek, looked to be the oldest in the room. He twisted a stocky finger in his beard and squinted at her. "Seems she can be of better use to us if she knows our situation."

Marek snorted. "I am in great doubt that we can rely on this woman for anything." He glared at her. "Woman, you are a friend of the Seren leader Kovim, are you not?"

"Of—the Emperor?" She fairly choked on the words. She did not want to visit this memory. Not now.

"You heard my question. Best answer before we all tire of the sound of your breath and one of us slits your throat."

If you were going to slit my throat, Mikel, you'd have found a reason to do it before now. She almost wanted to call his bluff. It would serve him right.

"You have asked me a very subtle question. There are many who would name themselves his friend to save their skin, yet I am sure the Emperor himself would admit to very few in return."

"Her riddles are unending." Marek kept a finger next to his mouth as if to keep words from flying out. "I would think you would have a greater respect—if not for me, for the show of force in this room. If you insist upon these aversions, I will be forced to ask you bluntly. Has he fathered children with you?"

She knew her face betrayed a personal disgust and probably a slight dose of anger. He should know better than to ask if she had made a whore of herself. Did he expect her to take that kind of accusation like a lady? He was mistaken.

Then she thought of it. A way to get out of this room full of faces who knew nothing of the cat-and-mouse game their Lord Marek was playing with her.

"I will tell you everything you wish to know…if I may speak to your leader alone."

Marek smiled at her, a distant, whimsical smile that said, *And here it is.* "You may, but you had better not disappoint me."

Instead of emptying the room, he tipped his head in the direction of a smaller chamber. The men who brought her rudely picked her up and hauled her. Marek pushed open the heavy door himself and waited while she was again deposited on her knees.

"Speak, Trzl."

She waited until the door closed behind the men. Alone in a room with him, he seemed to own the very air she breathed. His shoulders were draped with the fur of a wild cat and they towered above her like an omen. Had he really been this tall when she knew him before?

She carefully avoided his eyes, but her voice still came out timid and raspy. "As your man said. If you will tell me what is happening, surely I can be of better use to you?"

"I'll tell you enough. Bounty hunters the kingdom over are looking for you. Naturally, my men—being the fastest and best-trained, and our informants loyal because we pay well—were the first to find you. Bounty as high as yours brings promise of grain for the winter, sheep in the spring. You'll forgive my men for being angry that you were not Kovim's mistress." He watched her relief. "Or are you going to tell me what I want to hear: that Malcom is his, and five hundred coin in pure gold is ours to claim."

She sniffed once, more than a little pleased that his plans were going awry. "Malcom is mine. He is all mine."

"His father?"

"Hodran did not want him. He hated him."

"And your relation to the Emperor. Purely friendship?" There was a sneer in there, certainly.

"It was."

"I know there is more to this. You're hiding it from me."

"Am I?"

He sighed and walked away from her. "I know you are untrustworthy, Trzl, but as I said, the show of force in the room..." Marek waited for her to slowly glance up, just enough to see the curved blade on his waist and the long sword swinging near to the ground. The sword was light and thin, the old style of the Castle Guard. He must have kept it—or stolen it somewhere. "Well?"

"Nothing happened. Kovim tried to seduce me, but I would have none of him, and he asked Hodran to give me to him. I said no. Rumors started, I suppose."

"Oh, the Chamberlains can give their wives to each other if they wish? But by your own admission, you were not his wife to give."

"He wouldn't have done it," she said. "Hodran was never one to cower to Kovim. He was going to marry me, as soon as his second wife left."

Marek sputtered, something like a laugh. "And you believed him?"

No. But she didn't want him to know she'd been jaded by a skunk. "I was his favorite."

"His favorite." He stalked to a window. "Oh, you have come a long way. Out of the business of destroying peaceful kingdoms and into comforting the vermin who covet them. I am exceedingly proud of your exploits. You have the true heart of a saber tooth."

She threw her face up and looked him in the eyes. He let her look. His hair was grown out in a wavy mop that fell partway down his neck, his beard trimmed to less than an inch from his face—a counterpoint to his warriors and their bushiness. She thought she saw scars there, beneath the rough whiskers, cuts and gouges he meant to hide. His hair had turned darker, like the dirty sand of the southern rivers. Did the cliff air change a man that much? He did not look like Mikel. Not a thing like Mikel.

But the eyes—they were his. His soul was pulled deep and away, leaving them shadowed and forbidding, green and Orion-shaped.

"What happened to you?"

"I could ask the same of you." His face tipped to the side and out of the light. "What are you doing all the way out here, Trzl? Favorite of the Chamberlain and all?"

"I wasn't looking to be abducted by marauders if you're wondering."

"You have less secrets than you imagine. I know of your involvement in the border campaigns. You're not so innocent as you like to make out. What happened? Get a little too cozy with the new regime? Did they want more from you?"

That was exactly what happened, but she wanted to slap him for guessing it. "Does the Emperor want me dead? Because I know things?"

"I did not think it at first, but I am becoming convinced." He turned his back to her again and focused on the crackling fire in the grate. It gave her a chance to glance about the room, to look at the objects it contained and try to understand their purposes. But her eyes were riveted to his back as it rose and fell, as more words came in cold, brittle curiosity. "What use is your boy to them if he is not in line to be Emperor?"

"You have been away from The Four Cities a long time. It matters not whom the Emperor's son is. Kovim's family is not established as a king's, nor does he rule as one. We have done better than you think."

"We? You still call yourself a part of that lot?"

"I helped form them. They're still mine, even if I am not theirs."

His eyes narrowed. "I ask again, what did Hodran have you doing out here? Don't tell me you were looking for me."

"No. They think you are dead."

"So you say."

Trzl wanted to tell him everything—just as she wanted to listen to him and follow him about from painting to painting at the Derev Theatre a lifetime ago—but he was far worse than a loyalist now. She couldn't trust him. "I told you. Hodran hated Malcom. I had to leave before he was old enough to understand. Better he have no father."

Marek was quiet then, long enough she started to wonder if he'd even been listening.

"Marek?"

"*Lord* Marek to you." He knelt of a sudden, his eyes now level with hers. His hand went for her chin, and he held it still, looking narrowly into her eyes. Then he let go with something like a shove, pushing her cheek away from him. "Both you and your grandfather have always had an uncanny ability for getting whatever you want. I haven't a whit of patience left for you, as I've no way of knowing whether I am being played. I'll thank Allel you have a bastard son I can use to make you speak if you continue to pretend to care for him."

She reached for him in a pleading gesture, trying to keep her emotions in check. "Give me Malcom."

"Not yet. I will need more from you than this. And I will use Malcom to get it. Mark me." He reached for the door and then stopped. "You should be grateful I found you first. You would be in worse hands by now if any other raiders took you."

"I liked you better as a pompous Nersai," Trzl spat.

"So did I."

He opened the door and gestured for her to stand and walk out.

"The boy is worthless," Marek said aloud.

Skommek said, "But the price is still on their heads, even if he is not the Emperor's son. Surely a ruse—"

"If our purchasers discover that he is not, which they no doubt will, we will not get paid. Or worse, we will make ourselves enemies where first there were friends. I will not risk any more than we must."

Trzl was standing in the doorway behind Marek, forgotten, until Skommek nodded to her. "The woman—she is also useless?"

"Not entirely. She belonged to the Chamberlain of the Second City. She may have information we can use."

One of the men said loudly, "Can she get us the sequences to one of the Four Cities? Desert People will pay well for them."

Trzl shifted behind Marek, wished he would move, would let her go to a corner alone. Instead, he reached behind him and caught her arm in a tight, warning grip. "I greatly doubt that," his voice said, even, tempered.

Trzl was not so controlled. She felt herself gulping, her throat tight. He had just lied to his men...for her. What did he hope to gain by that? Were they untrustworthy? Maybe their situation was worse than she thought, and that was saying something.

"We've more ways of amassing food this winter?" someone asked.

"Our food is plentiful, as always, Gernan," Marek said. "And we've enough ore to trade for new sheep in the spring. You speak of luxuries."

Gernan said, "We tire of eating the eggs of cliff birds. Dermed wild-cat meat is tough and tasteless."

"It was good enough for all of you before I and my men made you feared and wealthy," Marek snapped back, then looked up at the aide that again shadowed him. "Tev."

Tev took out goatskins with charcoal sketches on them, motioning with a gloved hand. "Skommek and his sons will head north to trade for sheep, mounts, and wives on the next full moon, bringing with them one from every family who wishes to go. We have much in pelts and ore as usual, as the year has been good for them."

"Other than that?"

"Nothing to be done before winter. Food for the horses has already been arranged. Payment can be delayed—"

"You're forgetting the Cities," Gernan persisted. "If Desert folk pilfer what is needed to make fearsome war with the Cities, our folk will be paid for help in raiding them."

Tev looked tentatively at Marek. "We would rather not aid the Desert People, yes? They will leave many a dead commoner in their wake, and the city dwellers outnumber them ten to one. It would be slaughter."

Marek was in a foul mood. "They are fools to try to destroy the Cities." He pulled Trzl by the arm and handed her off to her escorts again. "Take her to her room. Bar the door and guard it."

"Where are you going?" Tev asked.

"To speak to her son. Maybe *he* can tell me something."

Trzl struggled against the arms that held her. "He can't. Malcom knows nothing about any of this. He was a baby."

Marek ignored her.

His men escorted her to a new room, one with a barred window and the skin of a large cat for a rug. If Malcom told him nothing, maybe they could go. Maybe this bounty was a misunderstanding. But would it make a difference? Marek knew what she did in the war. He remembered.

Trzl grit her teeth. Now that he had her, he would find a way to punish her. She knew he would.

{ 15 }
Uses

"YOU WANT TO SEE YOUR mother?"

"Yes." Malcom turned at the sound of a new voice. Its owner had a sharp nose and freckles, a mop of dark russet hair, and a clean-shaven jaw.

"Then come this way, boy."

The corridors of this castle were winding, confusing. It made Malcom feel smaller and smaller. These turning passages that came back on themselves and over each other until one was not sure just where they were. He knew this was an obsession from the time of the first Derev Orion, so this castle must be older than sin.

He felt especially smart right now. Here he was, solving the stuff of legends, things his friends from the hill country barely spoke of for fear of provoking the goblins.

He never really believed the legends, he told himself now. Mem-Mem told him that there were tales in this country that held no truth, and she owned books that had the right of it. (Goblins and faeries were real, though, of that he was sure. He had friends who saw them when they stayed out too late at night.) She also said that, near the sea, there were rooms fairly brimming with books and that someday they would go there. But he already thought he was smart enough.

"Why is there a mist?" Malcom asked. "In my village, when it rains, it also storms. Wild, with lightning."

"The rain in the cliffs is gentle," the man answered. "Storms only come in the winter, and then the winds drive everyone from their round huts and into the underbelly of the castle. The last Lord Marek did not allow his people to live in the castle at all. He was also a lousy fighter, and he did not train his warriors nor provide for his people."

Malcom frowned, trying not to become confused. "Where did *our* Lord Marek come from?"

"No one knows," the man said quickly, but he half-smiled and Malcom knew it was a joke.

They met Lord Marek striding toward them, and he cupped an arm around Malcom's shoulder, changing their direction.

Malcom shook him off. "When do I get to see Mem?"

The two men exchanged a look and no words, but Malcom could tell Lord Marek was not happy. He kept walking and said, "A little later."

"I want to see her now." Malcom was no child, but he knew how to fake a tantrum. He looked seriously at both of the men, hoping they might fall for it. They just blinked at him.

Marek said, "Do you want to go back to playing marbles with the boys, or do you want to come to the tower and discuss strategy with me and Pier?"

That was easy. "Strategy."

Pier raised an eyebrow at Marek, a gesture Malcom did not miss. He hardly missed anything.

They stepped onto the landing of the south tower and breathed in sharp, painfully cold air. Malcom looked over the side that dropped down into the mist...and promptly forgot about strategy. He heard the voices behind him, but he hardly cared what they said. There was little to see—and much at the same time. The vastness of the air could be felt, and yet there was nowhere to go from here but down. They touched the sky.

And it was *cold.*

Pier said, "Are you going to tell any of us how you know that woman?"

Marek's frown was in his voice. "I do not see a reason to."

Malcom glanced back and saw Pier nodding, running his hands along the edge of the hewn stone. Malcom ran his own hand along it as well. Ran it all the way around the tower, pretending not to listen. But they were talking about Mem now. He knew it.

"You would tell us if she were a threat to us."

"You have never questioned me before, Pier. You know I would tell you."

"Yes, but you never brought the enemy into our camp before now."

"I did not know it was she we were hunting—did not know she went to Hodran."

"But you are hesitant to be rid of her the quick and easy way."

Marek's voice grew quiet, and he leaned in close to Pier. Malcom was many feet away by now, but he heard the terse whisper. "It is not her I am thinking of. I do not want innocent blood on my hands."

"No, but there is all of our blood in the balance as well." Pier paused, and Malcom could feel his eyes boring into his back. "When Serengard fell, you sent a special guard out of the castle with a girl..."

"What of it?"

"...before we were overrun and your family was killed and most of our number slaughtered."

"By the Derm, the secrets you know will be the end of our friendship someday."

Malcom turned back and came their way slowly, not looking at them. Then he pretended to be distracted and left again.

He saw Pier smile oddly. "I hope not. But I remember this only because it was one of the few times you gave no rational reason for your actions. And you are behaving the same way now. *I do not want innocent blood on my hands?* I have heard that only once or twice from your lips and then only as an excuse for weakness."

"If you could hear any of the thoughts in my mind when I saw her, Pier, you would know my control is of the opposite nature. I wanted to crush her to a million pieces, but I cannot afford the luxury. *You* know. My father taught me the strongest restraint, the harshest of calm when facing decision. Only he thought my sister would be the one in the throes of it. I wish to Allel that she were."

"And now we both wish we had a true enemy in our grasp instead of just the Chamberlain's boy."

"Damn." Marek laughed, and Malcom's ears perked again. Did they think he was not listening? Then Marek caught his eye, and a tingly, icy feeling ran down to his toes.

No. He was supposed to hear this. That he had been nicer to Mem than he wanted to. That they thought she was a bad woman. That they thought his father was a bad man. He hadn't even known his father was alive. Mem wouldn't talk about him. Well, *was* his father a bad man?

Marek turned back to Pier, shrugged, but his voice was still grave, still intentional. "I wish I could have watched him walk out of the castle and bend his head to the stones. Seen him expose his neck to the first sword that dared. Maybe then I would believe in Serengard a little more, as Kierstaz did."

"The ax that killed Petrolai was one of that woman's friends, you know. Someone she ate bread with."

They were talking about the former King of Serengard, weren't they? Malcom froze in front of Marek, feeling exposed as he waited for his words. Like a target they were shooting at.

"I know."

"Don't you hurt my mem," Malcom growled at Marek. He didn't care that the man was three times his height.

Marek looked at him with a frank interest. "I'll try not to."

"I heard what you said. You don't like her."

"No. I don't."

"If you hurt her, I will kill you."

"Really, Malcom?" Marek turned to Pier, and for a moment, it looked as if he would laugh. "That is not something I would expect to hear from Otreya's grandson. How would you kill me?"

"I would steal your knife when you were drunk on mead and stab you in your sleep. I can sneak around. I am quiet."

"You are as different from your mother as you are from your father. You are honest."

He didn't know if that was true or not. "I want you to take my mem out of that dungeon."

"Already done." The man's smile disappeared. "I'll not hurt her. But in case I did, would you like to learn how to kill me in daylight? With a sword?"

Would he? Of course. "I would."

Marek drew his own sword, a long, glittering thing. He handed it to Malcom, hilt first. "Good."

MORNING HAD SCARCE BROKEN WHEN Tev—the short aide of Marek's—burst into Trzl's room. His eyes darted about the space for a moment, and then he told her bluntly, "Dress."

Trzl did not need to be awakened. She'd stared at the wall for hours, waiting for daybreak. There was a lone window in her room—a small tunnel in the deep castle wall. The only way to see out of it was to stick the entire upper half of her body into it, and there wasn't much to see once she did.

"Can I see Malcom today?"

"You are going to work with the other women. Away from here. Cutting hay in the highlands."

"What about Malcom?"

"He will stay. He is none of your concern now. You are dressed? Come."

Trzl followed the snobby little aide, though she felt like screaming in anger. She swore if she saw Marek today she would beat him with her fists. He would probably enjoy seeing her flail. Hodran had, but then, she never understood anything about Hodran.

The aide handed her off to a cliff woman. Trzl tried to break free of her grasp but was tossed immediately onto a wide, hairy creature that reminded her of an oversized goat. Her mount was led to the middle of a caravan of such animals, only a few horses among them.

The sky was a blanket of cloud, and Trzl could not tell how many hours they rode into the high grasslands. There were about thirty people in their company, and none of them spoke. When they did stop, the landscape had changed little, except that there was a strong wind and the jagged rockscapes that broke up the plateaus were steeper than before.

"Why don't you seek hay in the lower meadows?" Trzl asked one of them. She hated this country already.

The woman looked up at her, surprised. Was Trzl not supposed to speak? "We was bred for the harsh country. 'Side, there's bad men there."

Not so bad as your *bad men*, Trzl thought. "But why don't the men do it?"

"Men make war. Women make camp. The men would starve without us. When they are not making war, we boss them." The whole company of women laughed. They each added a quick joke, most of them in a dialect that Trzl could not follow. "There are raiders here, too, but we know how to fight them."

That seemed only to make her point more obvious. "If there are raiders in both places, then why do you not make hay in the meadows where the weather is warmer and the people are gentler?"

"In the rich land? I've told ye. There's trouble there worse'n we wish to see. Filthy Serens."

"But you are Serens yourselves. Or...were. Besides, there are very few in the hill country anymore. Most of them have moved to the Cities."

The woman at last looked puzzled. "The Cities? What are these Cities?"

For true? They did not know? Fine leader Marek was to keep them in the dark. But then, he was an Orion—what else should she expect?

"The Four Cities. The new Serengard?" Trzl spread her hands but received open glares for it. She ducked back down and talked while she worked. "There is work and safety inside the walls. Most of the farmers have moved into the Cities because citizenship is only granted if you are a dweller in one of them, and it's easier to buy food from the Drei anyway. There are only a few stubborn folk who build their huts and grow their alfalfa in the hill country."

"You're saying we could raid farther south? But we already have. You were brung in, weren't ye?"

There were a few snickers across the field. "That's so, Elna."

"I'm saying that no one would bother you there," Trzl said.

"That isn't so. There's gypsy folk don't take a liking to cliff people."

Trzl tilted her chin, mumbling, "Maybe if cliff people would leave them and their Seren friends alone on their pathetic little farms."

That brought a hearty laugh from the one called Elna. "And why would we be caring? There are few among us would call themselves Seren. My man—and most of the men about him—have always been folk who lived high above the stupid wars of the valley dwellers. We are far richer than they and proud of it. Serengard's troubles never meant much to us nohow."

It dawned on Trzl that very few—if any—of these people knew where Lord Marek appeared from. "Do Serengard's troubles mean anything to your Lord Marek?" she asked cautiously. "He is Seren."

It was the other woman's turn to shrug. "Serens have their uses. When they have superior swordplay. When they can mine ore from our own mountain. And when they travel with folk of the western mountains who know both war and medicine…"

The Drei?

Suddenly Trzl knew who the others around Marek's table were, who the sharp-featured man who brought her soup was. They must be warriors he acquired from Dreibourge. But he could not have hidden in Dreibourge. She and Kovim had searched there, turned the country upside down looking for loyalists; killed hundreds—if not thousands—of sympathizers. It was nothing to be pleased with. But what other course was there? The Drei were powerful people who studied war. They had to be conquered while they were weak.

There were no Orions there. They were all dead and gone years ago.

Mikel Orion must have been here all this time? Strange that he should trust these cliff people. They had bones to hide. So many bones. But then, Mikel was not much unlike them now.

Well, if this was his method of amassing loyal supporters, he was fairly terrible at it. What did he plan to do? March through the gates with a few hundred cliff warriors, a few Drei, maybe appeal to those in the southern lands who refused to understand Kovim's dream? Clearly, Marek had no knowledge of whom he would be fighting. The Army of the Four was eight thousand strong at the border and three thousand at the larger ports. Marek and his tiny gang of renegades, along with those Desert People they spoke of, would be dead within a week.

THE FOURTH DAY OF HAYMAKING tired Trzl enough that she slept. She would have liked to wake in the middle of the night and steal a horse, but she was always watched. Besides, it could not help her, and Marek knew it. It made her feel like something of a slave. They didn't feed her much, either.

Sleeping meant that she dreamed, and dreams were usually a curse to her. She dreamt that Marek was torturing Malcom for the gate sequences. She would yell, "He doesn't know! He doesn't know!" But Marek didn't stop, and the dream kept coming back.

Maybe she should tell him herself. Let the army deal with the fallout. If only she could be sure that she and Malcom could go home.

A week passed and then another. Trzl watched the moon fill out and wane again. The pack animals were loaded with hay and sent back down to the castle, but she was kept here, cutting and drying and binding. How much hay did they need? Or perhaps this was Marek's version of cleansing her... Of what? Of helping to establish the cities? Of what she did to knights that were loyal to him? That wasn't his judgment to make. And ten years was a long time. She had been cleansed plenty.

She was loading a pack animal when someone announced in a calm monotone, "Riders."

Trzl kept her face to the ground, pretending to focus on her work, but she was mostly thinking about a way to turn the tables and blackmail Marek. His people didn't know who he was. Surely that was worth something.

The voice grew more urgent. "Swamp People!"

"This far west? They must be desperate indeed."

"How many?"

"Five, six, seven—"

Elna, who was closest to Trzl ran at her, gesturing. Was she supposed to run? Hide? What did they want her to do?

The Swamp People rode in helter-skelter, nothing on their bodies but greased animal skins and a fine collection of heavy spears. The cliff women were prepared, their sickles and scythes easily converting to weapons. Instead of running for cover, they ran at the horses, at the men, tossing their blades and yowling like hyenas.

There were rumors that the Swamp People grew to resemble the terrible lizards they lived among. That they grew scales and their blood ran cold. Trzl didn't wish to see one of them, but she couldn't look away.

They snatched several pack animals by the halters and drove them off. Then one of them reached for a girl. He caught her, swung her up onto his horse. Trzl heard the screams, heard herself scream aloud at the sight. It was Sunn. They slept near each other and exchanged tales.

Then they were gone.

"Sniveling scum," one of the elder women said and spat on the ground. She went back to cutting hay.

"Why do they come here? What do they want?" Trzl rubbed her shoulders. There were raiders in the hill country and rumors of people taken, but it never happened near her. Those were the stories Rem, from her old village, told late at night.

"Oh, they only come around this time of year. Wanting to stock up for the winter, like everyone."

"Stock up on women?"

"Why not? That's why my man makes sure I know how to stab in the back with the best of them. Pity you are such a city sort, or you'd have learnt as well. Hadn't you any friends in the hill country?" And she laughed to herself.

Trzl did not think it was funny. She thought about it. No, she didn't have any friends. The village people were nice to her, but they were suspicious of her origin. She spoke far different from them and always bought things from the gypsies. Strange.

"Aren't we going to go after them? Bring Sunn back?" Several of them stared at her before she realized she had included herself in the suggestion. She would go herself. Readily. "Aren't you?"

"People make raids for slaves. Many get taken."

"Your men let them take their women?"

Elna laughed. "We women let them take some men now and then, too."

"Do *your* people raid for slaves?"

"We don't need to. We are rich enough. You may as well get back to work as you're two inches from being a slave yourself."

There were a few more chuckles, and Trzl grew furious. "Don't any of you love that girl?"

"I'm sure'n her mem loves her, but we learned long ago not to mourn them that was taken. There's more children to be had. Or did ye not know that?"

"Do you tell Lord Marek when this happens?"

"Why would we tell him?"

"We should go back to the castle. He will want to go after the girl." If he was still Mikel at all, he would.

Dead silence answered her. The women looked at each other uncomfortably, picking at their flowing robes of red, most of them swinging their scythes in idle hands. Trzl was used to telling people what to do, but she was far outnumbered. She kept her eye on one of the few horses. Close enough to run to in this heavy woven dress?

She hoped.

"If you won't go tell him, I will."

"No one is going anywhere."

She lifted the sides of her dress and ran.

{16}
Influence

TRZL WAS PULLED FROM THE horse by a cliff man with long hair and a dark tan face. The features were the same—small almond eyes, thin eyebrows, and rounded jaw—only this one was young and quite handsome. She had seen him before, arguing with Marek about wanting to join with the Desert People.

"Gernan? I have to speak to Marek."

"Sorry. You're going in your room, lady." His hands clamping down on her waist were rough and unpleasant.

"He will want to save her. One of the women was taken—"

That got his attention. He dropped her and whirled her to face him. "Who?"

"Sunn."

"Who *took* her?"

"Swamp People."

"Did they head south?"

"Yes."

"How long ago?"

"Not long. This horse was much faster than those stupid yaks."

He shoved her to someone walking by, one of the Drei. "Lock her up."

She would have liked to fight with them, but she had done what she could for the girl. And it had provided an excellent excuse to come back here. Maybe, if she was good, she could see Malcom.

As soon as the door closed behind Marek's man, she rinsed her face and took off her flowing red robe. It was ugly, and she felt dirty in it. Beneath was nothing but her clean linen shift. It was returned to her washed and fresh, but her dress was not returned at all. She wrapped her arms around herself and sprawled out on her catskin. She missed Malcom and her clothes and the familiar stubborn folk who lived in the villages...even the shyster gypsies. She wouldn't mind drawing all of her own water for the rest of her life if she could just be back there.

Alone. Safe. With Malcom.

She ran as far as she could, to the corner of the world, to protect him. At least, she thought it was the corner of the world at the time. Evidently, she could be found. She was supposed to be rid of Mikel. He should have died at the burning of Ashlin when all of the royal family was killed. The king, the queen, the crown princess, the prince, the Castle Guard. There were witnesses who saw him fall. True, they never found his body nor his sister's. It was assumed they'd been chopped into too many pieces to be recognizable before they burned.

She remembered that day all too clearly. The conflict within her—wanting him to live, knowing he couldn't—wishing there was some way to have the wonderful part of him kept alive and the horrible part dead. And afterward, deciding that she had never needed him or his stupid ideals. She had her own purpose and the means to carry it out.

But dead, he had become something other than a man. A beacon of sorts, something to measure time and meaning against. If she could not even outrun *him*, who was to say she could ever escape the other men she ran from? Or would Malcom be hunted by her demons, always forced to hide in the mountains like a maimed dog that no one loves?

Marek chose this moment to burst into her room—much like he had burst into her cell the first day. "Perhaps you should dress before you speak with me," he scoffed.

She tried to pull the plain white muslin up closer around her neck and glared at him. "If you would knock I would not be in my undershift."

"What's this about a girl being taken?"

Trzl suddenly wanted to cry. "They weren't even going to go after her, Mikel."

His face grew stormy for a moment. "I'd hate to have to beat you to make you use my name."

She knew that to be an idle threat. The most he had done was deprive her of dinner. She balled herself up, pulling her knees close to her. "It was terrible. You have to save her. I know you can do it. You have the skill with a sword to survive all the people of Ashlin."

"You told Gernan that I would bring her back."

He looked at her, and she realized it was a question. "Yes."

"I seem to remember your thinking far less of my chivalry." She turned away, and he let out a frustrated sigh. "You needn't upset yourself. This happens often, and I cannot convince them to inform me of it."

"Oh, goblins. They don't inform you of everything? That must be different for you, Orion."

Marek frowned, but he didn't threaten her this time. "Understand, they have lived this way for many years. They don't want war with neighboring raiders. There is a sort of code between them—they can take each other's people as much as they please."

Trzl felt more alone than ever. "If it was your child, would you allow it?"

"A youngling is a youngling, Trzl."

"So, you will go?"

"I will."

She brushed a tear out of her eyes, thanking Allel it had been a silent one. Then she noticed he was holding her brown linen dress—he had read her unspoken wishes. She reached a hand out for it.

He tipped his head at her, his eyes glancing over her undershift once more. "Not quite so flattering as the tulle you used to wear."

She tried not to let her puzzled frown turn into a smile. She did not recall him getting down to that layer.

"It would show when you got on or off a horse."

"Toss me my dress, if you would."

Marek walked toward her instead. "Can you lace this alone?"

"I can." Trzl turned her dark brown eyes on him. "I doubt you would know which part goes over my head and which over my hips."

"I know," he replied. "I have done it many times. She always asked me to lace her up."

"She?"

A sudden quiet fell on him, dampening the air. His touch grew rough, as if it were her fault that he thought of someone. He pulled the dress over her head, yanked on the fabric when it got caught on her hair. Felt her hips as he followed it down. Fingers pressed firmly against the bones. His breath came out in a short burst, and she waited, expecting something, anything. His hands were warm, and she was cold. It had been a long time—a very long time.

"I was contacted by some bounty hunters today." He sneered a bit as he tugged on the leather laces to her dress, pulled them a little too tight. "They offered me a chest full of gold for your Malcom."

Trzl felt him tie the laces but didn't step away. She froze, listening.

"There is still a price on his head. Some think they can claim it despite the risks. There is a price on your head, too."

She turned to face him. "How did they know you had us?"

Marek pulled a weapon out of the leather garb he wore, tested its sharpness on his thumbnail. "It would seem I am the first suspect when something goes missing around here. As I said, it is the way of this place. People are taken." He returned the blade to its sheath, and she began to wonder if he was taking her with him somewhere.

"Are Malcom and I to be your slaves now? Since we are useless?"

His face grew dark again. "Is that why you think I have kept you this long?"

She didn't know, but she didn't want there to be any doubt that she was willing to do what he wanted. She sank to her knees in front of him and caught at his fur cloak. "Don't keep Malcom from me forever. I beg you."

He pried her fingers free from his clothing. "I am not going to sell him to anyone. Not just yet. You needn't prostrate yourself."

"I will do anything." Trzl jumped up, savagely facing him, her eyes boring into him. "Anything you like. Take my body if it would give you pleasure and if it would induce you to return Malcom to me."

His mouth turned up at the edges. "Why, Trzl, I've been waiting some time for you to offer that. I'm surprised it was not the first thing on your mind."

It had been, but she wasn't going to mention it until she had to.

"Your body isn't enough to tempt me." He walked to the door, his hand hovering over the iron rung. "If I wished to take you, do you think I would have waited for you to suggest it?"

She smiled at him. "I'm not afraid of you, Marek."

"You should be afraid." His voice was dead serious.

"You're still lying to me."

"I'll stop when you stop."

MALCOM RAN INTO THE ROOM the instant the door opened.

"Mem!"

Mem threw her arms around him and squeezed him tightly to her, kissed his face and smoothed the hair out of his eyes. "Are you hurt? Did they hurt you? Did they keep you in a dark room?"

He blinked back at her, even squirmed a little. "I am fine, Mem. You know I am not afraid of the dark."

Mem looked up at Marek. "Thank you."

Something passed between the two of them that he did not understand. He grew suspicious. Had she promised to do something so that she could see him?

"He didn't hurt *you*, did he, Mem?"

She actually laughed, a happy laugh. "No, no. Needn't worry—Marek won't touch me."

Marek stayed in the doorway. He crossed his arms and said bluntly, "Say your goodbyes."

"What?" Mem looked up, clutching at Malcom's clothes.

"Malcom is coming with me."

"No."

"You wanted this girl brought back. Malcom and I will do it."

"You cannot."

Malcom could tell Mem was afraid of something else. That he would die? That was silly.

"You needn't fear for him, Trzl. I am training Malcom as a warrior. You have treated him as you were treated as a child—sheltering him from everything under Allel's sun. He needs teaching in the ways of the sword."

"He is *nine*."

"My sister was his age when she defeated a knight of my size in parry, and these are far more dangerous places. Did you think you could keep him an innocent little soul forever?"

Mem just shook her head and said, "As if you would know how to raise a son."

"I'll be back before sundown," Malcom told Mem proudly.

She just shook her head. He followed Marek out. A moment later, he heard her throw herself against the door and yell his name, stifled by a sob.

It was fine. Mem was afraid whenever he stayed out late hunting otters with his friends. She was afraid of so many things. That he would get lost, that he would be eaten by a wild-cat, that he would kill a swamp rat and acquire a taste for blood. None of those things ever happened.

They were not the only people going, and that disappointed him some. Marek motioned to each of his men, explaining who they were.

"Skommek, Gernan, and Colstadt. Malcom."

Malcom already knew most of their faces, but Marek had never let them do anything together. He knew Tev, the aide who was always somewhere near Marek. He was only a little taller than Malcom, like a runt, but he had the strength of a man—Malcom remembered from the night he had been dragged down to Mem's cell. Tev could easily be twice his age.

Skommek was *much* older. Gernan was muscled, and he wore a lot of weapons. Colstadt was wiry, with strawberry-red hair that came to his chin. He saluted in a foreign manner and said, "Welcome to our ranks, Malcom."

Tev rolled his eyes, shook his head, and sunk his heels into his horse. The others did the same, disappearing into a large, dark tunnel in the side of the castle. Marek waited until Malcom mounted and urged his horse forward before he followed them into the dark.

At first, it was too black to see. His horse knew the way, though, following the others instinctively, deep into the guts of the castle and down through levels of rooms that didn't show from the outside. They passed through large chambers lit by torches, some of which seemed to be stables since they were populated with more horses than cliff folk. Strange that most of these people liked to live in their woolly round tents in the cold but they saw fit to keep their horses indoors.

The ground beneath him began to slope, and then the horses were picking their way down set after set of stairs. Malcom grew frightened for a moment. Not for himself—not really. But the image of his horse turning an ankle and having to be left was not a pleasant one. Then he thought of the night he and Mem were brought here and realized these cliff horses must have been doing this for a long time.

Still, he kept his eyes closed tight.

They exited the tunnels long before they reached the bottom. He remembered, there was a canyon when they were brought here. This was no canyon. It was a footpath that led down a crevice in the rock, and it was steep and narrow.

The red-haired Colstadt threw a smile back at him. "It's easier than you think," was all he said, but it gave Malcom a happy thrill. He would keep his eyes open for this.

He took a moment to look around him, to see the sage green color of the moss that grew in abundance on stones that were a queer powdery blue. A million trickles of water came from somewhere deep in the rock, and the dark shadows of large birds soared above them. Below them appeared an endless stretch of gray.

"Is that the sea?" he asked Colstadt.

Marek answered from behind him, "No, the sea is fifty miles north. It is far harsher than this."

"I *like* this," Malcom replied. Colstadt's head snapped around as if he had spoken a dirty word, and Marek's eyes narrowed. Well, he did like it.

Gernan called back at him, "I've forgotten your name, boy, but I'd rather ride with you than these Drei."

Colstadt threw something at Gernan's head, and Gernan laughed loudly.

The horses ignored them.

{17}
Rescue

NIGHT AND A STORM WERE almost upon them when they found a camp. They came out of the cliffs and into the hill country—only it was still cold, and mostly just a rocky plateau. They left their horses behind a boulder and crept forward on their bellies. About a half a mile away from them, three campfires glowed against the darkness. Marek smiled slowly, causing Malcom to wonder how often he did this kind of thing.

"How did you know they would be here?" Malcom whispered, though the wind was loud enough to mask his words.

"Swamp People are addicted to water. It is a part of them. Even when they camp for the night, they must have a pool to dip their feet in."

That seemed strange. It gave Malcom a shudder.

"Pretend they are water nymphs," Colstadt told him. "Nothing frightful about it."

He nodded numbly, but he was still a little frightened. Marek pulled out a small sword of mirror-white steel and handed it to Malcom.

"For tonight."

That must mean he could not keep it. Too bad. It was a far nicer sword than the one he trained with yesterday. At least, it was a better shape.

"I am taking Skommek and Gernan and going around to the south. Tev, Colstadt, enter from the north and drive them toward us. Malcom, stay between their camp and our horses."

"Don't I get to fight anyone?"

"If they slip through Tev and Colstadt, yes, you do."

Malcom looked at the short, skinny swords strapped to Colstadt's back and the long one tied to Tev's leg and thought, *For true, no one will get past them.*

Marek and the cliffmen broke off without another word. Mem would be angry at Marek for leaving his side, but Malcom didn't care. His heart thrummed loudly as he slipped forward behind Colstadt. It took a long time to get close, crawling this slowly. He could have sworn it was an hour before Tev raised a hand to him, a signal to stop.

They were on the edge of the pool of water—about a half-mile wide and a quarter-mile long. Malcom couldn't tell if it was a lake or a pond or the product of heavy rainful. The Swamp People had built a rise out of mud and straw that provided a platform for their camp, much like what a beaver would build. Their huts were round and covered in strange, scaly skins, built in circles. In the middle of each circle was a campfire. The light of the fires lit the open area of their camp, and even from this distance, the detail was distinguishable. The people wore very little clothing. Their hair was long, their beards nonexistent.

How could they stay warm without shirts?

Tev slipped into the water, making tiny ripples, moving with stealth and ease. He jerked his head at Colstadt, then turned about and gave Malcom a slight smile.

"We'll be back," Tev whispered. Then they both slipped beneath the surface.

He watched for what felt like an eternity, huddled against the ground, listening to the storm coming toward them from the west. It rumbled and crashed against the cliffs behind him, and he knew they would have to pass through it on their way back.

Suddenly, there was movement. Gernan sliced down two men in one instant, making Malcom blink with surprise. Marek was on the other side of the same fire, a curved steel blade gleaming in the firelight. His hand was already closed around the wrist of a girl. He must have gone into the huts and found her.

One of the Swamp men tried to take Tev, but Tev stabbed him in the neck with something so small it could only have been a dirk. Malcom squirmed. He wanted one of those, too. He closed his hand tightly around the sword that Marek lent him and pretended it was his own. He wished he could be a part of their number. Desperately.

He tried hard to watch their every movement, to glean what he could. He was certain there was a reason behind every single action, like a play enacted by the gypsy folk.

He realized all at once why Mem had not wanted him to go. She was afraid, but not the same kind of afraid as when she let him leave the village with a friend. She was afraid of this—that he would *want* this. Well, he did. He didn't like hiding and feeling weak, afraid to set foot outside the village common. He wanted to be strong enough to protect one of his own. To rescue a captive. To fight for Mem.

The Swamp People appeared too drunk to fight. They had spears, wooden and fitted with huge dragon teeth, but nothing more happened. He squinted, blinked, and the exchange was over.

The first raindrops fell just as the cliff men came back through the water, this time not bothering to hide beneath the surface. The girl had her arms around Gernan's neck and her legs wrapped around his waist, but Gernan wore a fixed scowl on his face. He was furious...at Marek.

"They were slaves of theirs."

Marek disagreed. "They are a part of their tribe. If they ever weren't—"

Gernan shook his head, his long, leather-wrapped hair shaking with it. "They are slaves! Did you see how fearful they were? Tev, did you see?"

Tev just shrugged. Malcom stood and handed his sword back as Marek reached him.

"Well done," Marek told him.

"They weren't village slaves, neither," Gernan persisted. "They were northern folk, from above dragon country. I don't need them to fly the flag of a gray gull to tell."

Skommek, the oldest man, said, "No way of telling after they been south long enough. Leastwise they weren't ours. Didn't know a word of our language."

"They were afraid of *us*," Marek snapped. "Swamp People are no animals. They want to be left alone, same as we do. If they are not a part of their tribe, let it be on my head."

Gernan spit on the ground. "We should have taken them. They would have been better off."

Marek stopped. Heavy rain drops picked up their pace, the rhythm growing faster. "Understand, Gernan. We do not take people. Not anymore."

Gernan stepped close, hissing savagely at Marek. "I have trusted you and followed you into many a skirmish. You should maybe trust me this once."

Marek looked him up and down, then started to walk again. "I trained you in the Seren arts of the sword, Gernan, but you'll need a few more years before you can take me as your equal. When you are ready to challenge me, do so at home."

"I shall. But it will be too late for them," Gernan mumbled, loud enough for Marek to hear.

THE STORM PASSED QUICKLY, LEAVING shallow pockets of water and a clean sky of stars. Trzl laid her head back on one of the stones that bordered the parapet and stared straight up at them. Tev had bound her hands again, else she would have run all ten fingers through Malcom's nut brown hair. As it was, she must be satisfied with his head lying across her knee.

Tev kept a close eye on him, as if he might slip Trzl a weapon. Small chance. They couldn't get out of this place even if she were heavily armed and trained.

Marek polished the blade of a sword with bunched-up linen, the rag coming off red. She did not like to think of what they had done this night, but they brought the girl back. That, at least, made her happy. And it told her something she wanted to know—Marek would still listen to her. She could manipulate him if she worked at it hard enough.

"Have I told you the tale of the warrior in the sky?" She spoke to Malcom, but she raised an eyebrow to Marek when he looked at her.

"I know it." Malcom began to fidget. Maybe he was only resting on her to make her feel better, but she didn't mind. It worked.

"That the warrior used to come to a dead stop over Serengard, every night for three hours. The sky stood still. They say the centaur reigned over Dreibourge in the same manner, the woman over Aldad, the lion over Elloya."

"Glad to hear you've learned some culture." Marek's voice was still cold with her.

She smiled distantly. "The tale used to be true."

"It was never true, Trzl."

"It was. In the days of the early kings, when the Orion family had a stranglehold on the throat of Serengard, even the stars stopped to acknowledge it. The night of the spring solstice, the Castle Guard would burn fires to the sky—usually fires full of the crops of the people, tributes paid to them—thanking Allel for sending the warrior over Serengard and for bestowing another year of prosperity. But the opposite was true. The people suffered under the heavy tributes. The warrior stopped because he wanted the people to know that they needed to stand up and fight the Orions. Slowly, they began to fight the kings, and the warrior stopped for a shorter time each night until the reign of Petrolai. By then, the voice of the people grew loud enough that the warrior knew he was not needed, and he stopped only for a moment. Then the Seren threw down Petrolai, the last Orion, and the warrior never stopped again. The stars were free."

Malcom gave a happy sigh. She knew he liked the story, as much as he pretended not to care.

One of Marek's men, Pier, was staring at her. When he had brought her soup in her cell that first day, she thought he had a kind face. Now it was dark and glowering. And Marek was laughing, a mean, hollow laugh.

"If your story were true, it would mean that Serengard is weak now."

Malcom stirred, stood up, and walked quickly away from her. Trzl blamed Marek.

"The Orion was a curse."

"Tell me it isn't a curse to have thousands die in a bloody war—a war that served no purpose but to bring them under the still closer rule of dozens of men instead of one. At least then, they were subject to a whim. Now, there is treason and endless suffering—starvation, even. Before the stars were free, there was no such hardship within these borders."

"You say this—you who are a raider and make slaves of the weak."

"I make slaves of those who cross me. No one else."

"Why don't you have it out with me, then? Tell me what you wish to know so badly."

Marek slipped his sword back in its sheath and shifted, leaning his head back against the stone wall. "I've a use for you. But I've no mind to tell you until tomorrow."

"You have questions for me. You said."

"They can wait."

Trzl caught the tension in his voice, thought again of the lies he had told his men. Pier kept his head down, but his eyes looked up from under his brow, locked with hers. Watching. She looked back to Malcom, walking along the catwalk beside the castle wall, and gave Marek a shallow smile.

"Malcom is pleased with you, I think."

He nodded briefly in reply.

"I hope you will not teach him to be too vicious."

"Life here is vicious. You are a vicious woman in your own way, in case you forgot."

"You will...give him back to me. Soon. Won't you?"

Marek laughed, letting one of his arms languish on the stones. "Give him back to you? Can you even prove he is yours, Trzl?"

Trzl sat up, not finding it funny, and tried to climb down off of the step she was on.

"In all fairness, you do admit he was born out of wedlock." Marek stood, his hand outstretched. "Come."

She didn't mind being alone with Marek. But at night in his own castle? The thought made her cold all over, and her voice was hoarse when she said, "Must I?"

She shouldn't have for Tev stood and smacked her across the face. The blow made her cringe, although Marek stayed Tev's hand afterward. Another Trzl would have smacked the spindly boy right back, even with her hands bound. But she ignored him and followed Marek. No reason to pick a fight when she didn't have the high ground.

"Malcom?"

Marek untied the rope and seized one of her wrists. "You have seen him enough."

His steps grew faster as they wound through confusing corridors. The way became more and more narrow, the torches fewer and farther between. A sound grew from a whisper to a deafening pound the farther they went, and at last, she realized it was the rushing of water. She could not tell whether they had climbed higher or gone lower for the stone stairs led up and then down and around again. The path began to brighten with an eerie blue light. Around a final corner and it hit her in the face, making her blink. He pushed her into a room that seemed to glow with daylight, but it was only the moon casting a full whiteness.

He pulled her inside and swung her body about, until the recoil brought her close against him. She yanked on his arm, tried half-heartedly to pull away, but he cupped the back of her neck with a hand and drew her ear against his mouth.

"Are you ready to tell me the gate sequences?"

There was no use continuing to deny that she knew them. "What good will come of knowing?"

"Why did you not tell me when I first asked?"

"You implied that they had value. I won't give them up until I know of what value they are." And because they were good leverage.

"Curiosity on my part. Your Council of Four puts out a bounty on you at the same time as an interest in the gate sequences is sparked in bounty hunters abroad. My first guess is they must wish to tie up loose ends, and perhaps you know them. If they have any greater value, I'd be happy to hear of it."

"There can be only mischief and bloodshed if anyone breaks into or out of the Cities."

"In your utopia? Bloodshed? I'm shocked." He did not loosen his hold on her. "Yet there is more to confound. The Council of Four wants Malcom. Why?"

His other hand tightened on her wrist, and her mind shut down. "I don't know." She wanted to feel other things—the mist that fell on her face, the thrum of the falls pounding inside her chest—but all she felt was the hum of his closeness, seeping through his hands and into her body. Calming. Stirring.

"You insist on lying to me still? I'll toss you out in your village and let the nearest bounty hunter take you."

Did he think that was a threat? She would have thought the nearness of him, the knowledge that no one would hear her scream over the waterfall to be a better one...at least in his mind. "I *want* to go back to my village."

"Then you are a bigger fool than I thought. Do you know how quickly you would be dead? If Malcom is the only one they seek—"

That was a threat. There was nothing she was more frightened of than Malcom being alone in the world. "Hodran would not kill me."

"How do you know Hodran is even aware of this? You said he did not care about the boy."

"The Four always decide together. He knows."

His breath against her ear was warm, his voice lulling. She was exhausted, and she wanted to lean against him—wanted to be closer— especially if it would help him to believe her.

"I need to know if he will kill Malcom."

"Why do you need to know?"

"Reasons. Reasons I am not going to tell you."

That was all? There was more that she wanted from him. Right now. She slid her hand between the clasps of the leather wrap across his chest, felt a thin woolen smock beneath. She dug her fingernails in gently. He didn't move. Not an inch.

"He would not kill Malcom. None of them would. Otreya is as important a member of the Four as anyone, and Malcom is his grandson. He is safe." It felt good to have told him something that was pure truth. Maybe she could get some honesty from him in return. "What are you going to do?"

"We're going to a melee. Gypsies and rogues and gremlins travel together, and we are bound to learn something. One thing's had me curious—if you left years ago, how do they know what Malcom looks like? Enough to render him recognizable to the disreputable folk I hired?"

A very good question. Trzl laid her head against his chest and nuzzled him. "I don't know."

"Someone has had their eyes on him for a very long time."

That scared her, but not as much as it would have if she were alone in this. "I can't think who."

"Are you sure?"

That familiar warm feeling began to steal over her. Maybe it was because he had her in a dark corridor where he could do Allel knew what—yet he would not even let her slip her fingers inside his shirt. Whatever happened to him, he was still the same man she knew in Ashlin. Had he taken her down here to try to prove something to her? It was working.

"There is a reason they might want to watch him."

His grip tightened on her for a moment, and she knew he sensed the fragility of her trust. "And?"

"There is a crypt, in the caves of the First City. It holds all of the ancient books and records that were taken from the Castle of Orion, those that were not burned."

Marek interrupted, his voice going tight and hoarse. "Books? They did not destroy them? Are you saying there are some left?"

"Yes." She was annoyed at his excitement. She could not have cared less about the foolish histories that held far too many lies. "The crypt opens with the blood of the four council members. If something has happened to Hodran—or if he is missing, or if he refuses to open it—they might want to know where his children are. Just in case."

Marek ran a hand through his hair, his face blank with wonder. "Are you certain? They saved them?"

"I don't know what they saved. I know something is there. I don't see why they would want to open it."

"Trzl, you're not going to stay here."

She raised her head slowly. "What?"

"I can't keep you here, especially if you refuse to make yourself useful. You're coming with me to this melee. Malcom will stay here until I get some answers."

"Why do you need answers? It's not as if they are going to storm your castle."

"I won't have loose ends that might lead anyone here. My people follow me because I keep trouble at bay. At the very least, keep them free of these kinds of entanglements."

"But must you take me with you?"

"You are the bait."

"Oh." She didn't mind, as long as Malcom would be safe, and he would be. She let herself lean into Marek, run her fingers over the leather that covered him, the furs draped across his shoulders. He didn't seem to care until her hand touched his face. Then he grasped her wrist and pulled it away, his face twisting with some kind of pain.

"What are you doing?"

She honestly did not know. "I...I want you to know that I am grateful. For how you have treated Malcom."

"I don't expect gratitude."

"Well, if you've no reason to keep me here, why don't you let me go? I can do just as well on my own."

"Call it an inkling, but I don't believe you could have been thrown in my lap this conveniently without there being someone or something behind it."

"Are you calling me a spy?"

"Near as much." But he half-smiled as if it did not alarm him. "The eleventh or twelfth reason I find your charms grating."

You're afraid of me, aren't you, Marek. That's why you keep trying to make me fear you. *You don't want me close.* "You judge me harshly, when you are the one who brought me down here, unbound my wrists and dragged me through your castle in the dark like a regular savage."

He finally laughed. "I am no savage. Farther up into the cliffs, across the plateaus and into the caps, there you will find savages. This castle is the last outpost of Seren civilization. Beyond it... Beyond it, you would find a crudeness you cannot maneuver. But your son will, if I have any say in the matter."

{18}
Bait

HE BOUGHT HER A DRESS from a gypsy peddler, a brown velvet thing with turquoise trim. Even the money she had stolen from Hodran would never have gone to something this fine.

She could not help blurting, "How rich are you really?"

"Not rich enough."

"Not rich enough to afford a war?" She turned her eyes on him in question, still standing inside the dress stall. He put a hand to her elbow and guided her out of the tent, but he dropped it as soon as they were again in the open air.

"I'm still unclear as to why you think I'd have any interest in a war. One war was enough."

Trzl shrugged. "I can't imagine you turning around and selling those gate sequences once you had them. The temptation to use them would be too strong. Bloody man such as yourself."

She could not tell if he was listening. She was being ignored by the other folk at this melee, but holding the soft, lovely dress made her think that would soon change. *I am bait.*

"You're going to put me on display in some manner, aren't you? See if anyone notices me when I am dressed as a Chamberlain's wife?"

He lifted the edge of a tent and motioned for her to enter. It was full of wares at the front and several patches of bedding at the back. As soon as she saw the blankets, Trzl wanted to sleep. She had slept in the back of the wagon for an hour as Tev and Pier set it up, but an hour hadn't been near long enough to catch up on the day and a half of travel it took to get here.

Instead, Marek unlaced her dress, quickly, without lingering. She felt a strange hollowness, wishing that he had. A cheer went up from the village common and she knew what it meant.

"They are lighting the fire."

His hand paused on her forearm. "There will be plenty of mead to go around if you cannot calm yourself."

"I am nervous. I don't know why." She didn't, and it was frustrating.

"You needn't be," he said as he stepped back through the tent entrance. "No harm will come to you here."

It wasn't that.

She took her time climbing into her dress, taking inventory of Marek's weapons once more, hoping he may have left one in the tent that she could come back and steal. Surely he removed some of them from his person just for the night.

"You won't find any poisonous berries or little red hilted daggers in here."

She turned to see he had stepped back in. How long ago? His words slurred slightly, just enough for her to tell that he must have downed some mead. He remembered the color of her old dagger? Hodran had taken it from her. How she missed that fine piece of steel. The wish to explain the past ten years overtook her for a moment. Maybe he would be more amenable in this condition.

"Marek, I—"

He cut her off, securing her arm. "I'm no Lord Marek here. I'm a common man who can afford to spoil his lady—a lady who glowers and hates him and he must keep in sight all evening, lest she leave him or stab him in his sleep."

He led her out among the tents, through the crowds of revelers. Trzl saw Tev and Pier a good eight feet away as Marek tossed her under a canopy with a good view of the fire.

He perched himself next to her and shoved a wooden tumbler into her hand. "Have some mead."

She took it, more nervous from the fingers that brushed hers than from this dangerous thing they were attempting. "Did you fight in the war? Or did you hide in the cliffs and watch it happen?"

"I fought. Tev and some of the rest of us."

Trzl glanced at Tev, who was looking longingly at the dancers, and thought him too puny to have been much help. "Were you stationed on the border?"

"I wasn't stationed anywhere," he snapped. His eyes were serious. Maybe he had nothing to drink. Maybe he was just trying to make her comfortable. Well, she wasn't, but the mead was good.

"Did you follow Lomius and the Knights of Rilch? Karamov? Or did you lead the Desert uprising? I was curious about that. You always did get along with those folk."

"You know more about those battles than I do." His face was blank, but his eyes began to flicker. She was making progress.

"Tell me, Marek. Whilst you fought with the knights, with that fine sword hand and distinguished face, how did you keep people from recognizing you?"

He looked up at her sharply, caught her arm. "You will keep your voice down."

It was her turn to laugh. This mead was heavy and thick. "You—"

She pulled herself toward him, putting her fingers on his chest. He caught at the bare hand. She felt the heat of his flesh, and she knew he felt hers.

"I warn you…" he mumbled.

She leaned into him and kissed him, making his body go rigid. She was the one who pulled back, reeling with the strangeness of it, the feeling of his chest through the thin smock. His reaction was delayed, but when it came, it was bland and controlled—a tone Mikel would use.

"You are not going to get anything that way. I have told you. You do not tempt me."

"Liar." She swallowed, backing away, keeping her head tipped invitingly. "How could I not tempt you? Oh, I know. One of those ragged mountain girls is yours. Or maybe several of them?"

Marek stood abruptly. "There was one. She died."

Trzl waited a moment before she stood to follow him, back between the tents, among colored lanterns and gypsy folk who tottered with strange substances. A few turns to the right, and his arms grasped hers, pulled her close against him.

"He's coming."

"Who?"

"The man across the fire. He was staring at you."

"I didn't see anyone."

A faint smile played on his lips, and she realized he was not drunk at all. "I did tell you to drink mead and relax."

It wasn't until she heard the footsteps that she believed the man was coming or that there even was a man. The steps were soft in the grass and made the hair on her arms grow goosebumps. She trembled without meaning to. Marek slipped a hand into her hair and pulled her face up to his.

He kissed her. Gently. Carefully. Insincerely.

The air went dead and reeled about her. She knew he didn't mean it, but the simple touch and the sweet feeling of his hand curling against her neck made her want to trust him. To feel safe, if only for a moment.

Their pursuer rounded the corner and stood blinking at them. He held a club in his left hand, and his right clenched and unclenched shakily. By the time he reached for Trzl, Marek had knocked the club away with the hilt of his sword, clapped a hand over his mouth, twisted him by the arms, and shoved him into the grass.

Pier and Tev rounded the corner and picked up the body, dragging it back between tent stakes and wagons until they reached a quiet place in the midst of the dark, empty tents. Pier took out a small dagger and laid it against the man's throat, putting a finger to his lips to tell him to be silent.

Trzl felt a hard knot forming in her stomach, not sure she wanted to see this. "What are you going to—"

Marek stepped to her in one stride and placed his own finger against her lips. The gesture was similar enough to Pier's that she shuddered visibly. "Do you recognize this man?"

She shook her head.

"Trzl, look at me," he ordered. "What are you afraid of? You've seen plenty of blood and done many a desperate thing."

She didn't want to go back to Hodran. It was that simple. "Don't send me with him. No matter what he offers you. I'll pay it off, just don't—"

Marek didn't comfort her like she wanted him to. He looked straight in her eyes and said, "Don't be a fawn."

Pier said softly, "Marek."

Marek went to him, and both he and Pier bent down to hear the man's words. The conversation ensued in tones too low for her to catch, probably because they did not want her to. She heard Pier's voice the most. When they stood and released the man, she looked to Marek, but he was stewing and preoccupied. Tev walked past her with a glare.

"What did...you tell him?" Trzl asked.

"That we had you first and the bounty was ours," Tev snapped. Marek did not contradict him. Pier again looked at her strangely, his eyes hard as stone. They were not disappointed, that much was evident.

Marek said, "Get some sleep."

They must have learned all they wanted because they went back to the tent, but none of them slept besides Marek. Trzl stayed awake, staring into the dark, and she could hear the breathing of Tev and Pier—shallow and alert.

Sometime near dawn, Tev jumped up and left, reentering a few minutes later with another Drei from the castle.

"Sorry, Colstadt, no fire," Tev apologized.

"I don't mind." Colstadt settled on a sheepskin, his face wet from rain and sweat, but he stared at Tev for a moment before stating his business. "You have a problem, Marek. Skommek took the boy to trade with Anaqi for the bounty money. Gernan allowed it, even went with him."

Pier had clamped a hand over Trzl's mouth to stop her scream before Colstadt had even finished speaking.

"No no no," she mumbled into his fingers.

Marek gripped Colstadt's shoulder with an intensity she thought he reserved for her. "Where?"

"At the Forks, but I am sure by now the trade has taken place and they are gone."

"You could not prevent it?"

"Not unless I fancied fighting Skommek and Gernan and two dozen of their comrades. I could've killed them, Marek, but I'd rather not hurt my friends. I would kill Anaqi first, and I like Anaqi."

"Anaqi will not take the boy in himself. He will trade him to someone besides a gypsy."

"Which is why we must move quickly."

Marek left the tent, Tev in step behind him and Colstadt shadowing them. Pier waited inside the tent as Trzl struggled to stand in her heavy dress. He offered her his arm, which she ignored, the lack of sleep and fear for Malcom hitting her bluntly all over. Tears stung her eyes, and she ran after Marek as quickly as she could in the dark.

There was still a large fire in the middle of the common. The noise drifting through the camp suggested that the gypsies and villagers had stayed up all night. Trzl caught Marek by the arm as he was about to mount a horse.

"What are you doing?" she choked out.

He jerked away the arm she clung to. "Pier, take Trzl back to the cliffs yourself. Avoid challenging Gernan if you can. Tev, with me."

"Wait!" Trzl caught at his horse's bridle. "Take me with you."

"You've caused enough trouble," Tev snapped.

Trzl wasn't talking to Tev. "Bring him back, I beg you."

A bone worked in Marek's jaw. "I will bring him back. But I will not do it for you."

Colstadt remained behind for a moment, leaning his head down so he was close to her. "I'll do it for you," he grinned. Then he kicked his horse and they were gone.

Trzl turned to Pier. His face was somber but not sympathetic. "On your horse," he said softly.

MALCOM EXPECTED TO BE BROUGHT to Mem as soon as she got back. He did not expect to be placed on a horse with a hood over his head, to have strange arms hold him roughly, to ride horses all the way down to the dry riverbed.

It wasn't Marek. He knew Marek's voice.

He could hear the pounding of hooves, knew that they were many. He was a little frightened but not too terribly much. When this had happened before, they had been brought to a castle full of rugged warriors who taught him how to use a sword. It hadn't been that bad. Except that Marek was unkind to Mem that once…which was bothersome because otherwise he liked Marek.

Hours passed. He grew tired, clinging to the mane of the horse he rode, pulling away from the arms of the rider that held him. He must've fallen asleep, for he woke suddenly when the hood was taken from his head and he stared up at a man with a dark face and black beard. He had more jewelry than Malcom ever saw on a man, even a gypsy man.

"As promised," one of the cliffmen said from behind him.

Malcom turned to look, but someone took his face and turned it forward. He thought he spied Gernan, near the back. Was he his only friend here?

The dark man had others with him. They gave money to the cliffman behind Malcom, and then one of the dark people reached for him.

"Don't!" he yelled.

They did not heed him. He kicked and screamed until one of them stuffed a rag in his mouth and another bound his hands and feet. He could still see, though. He could see Gernan, at the back of the group, sink his heels into his horse and turn away.

{19}
COLLISION

GERNAN LOOKED OLDER THAN HIS twenty years—maybe because his brazen black eyes already had wrinkles at the corners. Their perfect almond shape placed him among the most handsome of the cliffmen, but beauty was not something they valued. Life above the meadows was about being as powerful as you could on your own plateau.

He met Marek's company in the outskirts of the swamps where Anaqi liked to deal, nearly running into Colstadt. Who gave Colstadt the right to ride in front?

"I only did what was logical," Skommek blurted, right to Marek's face.

Marek was already incensed. "You what?"

Fine time to forget that Marek has a foul temper, Skommek, Gernan thought.

Marek drew his sword and swatted Skommek's temple with the flat of it, lightning-fast, knocking him off-balance and off of his horse. "Where is Malcom?"

Skommek spit blood from his bruised cheek. "You only kept him for your bit of skirt. I tell you it is she who is a curse to us. She will bring death upon one of us, surely."

"I said she and the boy were none of your concern. I am certain I said that. Did I not say that, Tev?"

"You did." Tev did not seem very happy about any of this either, but Gernan knew the aide sympathized with their predicament. Marek was not acting himself. This dark-haired woman—she-devil, cursed thing—gave him a blacker mood than any he'd seen. It had been better when she was off making hay.

"Which way did Anaqi go?"

"You're going after him? Lord Marek, a deal of this kind—"

"Yes, I'm going after him." Marek sawed on his reins. "I wouldn't recommend bringing reputation into this, Skommek. You walk a thin enough line as it is. And you, Gernan." His voice lowered, and he pulled his horse up close. He looked for a moment as if he might spit in Gernan's eye. "You have a hankering for a fight with me? Or is this your way of reminding me that our terms will matter in ten years when I have lost some of my swiftness and you have gained some?"

Gernan smiled slowly. He liked Marek, especially when he was quick in the head like this. "Neither, my lord. I thought it was always your intention to trade the boy. Seemed right to take the chance when it was offered."

Marek closed his mouth hard, his gloved hand fingering the hilt of his sword.

Gernan added quickly, "I'd warn you against following Anaqi. He's surely traded the boy to the city army by now. They were to ride out and meet him, and he expects certain reward for his trouble."

Tev gave Gernan a piercing glare, one he did not think he deserved.

"Then you may have sealed your own coffin, Gernan," Marek said. "You're coming with me."

"With you?"

"To the Cities."

That made him start. He had never been west of the cliffs. He had been east, high into the cold country of the Caps and the summerlands in the clefts. He had even been to the settlements on the plateaus. But all cliff dwellers knew the valleys were full of giants and creepers and dark folk with endless muscle. He tried to keep the trepidation from his voice when he said, "What is the boy to you? He is the son of your enemy, and of a woman who'd mutilate us in our sleep—"

Marek was already swinging back for the cliffs. "It is for Allel to judge his parents' deeds. A child is innocent."

"With the darkness of blood reapers in his body. Didn't we leastwise kidnap him for such a purpose?"

"Before we knew why he was hunted. He is no child of Kovim—" Marek stopped abruptly. "I know where they are taking him. We need Trzl as well. And fresh horses."

Gernan frowned, watching Marek kick his horse into a gallop, head north again. "I'll not trade in my horse."

Tev circled around behind him and hissed to Skommek, "You bastard."

"Am I to be treated as meat leavings of a sudden?" Skommek answered. "I've done nothing shameful this day."

"No, and that is the worst of it. If you had challenged him, he could have lopped your head off and ended it. As it is you must be locked in a dungeon and watched. And to incite Gernan—"

Gernan would not take that in silence. "There was no inciting. I'm capable of challenging Marek my own self. 'Sides, I know you like me." He reached out and pinched Tev's chin with a calloused hand. A chin that was soft and tiny—a little point at the edge of a rounded face. His gesture provoked a quick snap of the teeth as if he had reached out to pet an angry dog.

Colstadt pressed his horse between them in seeming nonchalance, but

Gernan noted the edge in his gaze as Tev rode forward next to Marek.

He leaned in and whispered, "How long have you known, Colstadt? That our respected lord's boy is actually his girl—"

"You want to die now?" Colstadt snapped.

Gernan tossed his long, tangled hair back over his shoulders. "You would kill me over her, Drei?"

"She will kill you herself."

"But how long?" Gernan insisted.

"Seven years, gremlin."

"Huh." Gernan felt as if he'd been a great simpleton. If Colstadt had known that long, why had he not observed the young Drei casting his eyes at her before?

They both grew more and more somber as they neared the cliffs, the silence between them almost a tangible thing. He wondered what Colstadt was afraid of—if anything. He himself was afraid of being tortured to death away from home. It was a great disgrace to be buried away from your fathers. He prayed silently to the old spirits of the cliffs, but he only felt worse.

SMOKE FROM THE MELEE FIRE disappeared behind them far too rapidly. Trzl wanted to run—to follow Marek and get Malcom back—but Pier made her ride in front the entire way, watching her movements with emotionless eyes. He kept the pace to a canter, driving her back into the castle in less than a day. When he pulled her from her horse, exhausted mentally and physically, she thought he would send her to her room. Instead, another Drei appeared, one she had not met before. They escorted her to an empty chamber somewhere high in the castle— probably near her own for it had the same long, lone window as hers.

Pier appeared a few minutes later, looking tired himself. "This can go quickly and rather comfortably for you, Lady Chamberlain, or it can be long and somewhat painful."

"I'm sure I—"

"Have a care not to lie to me, Trzl. We all know who you are. We know with whom you were allied the day Ashlin burned, and we know Hodran of Neroi and his breed—would see them all rot in the Derm if we had our way. Instead, we get you. Sniveling little creeper that you are, climbing about our castle and taking note of whatever you damn well please. Do you think I do not know why you are here?"

"*I* don't know why I'm here." Trzl must have repeated these words far too many times in the past moon.

Pier looked to the other Drei and shifted.

A long, snakelike coil came from behind the man's back. A whip.

Trzl froze, staring at it. She wanted to curl up in a ball and go to sleep.

They walked toward her simultaneously, and she backed up, all the way to the wall, before they each grasped a wrist. She tried to struggle, but their hands outdid her in strength. It took only a moment to bind her wrists with a leather cord and secure them to a heavy iron ring in the wall.

"Tell me, do you have a purpose beyond bringing in the former leader of the Knights of Rilch? Some master plan you wish to play out? Because I tell you, it may be working on him, but it sure as the Derm will not work on me." Pier leaned in toward her face. "If you'd like to make yourself more endearing, you should speak now. You can start with the sequences to the gates of the Four Cities. That would be especially helpful."

Mikel led the Knights? She hadn't known this. No one knew. "I tell you, I have not seen Hodran or any of his cohorts in near upon six years. I have been in hiding myself."

"But your grandfather, Otreya. The Pitching Boar. He is close to

Kovim, is he not? One of the Council of Four."

Trzl stiffened, hoping this was as far as he wanted to take this. "I do not call that man my grandfather. I disowned him when I left Hodran, as I tell you, six years ago."

His eyes bored into her. "I know you know the sequences."

"You only want to know them so you can sell the information to the Desert People and start a bloody war."

"A war?" He laughed—a terrible, angry laugh—his face growing dark as Marek's had last night. "We already fought a war, Trzl, wife of Hodran. We spilled more blood than I would ever wish to see again. Thousands dead—some at the end of my own sword, some at Marek's— but far more tortured to death in Dreibourge, killed for little more than an allegiance to their God and their traditions. And for what? My country has had peace with the Seren since the reign of Tame. Now, at the whim of a tiny Seren who hates the Drei, we are slaughtered and starved." Pier waved an arm to the other Drei. The man uncoiled the whip, letting it drop to the floor and slither about.

This was a night for revelations, indeed. There were Drei in the Knights of Rilch, the picked force of Border Guard that fought her own militia? How many? Why then had the Knights lost? She shivered at the whip on the floor.

"You Dreis *do* all have a rotten side," she said.

"Trust me, I've a side far fiercer than this. If you refuse to help, I might get more cooperation by nailing your body to the gate of the Second City."

"You're mistaken. No one cares about me anymore, least of all the Chamberlain of the Second City." Panic began to set in. She had never been beaten by anything besides Hodran's hand. She did not know whether she could withstand it. And with Malcom gone and her strength at a low—

"No one but Mikel Orion, hmm? Since the first time he spoke to you,

you've been controlling him and causing him to do your bidding—with no heed to himself or any of us. He should have forced you to answer, but he does not see what you are. I do, and I care enough to make a thorough job of discovering your purpose." Pier took a knife out of his belt, sliced her velvet dress down the back to her waist, and peeled away the fabric.

Trzl scorned him, her eyes shooting daggers, an attitude she knew she could not keep up for long. "Do your worst and you will learn nothing."

He nodded to his accomplice. The whip hit her skin smoothly, and at the moment of contact, she felt nothing. Then the stinging set in. Just in time for another stripe. And another. The third drew a scream. The fourth drew blood.

HER VISION WAS FOGGY WHEN she woke. Had she slept? Or fainted?

Her back stung madly, as if a thousand hornets had sunk their tails into her. She tried to move, but it made her cry out.

"She wakes," the other Drei said.

Pier stirred, and she heard him stand up. Had he been sleeping as well?

"Don't touch me," she whimpered. She hadn't meant to say that.

"No cause for alarm." Pier brought her a bowl of soup that smelled faintly like duck. Her hands were still secured with the strong cord. He lifted the spoon himself and brought it to her lips. Trzl did not dare glance up into his eyes.

It was all rushing back to her. She broke down, begged him to stop. Told him she would give him the gate sequences. Cried like a child. Recited everything she knew from memory. Told him over and over that was all she knew, that she thought it was accurate and would he please, please leave her be.

She caught a glimpse of his hands. Hands that beat her with a snake skin whip, almost with pleasure, yet they were slim and long, scholarly in design. She would have liked to think pleasant things of such hands.

He fed her every bite of the soup, his eyes intent on her face, hers intent on the spoon. Then he walked away, still talking to her. At first she did not even listen. Yes, he was a loyalist. He was on the side of Orion in the war. He was bitter about what happened in Dreibourge. None of it mattered now. The Four Cities had their faults, but they were better than the alternative.

"...we had spies back then, but none were near as effective as your sort."

"I don't care." She didn't. She didn't care about anything but being cut down from this horrid iron ring and getting Malcom back.

He seemed genuinely surprised by this. "That is a change. If you don't care, why don't you tell me the rest of the sequences? Before I have to hurt you more."

"I don't know anything more, I swear before Allel." She heard the latch to the door being lifted again, the chain displaced, and she cried out.

"Goblins, Pier, get her out. To her own room before Marek sees what you've done." It was Tev. Did that mean Malcom was back?

"Marek should be pleased that I've managed to extract what he could not."

"Let him learn of it from you and not from her."

Pier was agitated. He cut Trzl down and allowed her to crumple on the floor. "He should know—"

Too late for Tev's helpful advice. Marek was there. Or his voice was. Heavy footfalls and the words, "Damn you, Pier."

{20}
Tгцтн

TRZL LET HERSELF GO LIMP. Someone lifted her, arms under hers, her back kept in the air. Someone with tall, built shoulders. Clean, smooth hair. Marek. She made a moaning sound and he stopped moving instantly, pressing his lips to her ear but saying nothing.

"I've learned the sequences," said Pier. "And that she is malleable with a little pain. Something you should have discovered the instant she set foot in the Castle of Marek."

"Do not explain yourself, Pier," Marek hissed through his teeth. He carried her up a few sets of steps, her stomach draped across his shoulder and his arms wrapped around her hips, into a room that was cold. "Light a fire in here."

Trzl could hear the fire spring to life in the grate, but could not feel its warmth.

"Marek," Pier tried to begin again.

"Out of my sight. Out. With Tev. You both have had your way this night. Rest my horse and get me a fresh one by dawn. And Tev, bandages and a poultice for open sores and bruising such as this. Ask one of the other Drei."

Marek laid Trzl on a large bed, one with four posts that curved and bowed outward in traditional Seren style. Her eyelids were swollen. She didn't realize until she tried to focus beyond a foot in front of her. She took it in lazily—the fire, the ornate rugs, the tall ceiling that wound up in a circular design of pinkish marble.

"Why are you—"

"Shh. No need to speak."

A tear dripped unbidden down her cheek. "Mikel."

"Not my name."

"Please."

It felt good on her tongue. And here, in this rich chamber that must be his, she should be allowed to say it. His hand smoothed the hair away from her face. It hurt where he had to tug it out of the scabbing, bloody sores on her back. Her head was cold and covered in sweat. She hoped she was not delirious, that this was not some dream, that he really was mumbling these words to her.

"Would that I was of a mind to beat Pier for this myself. It would do him good."

"He hates me."

"He thinks he has to protect me from faeries such as you."

Trzl drew in a ragged breath. "Malcom? Do you have Malcom?"

"Drink." Marek held a flask up to her lips and helped her choke down a few gulps. It was heavy liquor, stronger than mead, almost akin to the white brandy she had chugged with Hodran. It rushed through her body and warmed her stomach.

Her eyes looked up at him, more aware now. "Malcom?"

Marek took a deep breath. "Not yet. I need fresh mounts and clean disguises to get into the Cities. And I need you."

Trzl tried to sit up. "Yes. I'll come with you."

"You're not coming now." He traced a finger down her torn back, and she cried out sharply, buried her face in his bed. That proved his point. "Trzl."

Her head snapped around to look at him. "Yes."

"I need to know where Kovim would take Malcom and to what purpose. Tell me any weaknesses Hodran or Kovim may have, about the lay of the land, the troops, anything you remember."

"I told you how that crypt is opened. By the blood of each of the Council of Four."

"Something concocted by the Desert People?"

"Yes. If Kovim wants to open it without alerting Hodran and the other Council members, he could use his son's blood."

Marek let out a tight breath. "What if it is his great-grandfather's blood they lack? And who is the fourth member? Are all the Chamberlains also on the Council?"

That wasn't how it worked, but he was watching her face closely. "It *could* be Otreya's," she admitted.

He closed his eyes for a moment. "How much does it take for you to tell me you're the fourth council member?"

Trzl wanted to panic—to run from him. But there was nowhere to go. "How long have you known?"

"Since you said Hodran and Kovim fought over you. Not to insult your womanhood, but those two never valued it."

"You have to believe me. I haven't been involved since—"

"The rest doesn't matter. I knew you were withholding plenty. But if you want your son back, you have to trust me. It's your blood they want, and they've the next best thing. He counts for a hostage as well. He'll be heavily guarded."

"Do you think they will hurt him?"

"I mean to stop them before they have time." He whispered it, close to her cheek, his hands running through her soiled, matted hair. She closed her eyes and turned her face away from him, let him fan it out on the bed, start to untangle it. A boy came with the poultice and soft linen. Marek dipped the fabric strips in the concoction himself and laid them on her back. She bit her lip at the searing, burning sensation that came from the compound of herbs and alcohol and who knew what.

"Am I hurting you?"

She shook her head no, though it wasn't true.

"I was Lomius."

"Hm?"

"You asked who I was with in the war. I led the Knights."

She nodded but she already knew. Pier had revealed as much.

"You needn't fear Kovim's intentions in this case. The man we caught at the melee said the bounty was put out by…a specific member of the Council."

"By Hodran?"

"By Otreya."

Trzl gulped. "No, that…has to be a mistake." Her grandfather should understand that she wanted nothing more to do with Hodran and Kovim. That she'd had enough.

"The man insisted you were soon to inherit Otreya's powers."

"His powers?" She tried to laugh, but she knew Marek would see through it.

"He can manipulate. Very well." Marek waited, but she had nothing to say. "The man said you lived in the villages to learn the names and faces of the people, and that when you came into your own you were going to drive them into the Cities to slavery. He was no bounty hunter. He wanted you and Malcom dead as soon as possible."

Trzl knew what he meant about Grandfather, even as she fought to deny it in her own mind. "Do you believe such preposterous vomit?"

He became tense and grave at the same time. "I don't know what to believe of you, Trzl."

"I'm not a spy or a turncoat. I could never be that complicated."

"The Derm you couldn't." He stopped touching her for a moment. "You ran from me to my own nemesis—he was your perfect rebel, your hero of the day. Only too happy to take what you offered."

"You do not know."

"Oh, I know. And I warned you."

"There was a whole empire to consider."

"Don't pretend you helped anyone." A little of his Ashlin accent was coming through.

"Oh, and you did? By leading the Knights of Rilch into battle time and again, knowing it was a losing cause, that you were killing your own people? *My* people? I had to go to someone. I had to make the best choice I could."

"You never needed to go to anyone. You may have needed the protection of a man, though it seems improbable, but any plow boy would have served. You are far stronger than you think yourself, Trzl."

That wasn't what she meant. She never thought once of protection. Must he always be overly gallant? All these years that she thought him dead, there was one thought that drove itself into her mind. "If it weren't for your infernal discipline, Malcom would have been *your* son."

"If I had forsaken my discipline, as you call it, I would be no different from Hodran, and you would hate me as such."

"I would not. You were always different from him."

"Oh, yes. In case the man who wanted your body and your connections didn't take you, you could fall back on a man who wanted you for your soul. Allel forbid."

"Stop." She didn't want to be bitter about something that happened long ago. She wanted to be patient, to try to understand what he felt. "I wouldn't have fallen back on you. You made sure of that when you formed the Knights."

He let out a laugh that scoffed her. "Everything is not about you, Trzl.

For true, I'm glad you resisted me. You were a labyrinth of a woman, with men and powers you wished to please more than you could have ever cared for me. You and I weren't meant to be lovers. We aren't the kind."

That shouldn't have hurt, but it did. It struck her hard in the gut, and she wished she could stand, throw herself at him, pound his chest. "You loved *her*."

Marek turned fierce all at once, his voice going heavy. "Do not speak of her."

"Who was she?"

"No one you were ever fit to... She..." He was quiet for a long moment, and then words poured from him, words that must have been bottled for too long, coming out strong and angry. "She was perfect. She was like a fire that burns everything in the room, everything in her path, makes them bound to the brightness of the sky." He let his breath out slowly. "No one likes to have a ruler. I know better than anyone. But whatever you and your compatriots had against the Orion crown, there is something to be said for peace, Trzl."

She wondered what made him change the conversation to rulers and peace. Had *she* died in the war? Or in Dreibourge?

"When Skommek brought you here, I hated you for being alive. You, who used the lives of others as play things. And she, who would never dream of being half so selfish..."

Trzl felt something slipping through her fingers—something that had never really been there. "I never meant to use you that way. To destroy everything you loved. That wasn't why I did it." She bit her lip, and the admission burned. "I was...blinded. But I didn't have Malcom, then. Now I've lost him to people I can't trust. They're going to hurt him—"

Marek put a hand to her lips, as if she would hurt herself if she kept speaking. "You mustn't say these things tonight. I've told you, I am bringing Malcom back. He is not lost."

"I know you don't want to do this for me," she murmured into his hand. "I understand. I will repay you."

"I *am* doing it for you. Trzl, you've a son that I am near jealous of. He's strong and smart and unafraid. You did the best a mother could. Do not think for a moment I do not admire what you've done. I do, and I'll expect no payment."

His rough hands slid under her sliced dress with the herb mixture, light enough that she could barely feel them grace the skin, but a whimper or two came out.

"I'm sorry. I hurt you."

"It is not that." It was this. Him. So close.

Trzl turned onto her side, in spite of the pain from the movement, her vision still blurry but her mind clear. She reached up to trace his jaw, ran a fingernail down from his temple, around it, to his collar.

Marek did not resist her. She pulled on the laces of his shirt, pulled him down and toward her. His breath was even—and then it was not. She tugged once more, and his mouth was on hers. He cupped her neck, held her from moving away, his indifference dissipating. He was hungry, desperate. She kept her fingers tangled in his shirt, pushed back against him, forced him to brace harder, to kiss her harder. Her back hurt when she moved—hurt as much as a raw flame—but nothing hurt like the need to get closer to him. She knew it wouldn't last long, that soon he would shove her away as he always did. But here he was—raw, unbridled—for once. She couldn't miss this.

Marek didn't shove her. He let go gently, slipped his hand out of her hair, pulled her hand off of his shirt. He had one knee on the bed next to her, and he unfolded it and stood, distancing himself from her.

"I—" she started.

"Don't speak. Don't."

Trzl wanted to scream at him. Anything.

He leaned an arm against the bedpost. His hair fell in his face, hid his eyes from her. "You're hurt and exhausted and afraid for your son.

None of this… Tell me about the army."

"What?" she whispered.

"The troops, the outposts, where they are stationed. Tell me everything you know about the lay of the land. Now."

She didn't fight with him. Not now. He could say anything he wanted tonight. She was thirsty to hear him, to know him as something besides the image she created herself. "There are no military outposts, save at the borders."

"The ports?"

"Closed and guarded. Trade is at a standstill with anyone besides the Drei, as stability is difficult when so many of the people disagree on what to grow themselves. Whatever you do, you mustn't enter any of the Cities. You would be spotted immediately, no matter what disguise you wear. Everyone there is tallied and noted, even those who live in the country. The soldiers on guard know the names of everyone." She laid her head down again, exhausted. "They would take Malcom to the closest city, I think. Place him under guard. Probably those trading for him were of the City Guard at the First City, where Kovim resides."

"Is there a chance the gate sequences are changed as you claimed?"

"No, they cannot be changed unless they are rebuilt. It is a mechanism. As I've said, you mustn't use them. They would catch you immediately."

"Depending on what happens, I might be forced to sell them."

"You shouldn't. It would bring unchecked attention to anyone who knew them."

"I'm sorry."

"I am sorry I lied to you. I thought I might need to keep them…to reclaim Malcom from you."

Marek smiled. "You are as good a negotiator as any."

She had nothing to say to that beyond a deep search of his eyes.

He sat down next to her again and fixed the poultice methodically, as one bandages an unknown creature found in the woods. Yet, there was an odd sharpness to the words when he said, "Did Hodran ever lay a hand on Malcom?"

"He didn't touch Malcom. He isn't the kind of man who cares what children do."

"What did he do to you?"

She bit down on her lip and shivered. "Nothing."

"He did something. You used to be fiery and stubborn. There wasn't a frightened bone in your body. Now you try to seduce me even as you cower at my touch. What did he do?" He laid a hand on the front of her shoulder, the part with no cuts or welts on it. "You don't have to fear him. Not anymore."

She wanted him to say something else: that she could stay. "I don't fear him. I..."

"Tell me."

"I was afraid for Malcom. Hodran...he was with many other women. All the time. At first he would lie about them, and then he stopped lying. He didn't even care, and he thought he could still have me when he pleased. When I told him I was leaving him he went into a wild rage, and Grandfather said I needed to stay, then I decided I wasn't just leaving Hodran. I had to take Malcom away from all of them. I was the fool. For trusting him—ever—for thinking I could play that game."

Marek did not dispute her foolishness. "Did he hurt you?"

"He...hit me. Some. And I hit him back."

That strong muscle worked in his jaw, the one that meant he was keeping back something ferocious. "I'm sorry I did not find a way to kill him years ago. I came close. Many times, for many reasons. If I'd known he... I would have liked to spare you." He slid off the bed, released her hand, gathered things from around the room. More weapons and tools.

"You are leaving?"

"I must."

Trzl moved again, crying out with frustration at her immobility, not the pain. "I want to come with you. To get Malcom."

He stopped moving and stood there looking at her, his hand painfully near the iron ring of the door. "You have to stay. I'll be pushing a double pace or faster. You would—"

"Marek?"

He let out a heavy breath. His eyes locked with hers, like he knew what she would say. Like he was begging her not to say it.

"I'm not... I..."

He came back, kissed her once on the forehead. "I will bring Malcom."

{21}
Mission

GERNAN PLACED A HAND ON his temples before he ran his fingers down his long, tangled hair. He could not manage to calm his nerves in this short hour, and that was unusual. He was not a nervous man.

He was confident in his ability to kill with speed, but he hadn't fought with any Serens beyond the hill country. Marek must be from a City because he knew the Seren arts of the sword, but who was to say Marek's incredible skill was not average at best in his own country? No one could say, and that was what worried him.

Rescuing four captives from some Swamp People would have been easy. Marek counted Gernan's eagerness to take them from the Swamp People as a part of his naivety, no doubt, but Gernan was three years younger than Colstadt and far more sober. He did not like the look in the eyes of those women. They were scared. Perhaps Marek was right—they had been scared of *him*. The thought made him uncomfortable. He *wanted* to be feared by men. To be feared by women was rightfully unsettling.

When he saw Colstadt, he said, "Where is Marek?"

Colstadt shrugged his shoulders and tightened the straps on a bedroll.

"You are coming?" Gernan was impatient to be moving. "What is your hand in the devil-woman squabble?"

"I want to." Colstadt said it in a cool voice, one that couldn't know what is involved.

"You ever been out beyond Dragon Country?" Gernan asked.

"When I was a boy. My father was an excellent thief back when Dreibourge could support them."

Pier came into the predawn glow atop a fresh horse, offering a dry laugh. "Nearly an age ago now."

"We are not going to Dreibourge." Colstadt shifted uneasily. "Serengard is still beautiful, I am told."

Gernan wanted to laugh as well. "And frightful," he added, though he really didn't know.

Colstadt's slim, young face grinned. "I tell you, I am more ready for this than any of you. I've long wanted a chance at some of Kovim's goblins. Don't attempt to deny that you've wished for the same, Pier."

Pier gave a bemused smile, but Gernan saw that it was a forced expression. Pier was afraid as well.

Gernan was among the bravest of warriors, which made him one of Marek's choicest men. If he could play this well, he would gain still more favor, enough to one day challenge the Lord of the Castle, as was the way of it. Become the next Lord Marek. It was not that he lusted for power overly much—well, perhaps that was part of it—but he knew the ways of the cliffmen better than Marek. He wished to make them stronger.

Marek at last emerged from the castle. He brushed past Colstadt to the one of four saddled horses, ran his fingers over its flanks.

"Where is Tev?" Gernan asked innocently, gaining a glare from Colstadt.

"Not coming." Marek was quiet, feeling the horse's side.

"Skommek?" Pier continued.

"Staying. You need a horse, Gernan?"

Gernan nodded thanks, his bearing submissive if nothing else about him was. "I have my own horse."

Colstadt swung into his saddle with a flourish, smiling at the excitement of the impending danger, his hair falling across his face almost ridiculously. Gernan wondered if he looked like that as well—all young and stupid. He hoped that if one of them got themselves killed, it wouldn't be him.

They all urged their horses, the Drei sitting straight and tall, Marek and Gernan leaning forward and whispering in the ears of their elegant beasts, explaining where they were going and why. Well, on that score, they were neither of them like their own folk. Marek always said it was only the Desert People who knew the importance of a bond with a mount. Gernan kept whispering, all the way down the tunnels, telling his horse about the Cities, the creepers, the terrible things they would witness. And that Gernan would bring her home safely and give her a fresh, sweet root for a treat.

They sprung from the cave mouth and into the dry river bed just as light flooded the top of the cliff, bouncing off the stone surfaces until it lit their path on the canyon floor. The cold morning air welcomed them with a blast of wind that hit them in the face like a splash of water.

Gernan rode out in front of the others, waiting for Marek to meet him. It took only a moment; then their horses were neck and neck, an easy gait set so they would not tire. Gernan narrowed his eyes and glanced over at Marek. Their eyes met for a moment—a moment long with doubt and suspicion, but laden with a respect for the other.

This Marek was the first to come from the meadow lands, come to challenge their very own Lord Marek with a dozen Drei behind him and desperation in the way he gripped his sword. Yes, Gernan knew the drive and the need. If he were to guess, Marek had been somehow forced into leading his group of Drei, but he must have chosen to take the cliffs. Gernan would love to do both.

Marek had better watch his back.

ℨ

TRZL WOKE TO FIND A tall, elegant woman changing her bandages.

When did she drift off? Had Marek been here? Had he touched her, spoken to her? Or had she been dropped in here by someone else and dreamed the whole thing?

"Lord Marek left this for you."

A tiny bag of arabica beans. Yes, he had been here. The realization brought more unreasonable feelings to her overtaxed mind. She had a vague recollection of having thrown herself at him again. Had she?

No. Her lips remembered. He had kissed her.

"How long have I been asleep?"

The woman smiled a little. "Few hours have passed."

It was preemptive of her, but things happened fast in this place. "Do you have children?" Trzl asked.

"Yes. Two of them, another on the way." She patted her belly, the inevitable glowing smile converging on her face. "You have a son, yes?"

"Yes." Trzl nodded, wanting to sit up, to move. But it would probably hurt too much. "Marek has gone after him."

"I know. We all know." The woman stopped straightening things, leaned down and looked Trzl in the face. "I am sorry for you because if Lord Marek dies or doesn't come back—or any of our men do not come back—you know it will be you that we will blame."

"What have I ever done? I was dragged here against my will."

"Lord Marek should have sent you back where you came from. He led his men to think that he kept you in order to gain something valuable, but in truth he had other reasons, I think, far less useful. And I bless Pier for trying to learn what you might know. To extract something of value from a prisoner who has meant nothing but trouble."

Trzl made a quick guess, let it spill out. "You are Pier's wife?"

She nodded bluntly. "Yes."

"You make good soup."

"Glad it was to your liking."

"I do not see that there is anyone to blame but Lord Marek then."

She shook her head. "My husband knows him better than I would like to, and I tell you Lord Marek has the right to be weak for a woman now and then. Today it is the woman I blame."

Trzl looked up at her awkwardly. "Are you going to beat me more?"

"I've a mind to. But I am not good at that sort of thing. Tev ordered me to change your bandages, and Tev is master. Leastwise, he is now."

Trzl frowned. She could identify Pier as a man of a breed she knew. Determined, predictable. This woman seemed likely to stab her in her sleep if it seemed good to her at the time.

"Why does Lord Marek live here?"

"Same reason any Dreis are here. Hiding from the Cities."

"And the rest? Those who are not Serens or Dreis. They have always lived in the cliffs?"

She stared at Trzl as if she were stupid. "We lived here under the last lord. All the Dreis came with the new Lord Marek."

"You are not a Drei, yet you married one."

"I do not think myself a Seren either. I was born here. I've a right to marry whom I choose, though there's some of my blood look down on that." She stood to leave, apparently finding Trzl's conversation dry. "Have you anything else you will be needing? I ask because I was told to."

Trzl shook her head. "No, thank you. You have been kind."

She answered with a grunt. Well, Pier picked one that was fine to look at but certainly knew how to be frosty. Like him.

Trzl tried to think back to the days when she was afforded the luxury of expressing her feelings about anything besides a burnt loaf of bread or the price of trowels being too high. Ever since Malcom's birth, everything she did was to get something. Something to give to him, something to protect him. She could not afford to dislike someone, could not afford to burn ties with anyone save the pure monsters. She might have to ask a favor of any of them someday.

It wasn't something she was prepared for. It was an instinct she had to obey, and when she did, living every moment for someone besides herself brought a freedom, a deepness within her that could not be stolen. No matter how many people disliked her, laughed at her, misunderstood her.

Malcom was everything to her. If Marek came back without him, she would go for him herself.

She slid off the bed, much as it hurt, and straightened herself into a sitting position. It really was not that bad. The fire had burned low, and she shivered, tried to pull some fabric up around her shoulders from behind her. There was a large, woven blanket that served, the one she'd slept on. It was deep royal blue with something the color of gold on it, certainly not made by these mountain people. Perhaps it was one of Marek's many plunders. Well, it was warm.

She tried to stand, but found that her knees buckled immediately. She would have to sit for a time and get used to this. She surveyed the room, tried to find things that would lend themselves as weapons. He must have many stashed in here if she only knew where to look. Certainly not under the bed. In that chest? In the wall?

Think. He took half a dozen of them the night before, sequestered them all over his person, had he not? Where did he take them from? There was furniture in here, rugs, loose stones. She just needed to search it all. And before she could do that, she had to stand up and walk across the room.

GERNAN DIDN'T LIKE BEING THE expendable one. Not knowing the country or the enemy they chased made him feel inferior—something new for him.

"These are from the city," Colstadt told Marek somberly. "See? Shoes on the horses. And good shoes, not rough-hewn like the meadow folk."

Marek slipped off of his horse and circled the pattern of hooves. "Anaqi continued south instead of returning to the hills."

"Looks like," Colstadt agreed.

"Why are we wasting time with Anaqi?" Gernan drew his horse up. "I could have told you which way Anaqi went myself."

"I wouldn't have trusted you to be accurate," Marek said.

Gernan thought that rather harsh. He shoved a long lock of hair away from his chin and insisted, "I would have told it true. You know I have no great love for Anaqi, though it pleases me that he deals with the Desert People." He cast a glance toward Pier and received a blank stare in reply.

"I don't care where Anaqi does his business, but where he goes after his supposed trade indicates whether he succeeded in unloading his merchandise," Marek said.

"Seems he did not?" Pier asked.

"Not if he headed to Neroi."

"The Second City," Colstadt corrected.

Marek smiled distantly. "The Chamberlain's palace is somewhere between here and there, is it not?"

Pier suddenly grew animated. "Marek, you are not—"

"By the Treacher, I am."

"He will know your face," Pier protested.

"As if I'd give a hanged goblin."

"You're a fool, or today you are. Trzl is doing this to you. Her child is the offspring of an enemy—both are better left to their own devices."

That is what we have all been saying, Gernan thought wryly.

"Shut it, Pier," Marek snapped. He was mad at Pier about something, too? "Before I do something we'll both regret."

"Admit that she has power over you, and you can end this trouble by making wife or slave of her, whichever pleases you," Pier suggested. "You are lord over her. Keeping her happy is not a necessity."

"Says a man who sees to his wife's every whim," Gernan put in. He refrained from mentioning that if Marek took a slave woman, it would make him quite the hypocrite.

"My wife was never a captive," Pier said. "She is loyal to me of her own wish. Besides, it is different when she carries a child. She would kill me in my sleep if I did not bow to her."

Marek ignored them, riding ahead in silence.

{22}
Tempers

THEY STOPPED FOR A BRIEF rest in a glen, and Marek told them to sleep until sunset. The horses needed water, as well as an hour to eat and let their stomachs settle. Gernan did not sleep. He spent the time watching over his horse, stroking her nose.

"You know we'll have to trade the horses out under cover of dark," Marek told him.

Gernan stuck his chin in the air. "Not mine, you won't."

"Don't tell me you brought your favorite animal," Marek scoffed.

"She goes everywhere with me. You didn't notice?"

Marek looked away, still troubled. "Not today."

Gernan wondered if indeed the woman had put a spell on him. He knew the Seren and the Drei did not believe in spells, but the cliff people knew they were possible. Perhaps a Seren woman could have learned the way of it.

"Is it true that you feel love for this woman?"

Marek turned molten eyes on him. "She fueled the fervor that killed my parents, my cousins, my friends. She did it with little remorse. Tell me—could you love such a woman?"

"Easily. Women do not need to be good. It is men who make the decisions that determine life and death."

"Ah, you easterners. Terribly impractical sometimes. Women build or destroy men. They influence as much or more. Without them, your men are nothing."

Gernan grinned. "So I hear you say it at last. You think we are nothing. Ha."

"Well, you were until I taught you how to use that sword."

He narrowed his eyes, then realized it had been in jest. Marek was entirely too moody right now. "Do you fear me?"

"I don't fear you, Gernan, but I'm not going to leave you to fight with Tev for control of the castle."

"You left Skommek."

"Skommek is not ambitious. You are."

That much was true, but Gernan hated to be clear as stream water in spring. He wanted to be confusing, as thunderclouds. "I wonder that you have always trusted Tev, and you cannot trust me, who has always been ready to aid you. What is she to you, I wonder?"

He expected a violent reaction from Marek, but he was either not listening or intentionally ignoring. He looked off to the west, a strange resignation coming over his features. He sat there just so until the sun slipped below the horizon, and Gernan saddled his own horse, smoothing back her mane and muttering softly. Then Marek stood and wordlessly reached for his horse's bridle, rubbing a hand over her flank before swinging on.

"An hour was not enough rest," Gernan said.

"Our quarry has undoubtedly changed horses at some crossroads and continued on with twice our speed," Marek replied.

"If you will stop in a village—"

"No."

"I can get us information. We will find them much faster. You want to bring the boy back, seems right we must take risks."

"Risks? Not Marek's code. Not anymore," Pier said from behind him. Marek did not respond. Pier pressed him. "The tactical move would be to enlighten the Desert People of the gate sequences. Let them raise fire and mortar. Our slipping in and out of the cities would then be a small matter."

"You know they would succeed only in storming the outskirts," Marek said. "There will be no taking on the Empire. They are not the kind to conquer for any reason, and bless them for it."

"Would that Tev would sell them while you are away. It would be righteous." Pier's face wore a hardness that said he meant every word. Gernan kept silent, not wanting to step between something that was looking more and more personal.

"Thank Allel I do not measure righteousness by your standard," said Marek.

"When we get the boy back, we should certainly sell him, Marek. And the woman, too, if she is worth anything at all."

"You have done quite enough concerning the woman." Marek looked as if he would like to strangle Pier. "Mount up."

Colstadt was still sleeping. Marek rode over beside him, letting hooves shake the ground, making Colstadt start, jump up and reach for his bedroll. He looked about him as if to say, *You did not see me sleeping, did you?*

Gernan would have laughed, but he could sense that he did not have allies in the two Drei. He had a vague feeling of dread in his gut—like they were already caught in the claws of a retching machine of old, their hands and feet useless. Pier knew it, too.

THE AREAS BETWEEN THE CITIES were an odd sprinkling of farmers that grew lesser crops, such as soybeans and erinweed. Most of it was now restful and full of grass as the country folk fell to the allure of the Four Cities and left their little stone houses to turn mossy and damp. It was all a well-orchestrated cause and effect when the other Chamberlains spoke of it, with their fine-robed gloriousness, but Hodran found himself bored endlessly by that kind of talk. After all, he had endured ten long years of it.

True, they built much out of those high-minded ideals, but when could they say enough? Kovim wanted to keep things moving forward, especially in regards to Dreibourge. And, if Hodran were to wager, Kovim had his sights set on the desert kingdom next. He would find that to be more trouble than it was worth.

So long as Hodran did not have to lead any more bloody campaigns, he would be happy, but he did not see that happening. It was already difficult to balance his duties as Chamberlain and one of the Council with his undying need to get under the skirts of his citizens.

He was chided for his weakness by his fellow Council members, every month when he made the journey to the First City to settle important affairs. He paid them no heed. He'd even started a recent binge of indulging in illegal slave purchases, something he had never allowed himself before. He usually liked to win his ladies, have them believe they were lucky to be with him. But he was getting older and had less time to pursue his greatest passion. With all his power, he really ought to have more freedom to employ in seducing pretty women.

He was having a glass of fine berry wine, alone on his balcony, when the knife came across his throat. The theatrics gave him pause but only enough to bring a laugh.

"Oh. Whose husband have I offended this time?"

"No one's husband, my friend. I come to settle an old debt."

Hodran started at the voice. The voice of a Drei. He hadn't slept with any Drei, but he had killed a few of them. "Who are you?"

"A friend of a friend. One you should not like to see again."

"I am honored." Hodran kept his tone even, smiling to himself and reaching up to adjust his slightly graying hair. "To what do I owe the privilege? Please, sit down. Have some wine. Remove that unsightly instrument from my throat, and we will speak like gentlemen."

The Drei let up on the blade a slight bit, but did not sit down. "We shall if you wish. But I warn you, I have a man behind me with an arrow pointed at your neck."

Hodran shifted in his seat, hoping his face did not look too terribly green. The Drei stayed hidden behind him. He kept the blade a few inches from Hodran's skin, causing him to gulp. "Do I know you at all?"

"No. I am with a group of bounty hunters whose prey was recently stolen from them. A boy by the name of Malcom."

Hodran was puzzled. "You said—"

"Yes. Trzl sent me."

Hodran cleared his throat, surprised. "Trzl is alive?"

"She is alive and pondering why her son was rudely taken from her."

"It was not I. She will tell you plainly I did not care for the boy. Girl was enough trouble to me, as it happened. I'll pay whatever price she wants."

The Drei moved, just enough for Hodran to make out long, slender fingers with perfect nails. Skilled fingers, no doubt. "She wants to know what happened to the boy. There was a price on his head, put out by the Council, or someone with equal power."

Hodran was, again, genuinely surprised. "It is none of my affair."

The Drei rose slowly, but the blade came up quickly, enough to make Hodran jump. "We shall see about that. Tell me about the crypt in the First City."

Now Hodran did turn a strange shade. He could feel the blood draining from his face. "The crypt? This has something to do with the crypt?"

"Trzl thinks so." One smooth slice down the edge of his neck promised that the next would be horizontal. It made him sweat. "Would the Council of Four want to open it without your knowledge?"

That is exactly what they would like to do, but the only occasion to do so would be a deviation from their original plan. A complete reworking of the Council, the Chamberlains, the Cities as they knew them. But he was not about to tell this strange friend of Trzl's the ins and outs of their overzealous blackmail schemes. Kovim could be playing him in more ways than one.

"Kovim has sent you to scare me, has he?" Hodran ciphered obvious surprise in his enemy. That boded well. "Understand, I am no enemy of his, but if he thinks he can use Trzl or Malcom to get to me, he is sorely mistaken. The boy and his mother can go to the Treacher, for all I care."

He could hardly wait until this creepy Drei left him to his own devices so that he could set out for The First City himself. Going to try to open the crypt without him, were they? By the Derm. He would show them.

The Drei turned to leave. "You might as well sit here in the air for awhile, Chamberlain. Don't bother calling for your guards. My men and I cleaned them out on our way in here." He leaned in with a dry snicker. "Enjoy your wine."

THE PALACE WAS OF NEW construction and strange to Gernan's eyes. Certainly not practical—not even designed for easy heating and cooling. There were a few dark corners, hidden passageways inside that allowed the guards to mobilize themselves quickly. Marek seemed to know instinctively where they would be. Or perhaps he had been here before?

They only killed one guard on the way in. Marek knocked two out cold, strangling a third with his bare hands when he refused to lose consciousness. The man might not even be dead. They opened a clean trail into the southern face of the building and held it while the two Drei slipped inside to locate Hodran.

Gernan felt a surge of confidence. The men in these corridors were not frightful. Some were slightly taller than him, but they weren't half so muscled. Their clothing was not conducive to moving quickly, although the armor looked effective enough. He guessed that was why Marek went straight for the head. Still, Gernan would feel much better if they could kill a few more of these soldiers. Just run at them, yelling, bury a knife in their chests. Something.

Gernan saw that Marek was on edge, almost excited. A breath of the air about him said he longed for a chance to scrap with this Chamberlain. Did he lust for power in the same manner as the lords of the Caps, those who lived higher up in the cliffs? He had never betrayed as much in his years as Lord Marek. The man was hard to read.

A few minutes, and the Drei were back. They made no sound as they reappeared, their feet as silent as their breath. *That* was more frightful than these soldiers.

Marek jerked his head in the direction of the gardens and the road. Colstadt led the way, slipped ahead, looking like a fox slinking about with his red hair.

Suddenly, there were four guards upon them, coming head on. Colstadt took his short swords from his back and sliced the first two across the throat, causing them to crumble in the dirt, not enough breath left to gasp once. Gernan was shocked at the sight. He never saw Colstadt use those swords in anything but training—never saw him wound a man at all, for that matter.

Marek pulled a short blade from inside his clothes and stabbed the third, while Colstadt killed the fourth with another slice at the neck.

It was over too fast for Gernan to move. By the time he stood and glanced behind him, the four soldiers were dead, and Colstadt and Marek had dashed ahead again. Pier slipped an arrow back into his quiver, and Gernan realized he had been aiming into the fray, waiting for a clean shot.

They caught up to Marek and Colstadt just as they crossed the road and made it into a thicket. The land sloped quickly upward, but Marek led them along the length of it for nearly a mile until they reached a stream. They were not pursued, but they were not tired either.

Interesting. His chest was accustomed to the thin, meager air of the mountains. Here, in this rich, fertile land—miles lower and full of the gifts put out by plants—each breath filled him with inhuman vigor. The northern folk suspected it was a curse of the valleys, a spell of the goblins and faeries who lived in the meadow lands, but this was making him wear a splitting grin. His people would be superior in this climate. *Superior.* This was why the Serens were afraid of them—the real reason.

He glanced quickly at each of them, wondered if they all felt this strength. Pier wore his typical blank expression, and Marek looked all-out angry. Gernan knew his grin looked stupid, but he didn't care. Colstadt was the only one who was gaping, wide-eyed. Had he never shed human blood before? Gernan wished it had been him. He wouldn't have minded.

Pier said, "He knows nothing of the boy."

Marek's eyes narrowed. "You are certain?"

Pier nodded. "I've tortured enough men to know."

"And women."

"She brought it upon herself."

"She always brought everything upon herself, but that's no excuse for you."

Pier changed the subject. "We'll loop back around to the horses. Then we'll find somewhere to trade them in before we swing south to the First City."

"Not my horse," Gernan said.

"Your own loss, Gernan," said Marek, "or you will kill your animal. We cannot stop in a cave when they tire as we cannot afford to lose the time. This is what is done when ground must be covered."

"You care nothing for your mounts for you have ten of them. My sweet gazelle has been mine since I was a boy. She is true."

Marek clenched his jaw stubbornly.

Gernan backed down, grumbling, staring at the ground. "Let me leave her in a village? I will trade her to someone of my choosing."

"Get it done within the hour."

Colstadt was still silent, staring. Perhaps only from exhaustion, but Pier was nodding toward him as if to say, *What are we going to do with this one?*

Colstadt was three and twenty, and it was a safe guess he had not killed a man before today. Or maybe he had long ago…in the war? Their only skirmishes had been with rogue Desert People and rival raiders from the other far reaches, and those conflicts seldom lasted long enough for much bloodletting.

Gernan did not need experience. He had slain a few cold dragons and a few mammoths in his day. A few men were not much different. Stab, slice, wipe the blade.

{23}
Rivalry

HE MADE CERTAIN TO USE the entire hour allotted him, mostly out of spite. It took only a few minutes of surveying the closest little cluster of houses to find a young stable girl who fell in love with his sweet gazelle.

"I will pay you to keep her for two weeks. And to give me any rotten old mount you have sitting in these mucky stables."

The girl claimed her stables were not mucky, and if she treated the horse well, could she ride it?

"You must understand that she is a spirited animal. She will run away from you if you do not speak to her all of your plans. And I will pay you handsomely now and handsomely when I return." He saw fit to lean in close and threaten the girl. "Sell my horse to another, and I will come for you."

Come for her and do *what*, the stable-hand did not ask. She nodded emphatically. Gernan smiled at her then and stayed awhile to tell stories about his horse and to reassure his pretty that he would be back for her, his sweetness, and not to miss him too much.

"Keep her locked up, or she will run away to be with me." The girl was wide-eyed with the magnitude of her task by the time he left, but still more wide-eyed by the nice little bag of gold he left in her hand. "Buy your mother something."

"I will," she said.

Gernan met up with Marek at the edge of the woods. Seemed he had traded their lovely mountain horses for mixed bloods.

"These were all you could find?"

"I'm incensed enough about it," Marek muttered. "What I wouldn't give for a few desert warm bloods just now."

"Where are the Drei?" Gernan asked, immediately suspicious.

"Scouting. There are several watch towers between here and the sea that we must avoid."

Marek kicked his horse, and Gernan rode behind him for awhile, none too eager to share his company. Colstadt and Pier joined them a few hills later, Colstadt holding his shoulders straight.

Pier drew himself up between them. "You are certain Trzl is not lying about the importance of this crypt? Hodran is convinced Kovim is using her against him. We shouldn't be stepping into a Council squabble. I'm not so sure the bounty was not a ruse."

Gernan said nothing. This was for Marek to answer, surely.

He brewed for a moment, then said, "Trzl has lied plenty, but she kept nothing from me when she knew her son was in danger."

"But did *you* extract the gate sequences? No."

"You would trust your information incurred by the whip, and not mine, procured by other means?"

"I would."

Pier could be such a jackass.

"You underestimate Trzl," Marek said. "Pain may wound her, but her child's pain wounds far deeper."

"If she is working for Kovim all this time…if she has made a deal with him—"

Marek held up a hand. "We extracted her from a village she had been hiding in for six years."

"She claims it was six years. Just how intimate was your bedroom chat?" Pier sneered. "I dare say she could lie to you as easily as to anyone. Me—I made sure of my information. Nothing like convincing someone they are going to die."

"You can stop boasting now, Pier. If your subjugation of a skinny little girl is something you are proud of, I suggest you find some birds to speak to."

"She is probably working for herself," Gernan said.

"Trzl is always working for herself," Marek retorted.

"I am meaning that she wants to destroy her old lover and his folk, so she plays the victim to you, knowing the Emperor wants her boy, and you come to blows with the Emperor just to retrieve him for her."

Marek shook his head. "She does not know me nor would she have known where I was."

"So you would like to hope, but there are gypsies this country over who might have whispered, and she succeeded in securing your help. What did she do for you, I wonder?"

Gernan knew better than to snicker along with his suggestion, but Pier did not.

HODRAN HAD NEVER ACQUIRED AN inner knowledge of Trzl's strange mind, but he did understand Kovim's, to a degree. Hodran had been recruited into this scheme to the dissolution of his own, subjected to the opinions of others and held accountable to a troop of rebels who were unpredictable at best. To be then distrusted and ignored when something important was afoot? It didn't figure that Kovim would ever doubt his worth. He had always been helpful, even when they were at an impasse.

Blackmail was his finest tool and he was ridiculously good at it. It was the reason they built the crypt—to hide the collective dirt they had amassed, not only on the royal family and their supporters, but also on each other. He had assumed he had the best of it, really. That they would play this game until they forgot about it and enjoyed their separate lives in their own halls of power.

But he knew what else was down there. He knew the books from the libraries of Ashlin had been preserved inside. The Books of Orion and the original copies of the Books of Derev. He knew the power these chronicles held and what they could evoke in a people long connected to the Orion family.

Hodran ran a hand across the shallow cut the Drei warrior had given him. He wondered what served to anger this particular man that would recruit him to a cause of Trzl's. Did he think any of them could be bribed to change the situation with the Drei? He should know there was no point in engaging Hodran in any such scheme. There was nothing he could do, no matter what they managed to drag out of the crypt.

He was a little afraid when he called for the keeper of his palace. He did not want the request to be met with the silence of fresh blood.

To his relief, a serving maid came running. "The keeper will be here momentarily."

"Where is he?"

"There has been an incident... What it is, I am not sure."

Hodran smacked the girl lightly to let her know he was done with her and went in search of his guards. He found them clustered around four bodies. He knelt to examine the wounds. Three of them were cut at an angle that only a one-edged short sword could manage—something he had only seen carried by the Drei. Another was stabbed cleanly between the ribs, in the manner of a Castle Guard duel. This was curious. Where did Trzl suddenly acquire friends with the training of the Seren arts?

"By the Treacher," he swore. At least none of his best had met this fate. He gestured to his keeper, ignoring the mess in the middle of his garden.

"Someone crept inside," said the keeper. "I am having the house checked—"

"They have departed, I am sure. These are the only casualties?"

"Yes."

"Good. I need a picked force mounted and prepared immediately. We received a summons for the First City. This time, alert the army of the Second City and have them ready to act if I so demand. Also, the watch towers. Tell them I am coming and not to be alarmed."

"As you wish, Chamberlain."

Hodran went to his armory alone. He chose swords from among the newest and finest, leaving off the old Ashlin-style weapons that Kovim and Otreya abhorred greatly. No need to stir up any more bad blood than was already stirred.

THE FIRST CITY HARDLY RESEMBLED its origins as the port city of Berekst. Colstadt remembered the place as quaint and bustling, far too small in size for the amount of people pouring in and out of its crumbling walls. Streets mirrored the wharfs they ended on; dykes and warehouses and bawdy fish taverns made up the majority of buildings, complete with a fortress by the sea that housed soldiers back in the days of Altrun Orion.

They slid on their bellies through underbrush. The last time Colstadt was here, he had tried to stowaway aboard a ship bound for the Caps. That was before the rebel army took the city. Before his father died and he joined Pier at the border. Before his hair turned dusky red and he had to shave his chin to stay handsome.

From here, they could see that the walls were now high and smooth, encompassing twice the land and half the color.

Pier raised his head. "They have reinforced the guard presence as well."

Marek nodded. "I'd assumed as much. Kovim is a smart dictator, and he has useful allies."

"And look at the gates. You would think he expected to be attacked *here* when any fool can see this would be the last place he could expect the Desert People to land. It is far too sheltered. I wonder if all the cities are as guarded as this one?" Pier sounded squeamish.

Marek nodded. "More than likely. He's made no bones about his fear that someone will try to take his Cities from him. As if anyone could. He has the Seren strapped down with a million cords."

Colstadt heard the bitterness in Marek's voice. Bitterness he and Pier shared, but Gernan would never understand. "Does he conscript everyone for the army? Where are the commoners?"

"There are no commoners anymore," Pier answered, a weathered tone to his voice. "They are known as citizens. Milliners, tradesmen, tailors and book-keepers—all of them leveled. The Empire is a machine now, running on ideas, as they would put it. Who is to say how long they will love it or when some of them will tire of it and wish for the return of an Orion? Not that the wish will do them any good."

Colstadt ducked his head. These were some of the things they never spoke of because they ran too close to secrets. Secrets he often wished he did not know—for if he didn't, he could be brothers with Gernan and have nothing between them. Instead, he knew firsthand that Marek, Tev, and Pier once fought with the Knights of Rilch. That they hadn't even trusted the Serens they fought with. That the few outlaw Drei scraped together by Pier were their last friends in the world.

He had discovered Tev was a woman on his own. She had been angry, smacked him and threatened him, but he often thought she was relieved that some of them knew. Not that she said much about it. But she told him her thoughts occasionally, and he savored each one.

"You need a closer look?" he said casually, his heart pounding. He was ready to use his short swords again, although he much preferred his bow. Much.

"Not sure that's the best idea." Pier frowned.

"I'm the one for it." Colstadt swiped a hand across his clean-shaven chin to prove his point. His hair was the right length, too.

Marek narrowed his eyes, thinking. "How many Drei live in the Cities, Pier?"

"Plenty, now. But don't you think I'd be—"

"No."

There was more to this. Pier's face was recognizable to someone? It must be a good story, whatever it was.

"Colstadt, you know how to—"

"Use my former accent to convince the guards I am a poor farmer from Dreibourge looking for work on a Seren grain farm. Yes, I know." He unstrapped his short swords from his back and tossed them to Pier. "Keep these?"

"Of course."

"Meet back here by sunset," Marek told him. "And Colstadt, stay on the outskirts. Trzl said they have tallies of who may enter the cities and who may not."

As he slipped away, he overheard Pier say, "I know the sequence to that damned gate."

THE EMPEROR WAS VERY SHORT. Malcom expected more of a man, for the terror he struck in those of his village—and for the way Mem always shushed the people who spoke his name. The soldiers who brought him wore heavy helmets that covered their features, and they forced Malcom to wear one the entire journey. It hurt his neck and made him wish his hands were free so he could pull it off and toss it to the ground.

He could think of nothing else besides finding some food; yet he was forced to meet the wretched Emperor. He stood with his shoulders thrown back, causing the Emperor to lean toward him and ask, "Are you afraid of me, child?"

Malcom squinted, realizing that this man's face was actually familiar. He had seen him once, when Mem thought him too young to know what was going on. And true, he hadn't known, but he always noticed when she was unhappy.

Malcom said, "No."

That made the Emperor laugh, a crinkling laugh that was far too gruff for his lithe, youthful figure. "Good. I would hate to scare a child. I am a good man, you will see, much more reliable than your father is."

Malcom looked puzzled but said nothing. The Emperor was seated in a high-backed chair against a wall. The room about him was white. Not white marble or white stone, but wood that was finished white. It was sparkling and new. Malcom wondered if perhaps he had been taken all the way to the land of faeries and goblins. This looked like somewhere they would live.

"You do know who your father is, don't you, Malcom?"

Malcom shook his head, pretended to forget the words Marek and Pier had spoken on the parapet.

"Ah. It is just as well. Your mother wanted to protect you from such scum, and I do not blame her. How is your mother?"

"I don't know."

"You don't know? Have you not been with her? Is she still alone somewhere, waiting for me? I know she ran away because she was dubious of my attention, but in all honesty, she should have been used to it. She was born for greatness, your mother."

He lit something that smoked. Malcom had heard about this new fashion, but he had never seen it done. He continued to stare at the Emperor. "Are you going to sell me?"

"Where would you hear such a thing? People are not to be bought and sold. That is an old tale of the hill people, and one you should not be listening to."

"I don't listen to them mostly. But I've been bought twice this fortnight."

"Well, no need to worry that it will happen again. I've a few short tasks for you, and then you can be on your way." His eyes narrowed, studying Malcom, as if he might have something else in mind for him. "I am disappointed that the price on Trzl's head seems to have gotten lost in translation. I would have liked to see that little desert pepper again, as would another man I know. Last time I spoke to her, she threatened to cut off my tongue if I spoke another word."

"I remember," Malcom said.

The Emperor started, as if Malcom had struck him with something. He walked up and leaned toward Malcom's face. "You do?"

"Yes." Malcom wanted desperately to spit right at his nose, but he wasn't sure what might happen if he did. He had never been in this vast of a city, nor had so many soldiers about him at once. Who knew what the rules could be?

"Well, my boy, we will not waste any time. You will see why you were summoned here, and then you will be allowed to go. Not home, of course, but there are plenty of fine warehouses where one of your age could find himself happily employed."

{24}
Escape

TRZL WAITED AN ENTIRE DAY and night for her door to open to anyone besides Tev. She knew better than to take on someone who had ridden with Marek in the war.

Enough time had passed for her to regain some strength, to search the room for anything Marek might not have taken. She knew she was breaking faith with him. She wanted to choke on her own thoughts, to change her mind and stay, but she could not wait any longer. If Marek failed to bring Malcom, there must be an alternative. Something.

She kept seeing it a million ways. Malcom in the hands of Hodran and Otreya for Allel knew how long and the Treacher knew what. Marek, dead, cut in a dozen pieces. The vision of a man of his strength lying broken and beaten made her shudder, but she ought to be prepared for the reality. Before this was over, she might have to grovel to someone worse than Marek for help.

There was some rope that tied back the curtains on the large, ornate bedposts. They made her think briefly of Dremir—and the last time she had seen him—sentenced to be beheaded in the square of the First City.

When she had asked him what for, he had chuckled bitterly to himself and said, "Politicals have no use for fanatics once they have done their job."

He'd been coiled in the corner of his dungeon, the most subdued Dremir ever got.

"I know why they sent you down here," he had spat at her.

"They?"

"The Council. You work for them. Like a parrot who is given treats for speaking words."

"No one sent me. I heard you were here and I came myself."

"How did you hear?"

"Hodran. He was boasting to some friends. What are they going to do with you?"

"Kill me. On a block. Claim I attacked a woman. You, much as you hate me, know I am not evil. It is they who are done with me. I'm just a cask of powder, now, waiting to explode."

"I thought you believed in all of this. In Kovim."

She would never forget the way Dremir had pulled himself close to the bars, close to her face, looked deep into her eyes.

"I have always believed, stronger than anyone. But that is why they cannot have me around. There will always be good and bad folk on each side of every coin, Trzl. You—I think you fell on the wrong side. But you might be a good folk. Depends what you decide to do."

He had looked at her narrowly, and then laughed, "Have a fine day, Councilor."

When she had finished climbing the stairs, pulled her cloak heavily over her face and stepped into her carriage once more, she had noticed her sash was missing. The next day she was told Dremir used it to hang himself in his cell. A part of her rejoiced that he had not met the block, not been falsely accused, not had people shake their heads and agree with his condemnation. It was one thing to bring about the ill fate of a stranger—another to stand by as one's friends were dismembered.

The memory caused her to tremble now, holding this rope in her hand. She did not want to harm anyone with it. But she might have to.

When at last the door opened to a girl younger than herself, come to change the bandages, she let her do her job first. The cool, fresh poultice on her back brought a shot of energy that made her shiver comfortably. She knew she should rest longer, let it heal. If she started to move now, it would break open the scabs, and she would be wrought with pain again in a few hours.

No. Time to do this.

She caught the girl from behind, pulled the rope up around her neck. "I'm not going to hurt you. I just want you to knock on the door and get them to unlock it. I have to get out of here."

The girl did not act frightened. Not a good sign. She did as Trzl ordered and knocked on the door. "I am done," she said simply.

Trzl pulled the shredded sleeves of her dress up over her shoulders, freeing her arms so she could use them. She swung around as quickly as she could, grabbed the weapon of the guard who manned the door, and swung it into his face.

"Do not follow me," she hissed at him, hoping her swiftness would be enough to frighten him. She ran to the closest corridor. It appeared empty, and she continued down it, kept her feet as light and soundless as she could. She had scarce gone down two staircases when her legs began to feel weak, and she was afraid for a moment that she would not make it to a horse.

Then she heard the echo of shoes behind her, a yell. A fresh shot of adrenaline filled her, and she charged down another few flights. As long as she kept moving steadily downward, surely she would come to the dungeons or the horses. Something she recognized.

Her nose found it first. Horses. To the left and down. There were two torches lighting the hall between the stalls. Horses inside chewed their hay thoughtfully. She slipped into the first stall, took a tall, blond mount by the halter, and climbed on without a saddle.

One hiss and the horse took off down the tunnels, danced down rocks in a dark dream world all its own. Trzl laid her head flat against its neck and murmured words to herself. She wasn't sure why, perhaps because the dark made her want to hear a voice, even her own, to not feel alone. Mixed with the sound of the wind, the pounding of hooves, the ripple of the horse's muscles beneath her, the ache of wanting Marek, the tenseness of fear for Malcom... It all became a smooth, dark feeling of loneliness, one that stretched into eternity with no resolution.

And then they burst from the mouth of the cave into bright sunlight and a smooth floor of rock. She thought she should slow the horse now that she could see the treacherous ground she galloped over, but the air was moving fast and she needed the speed.

She let the horse have his freedom and snuggled against its neck, praying she made it out of the canyon before nightfall.

COLSTADT FOUND TWO OF THEM sleeping. Pier alone was awake, keeping watch. He looked as if he was very much through with this gremlin chase.

Colstadt kicked Marek's leg lightly. "The Council hall is on the western side of the city, near the wall. Actually, rather close to the coast."

"Is Kovim there?" Marek asked.

"It was impossible to determine for sure, but from what I heard, he doesn't leave often."

"The crypt?"

"Where you told me it was. The city folk know about it. They think it holds old relics from Ashlin. Apparently, it is not heavily guarded because there are some vicious birds…"

Marek snickered. "Gherra birds? They are not vicious. Clever, Kovim. Do they not have pirates anymore? Berekst used to be an occasional target for…"

"Near as I could figure, they hung a few too many pirates, and they don't come around anymore. Wharfs are only for fisherman."

"Dermed."

"There are questioning points at every quarter, but they are sloppy at the wharfs. We can walk right around the embankments and come up from the shore."

"Excellent." Marek handed Colstadt's short swords back. "We move as soon as darkness is complete."

"And why do we assume the boy will be near this crypt?" Pier asked.

"His blood opens the crypt. As Hodran's son, it is Trzl's only guess as to what use Kovim would have for him. If nothing else, this will afford us a decent entrance to the city, and under cover of night, we can hope to locate Kovim, hope that Malcom is with him or will be soon. We take Colstadt's suggestion and skirt the wall, coming in at the coast. Let's get out of these weeds and down to the water. Colstadt?"

Colstadt led the way, trudging through the brush as quietly as possible. It would take hours to get there stealthily, of that he was sure, and it would give him too much time to think. He wished Tev were here, especially if this were his last night alive… But then, he wouldn't want her to die with him.

"We would do so much better if my own sweet girl were here," Gernan grumbled, still trying to blame Marek for his lack of fine horseflesh. But they would've had to leave the horses at the edge of the brush anyway.

"You would have her sniff our way in, as a dog would?" Colstadt tried to joke, but Gernan flashed a glare his direction. "I am glad I don't own a horse. She sounds as if she were as much trouble as a woman. I'll take a woman. Far prettier."

"You don't know beauty, leastwise not when it smacks you in the face," Gernan said.

"And your own sweet girl? So sweet that she has no name."

Pier hissed at them, making a signal to stop. "Silence."

After pausing for a minute and hearing no sound, Colstadt led them down into a gully that smelled vile. A heavy mist was falling with the evening. Everything looked strange in the fog, especially the heavy iron bars that cropped up without warning inside this murky mess. Colstadt had no guess as to why the bars were here, unless they were braces for a building that no longer existed. The muck was thick, and it tangled about their legs in an attempt to pull them down.

Colstadt had a heightened sense of awareness, one he recognized from dark nights before the cliffs—like those when he indulged in a long, tall shot of desert arabica—but with that came a weakness for dismissing the little things. Like the rock he tripped over and the iron bar he ran into in the fog. Twice.

Gernan trudged far ahead, moving quickly in condemnation of their caution. So long as he made no noise, it would not be a problem, but Colstadt saw that it made Marek uneasy. He looked jumpy. They all looked jumpy.

"You know he would like to supplant you as Lord Marek," Colstadt whispered, finding it impossible to keep quiet. "You will teach him everything—and then Gernan will use it to usurp you, to someday kill you in a fair fight."

Marek actually smiled. "Maybe in a few years. When I am a bit older, a bit slower, and Gernan reaches his pinnacle of strength and skill."

"It does not worry you?"

"I would much rather fight Gernan than you or Pier. At least Gernan fights as a Seren does. I will never rival the swiftness and cunning of the Drei."

That made Colstadt smile. "War and medicine. We Drei are

exceedingly proud of our knowledge, but it doesn't mean we cannot be outdone. You were one of the Knights, with the training of the Guard. Far better training than I."

"Do you want to supplant me? Given a few years I would hand it to your lot without contest."

Colstadt would be lying to himself if he did not admit that incited interest. "Would you not give it to Tev?"

"I would if he wanted it."

"Why did you not bring...her?"

Marek looked at him sharply but did not scold him. "Tev has been with me through enough battles, and this one does not involve her. You haven't an inkling of what she's had to do."

Oh, but he did. He'd seen her fight. Tiny, precise, and willing to deal with any threat, whether it concerned her or not. He couldn't help but think that Marek was making an admission of a sort by leaving her behind. An admission that he meant to die here.

Dermed, he missed having her with them.

Marek stopped walking and blew air threw his teeth. "Have you spoken to her?"

Well, this was embarrassing. Were his feelings that obvious? "I did. She threatened to kill me."

"You'll find me equally happy to kill you if you lay a hand on her."

Colstadt thought he was being laughed at, and that was not amusing. "I would never hurt her."

"Be careful who you claim to love. You may have to choose between life for her and life for yourself, only to learn that your choice accomplished nothing and she dies anyway."

Colstadt gulped, staring back at Marek. This was more than he heard from the man ever. It wasn't as if Marek had to tell him. He remembered Marek's wife. Who could forget her?

"You'll find Tev to be all pain as well but of a different sort. You've been warned."

Colstadt would have liked to argue, but they were at the sea.

Gernan was already easing his way down a sand slide. "We will have to go beneath the surf, just along this bar, and come up on the other shore."

"The surf is stronger than you think," Marek said.

Gernan laughed. "It is far gentler than the surf at the entrance to the Caps, and I've sailed that before. See how tame it is?"

"It looks tame. To trick you."

Marek took everything heavy off his person, save his weapons and his first layer of clothing. Colstadt silently did the same. He would have been as excited as a child to touch the south sea again were it not for the vastness of the City and the contrasting meager size of their company.

Pier had one more argument before they made the beach. "Did you think, Lord Marek, that if we are late, which we probably are, the boy is likely dead already?"

"We'll learn the truth of it ourselves."

MALCOM WATCHED THE LIGHTS OF the soldiers with widening eyes. They went steadily downward, deeper and deeper into layers of rock. He was no longer afraid of the long passageways in the Cliffs of Marek because he had friends there, but this was different. He did not know these men.

He shivered. It was cold in here, and there was nothing to keep him warm. As they came around a corner, there was a sudden draft, accompanied by a loud roar that grew greater and greater.

The sound of the sea hitting rocks.

{25}
Сомбат

GERNAN ROLLED ONTO THE SAND and coughed up a few gulps of sea water. He was not an excellent swimmer, but he was stronger than those two Drei. He'd always known, he told himself—ever since beating Colstadt in a close arm wrangle.

Marek motioned to keep themselves hidden in the water a moment longer. There were torches up there. A sentry, maybe two.

Why was there not a guard on the beach? It did not sit right.

"What are we waiting for?" Gernan hissed to Marek, having to raise his voice above the surf. This was beginning to look more and more like the trap he thought it was. A curse was a curse.

Marek only shook his head. He leaned over to Pier and spoke softly, too softly for Gernan to hear.

"A moment. Stay." Marek slid out of the water and disappeared up the beach. Gernan snorted to himself. Did Marek think he was the only one with a stomach for danger?

Gernan rolled out of water and waited on the wet sand.

Marek came back within a few minutes. "Two sentries on the beach, two at the top of the cliff."

"The two on the beach?"

"Dealt with."

"They have the boy," Colstadt said. His voice was so low it sounded like the coo of a dove. His eyes must be overly sharp. Gernan could not see a thing.

"You are sure?"

"I am."

Marek gritted his teeth. "Then we go."

⚔

MALCOM UNDERSTOOD WHY THEY SAW fit to shackle his ankles, but he did not understand why an aide insisted on rolling up his sleeves and washing his hands. The Emperor was doing the same, as was an old man with a handsome face and a beard.

Then came a sharp knife, and Malcom tried not to be squeamish.

Were they going to kill him?

No, they held it out first to the Emperor. He sliced his finger across it, a deep slice, one that bled nastily. He held his hand over a little rock shelf that was illuminated only by the torch of a soldier.

But then the aide wiped the knife with a cloth and held it out to Malcom. Malcom stared at it, frozen. Two men seized his arms and nicked his palm in the same manner. It hurt badly, but Malcom did not cry. He grunted, glaring at the men who held him. They forced his dripping hand over the rock shelf as well.

"You are a good boy," the old man said, calmly cutting his own hand and following suit. "It is time to do this, Kovim. You were wise to agree to it."

The Emperor frowned in return, as if he was not sure he trusted the old man. Malcom did. His face was much kinder than any other here, and his eyes reminded him a little of his mem.

"All right," the old man said. "We have everything we need. Open it."

The Emperor ran his fingers together. "The key," he said. An aide handed him a large key made of iron and he shoved it into the lock and turned it.

There was a rumble as stone tumblers moved, and then a cavern opened in front of them. Two torchbearers stepped inside, shining light on stacks of bound books and tools. The old man drew a long breath, his eyes going bright with an odd shine. He turned back to Malcom, holding a clean, white cloth.

"Here you are, my boy. That blood of yours is more important than any of ours. Don't spill too much of it."

That didn't make any sense. The old man stepped inside the crypt and reached back for Malcom, but then there was a noise in the dark, over the sound of the surf. A thud. The old man's eyes narrowed, and he tugged on Malcom's hand.

"Come, my boy. Things to be done."

Blood from his hand seeped onto the cloth and made him a little dizzy, but he followed, more puzzled than scared. Soldiers entered behind them. Light from a torch flooded the inside of the cavern, and Malcom saw that the walls were lined with weapons of copper-colored steel.

The old man focused on a massive stone chest, then gestured to two other soldiers. "Open it," he said.

Malcom felt his spine tingle as they pushed the lid up and off. The contents seemed to glow even before the torchlight fell inside the box. There were scrolls—and lots of them.

"Do you know what these are, Malcom?"

Malcom didn't, but he felt somehow that he should.

"No matter." The old man smiled, reached inside and took out a solid silver pendant. It was delicate filigree with a teal topaz set into it that was almost the size of his fist. He placed the pendant around Malcom's neck. It wasn't heavy, but Malcom felt as if it would burn through his chest.

The old man opened one of the scrolls and took the cloth from his bloody hand. His eyes locked on Malcom's. "I'm not going to hurt you, but you must do as I say."

Malcom nodded slowly, not sure what was happening. His whole stomach was in knots and butterflies, and the old man hadn't let go of his hand. He pulled it toward him and squeezed it.

"Ow!" Malcom yelped.

The man didn't stop. He squeezed until Malcom's blood ran into a trickle and fell in heavy drops from his hand, onto the scroll that lay open beneath. Malcom stared at it and noticed stains he hadn't seen before. Blood stains. From someone besides him? He tried to pull his hand away, but the man just kept squeezing.

There was a vial of some sort in his hand. Malcom hadn't seen him grab it. Had it been in his robes? The man tipped it upside down, and the contents landed as a dark powder on Malcom's arm, mingling with the drops and stains on the scroll beneath.

The man's eyes were bright aqua, twinkling. "This is it, child. Your destiny. Where your father failed, you will succeed."

Malcom didn't know what he was talking about. His hand throbbed and screamed at him, his head felt light, and the pendant about his neck was a heavy weight on his heart. "Take it off," he rasped.

"Soon enough."

The air was smoky. Not wood smoke. Something else. Malcom could hardly breathe. "Take it off now!"

THAT COLSTADT WAS THE FASTEST climber was a surprise even to him. He passed Marek on the way up, waiting for him at the first outcropping to be sure he was not outrunning them. Marek reached him, checked to be sure he still had all of his weapons in place, whispering to Colstadt to do the same.

As soon as Gernan pulled himself onto the ledge, Colstadt began to climb the next portion of rock. If this was his last night alive, he wanted to stay alone with his thoughts. He had trouble believing Tev was all that complicated. She lived next to him as a warrior, barely speaking, offering slight sarcastic commentary when she did. If anything, she should be easy to understand.

Colstadt pulled himself onto the rocky ledge at the top, and he could see the glint of steel helmets somewhere in the dark. The soldiers were clustered at a cliff wall a mere fifty yards from his entrenchment. He reached a hand down to help Marek up, then Gernan, and finally Pier, gesturing to each of them to be quiet.

He'd been right. They did have the boy. The crypt must be right there, immediately behind that group of soldiers.

"I count maybe twenty," Pier whispered.

"If you see twenty, there are forty." Gernan was learning.

"And two sentries." Pier nodded toward them.

Colstadt pulled out his set of short swords and checked the edge on his thumbnail. Not that he really needed to. It helped him focus. He saw Marek do the same with his curved blade and a couple of daggers. Finally, his long sword—dark Seren steel.

Marek raised a quick eyebrow to each of them. "Pier, Colstadt, take the lookouts."

Pier pulled his bow from his back, snapping angrily at the wet cord. He nocked an arrow, one of his own, hand-crafted from cedar.

They let their arrows fly. Pier's felled the first sentry instantly, swift and silent through the neck. Colstadt's arrow hit, but it was too low, embedding itself in the second sentry's shoulder. Pier swore, as did the other two. The sentry fell to his knees, grasping his wound. Colstadt nocked another arrow immediately and released it, hitting the man in the chest this time, making him incapable of raising alarm.

Time to move.

Marek sprung forward, his curved blades pulled first. Colstadt was right behind him, taking the left flank. He would fight his way to the outside of the cliff, working his way back through those he felled to make sure they were dead.

GERNAN COULD BARELY HEAR THE Drei running in front of him—quiet, because they wore the soft leather boots of a Seren today, not the heavy steel soles of a cliffman. He felt a flush of strange power. Something broke inside of him to give place to a wildness, a brutality.

A brutality that he needed. Or did he only want it?

The first slice of sword against skin was Marek's. A quick slit to the throat, and the life drained from the soldier's eyes so quickly that Gernan did not have to glance at the fallen body. Marek killed the next one in the same manner.

How? They wore metal armor that covered their entire bodies. Gernan could scarce see an armpit or a knee socket. How did they move?

He rammed into a big soldier with a puffy face. The man had his sword raised to shoulder height, a quick and easy slice if Gernan did not dodge it. He did, barely managing to hit the ground and causing the man to trip over him. These grunts were far too loyal to be conscripts. If one could not reach the neck, there were few soft spots on their person. Superior weaponry and superior armor. It was even rather light—Gernan could tell. Pier's arrows only cut through half of the time.

Gernan fought his third man for a few seconds before he managed to stab him at a break in the armor layers, right through the stomach, a move that required he step in close. He had to heft the wounded man out of the way with his shoulder before he could meet the next foe.

Marek hacked his way through with a calm docility. It was tempting to stay behind him and catch those he missed, but Gernan brought himself around on his right side, charged forward with a loud yell. He was a true cliffman—he fought like a wild cat.

All Gernan could see was the dark, patterned coats of the soldiers. There were stripes across them, three or four in a row. The weakness in the armor, right at the waist, proved itself an easier mark. Yet even Gernan hated to stab a man in the gut. It was a slow, painful way to die. He swung his heavy broadsword in wild arcs about his head, ignoring the fallout around him. Blood splattered everything, especially eyelids, until it was hard to see.

But there was a bright cluster of torches, and when the bodies parted, it was enough to catch sight of what Colstadt had seen from the beach. The boy, in the middle of it, his arm held tightly by a short, balding man. In a moment Malcom's eyes locked with Gernan's, and they relaxed. Malcom was afraid of the men who held him, but he was not afraid of Gernan.

Four men sprang in front of him, and he swung his sword once more, hitting armor and flesh and bone, not caring when he felt nicks in his own skin. Marek was next to him again, his sword slipping into weaknesses in the armor and back out again—clean, simple. Someone got a swipe in on Marek's left forearm, slashing through the leather chap. From the way he buckled, Gernan would guess he had been cut there before, but he came back up, dropping his sword and using a knife to deliver a quick cut across the soldier's neck.

The short man in the fine, simple robes was left exposed. The Emperor, was he? He stood facing Marek, puzzled, studying his face. He wore no armor and carried no weapon. Gernan didn't care, not this time. He drove his sword through the man's heart, grabbed the gaping Malcom, and tossed him over his shoulder.

"Do not wait for us," Marek yelled at him.

Gernan, for once, did not argue. He was gone into the mist.

{26}
Reɲelatioɲs

COLSTADT STOOD ON THE SIDELINES, his short swords dripping as the soldiers clustered about their dead leader, building a circle that encompassed him, the corpse, and Marek.

Gernan and Malcom were well away. There was no sound from the shadows where Pier had hidden, filling the air with endless arrows. Was he dead?

Colstadt did not have a scratch on him. He was breathing heavily, looking around him, daring one of the red-coated guards to move. Were they red? Or purple? Someone waved a huge torch in Colstadt's direction. Purple.

"Well," said a voice from behind the soldiers. "Mikel? A friend of my granddaughter's. She spoke of you."

Marek tensed visibly, and Colstadt felt his uncertainties give way to foreboding. *Granddaughter?*

A ripple went through the men assembled, one that wasn't quite fear and wasn't quite confidence. And then the owner of the voice stepped out.

A tall, slim man with a white beard.

"I knew I would see you again. I always wondered just what kind of loyalist you were. Apparently, not the kind who forgets about his lovely, lonely little monarchy hovel. Named after the prince, weren't you?"

Then Colstadt knew who this was. Of course. Otreya. The people said he could read minds and inflict curses. It sounded like a load of rotten squash to the Drei, but Marek was transfixed. He breathed in and out in silence, his bloody left arm resting against his side, his other arm clutching a knife.

"You must be happy now, mustn't you? Kovim is dead, and you believe the Empire will die with him. Ah, but it will not be. Something of this strength never dies." He tipped his white head. "You remind me slightly of the prince himself. A man I believed to have met only once, in the dungeons of Ashlin, but now I am not so sure. They never did find his body, did they?"

Colstadt's eyes flickered sharply over to Marek. *Move, won't you? Say something.* But he was beginning to dread that even he and Pier had been lied to about their purpose tonight.

Otreya laughed gently. "Do you know you are not of Orion blood at all, Mikel? You and your father and your older sister. They died for nothing, and you defended them for nothing. Serengard was always an illusion for generations. The secrets are still alive, though. In there."

He turned slowly back to the crypt, his eyes still locked with Marek's. Then he lifted his hand and the cavern behind him burst into flames.

"Fortunately for you, I have something to gain by burning them. And, in any case, you will be dead soon enough."

Finally, Marek moved. His right hand dropped the knife, darted quickly to his sheath, and drew his long sword again. Still, no one else blinked. They watched.

"Do you see this blade?" Marek said it quietly, directly to Otreya, but the silence of the others let the words hang in the air.

Otreya chuckled. "I see it. Seren steel has been illegal now for many years. Or didn't you hear? Everyone found possessing a weapon of Seren or Drei steel was put to death. Your Castle Guard will thank me someday. Such—"

"*This* blade has been close enough to take your granddaughter's life many a time. And you don't care. Perhaps it should take yours?"

Colstadt did not wait for a clearer order. The air around him erupted with purple-coated soldiers and torches that had fallen to the ground. They didn't need them. The scene was now lit by a reddish glow from the crypt door. He saw Marek pounce into the din, straight at Otreya, but the soldiers did not move to protect him. They went for Colstadt.

His legs tangled in arms and swords; he fought to maintain control of the air immediately around him and succeeded for a moment. Then he got shoved to the ground, a man poised over him with the point of a sword aimed at his throat. Feet stepped on his short swords, pinned them to the ground. He had only a long dagger left, and all he could do with it was hack at the man's legs in a wild, flailing motion.

Then the man fell, stabbed in the back by Marek, opening a space around him. Colstadt was quick on his feet, and he bounded after him. They beat a desperate path back through the mob.

Someone brought a heavy weapon down on his shoulder. He felt his entire right side go numb, feeling slippery and strange, but he kept running. Had to keep moving.

They pulled into the relative safety of the darkness and toward the cutout in the ledge. Pier was still there, his stash of arrows near exhausted. He had felled enough of their pursuers to convince the rest to turn back. They were not followed. Were the Emperor's men afraid of the dark? Or did they see no reason to pursue them now that their leader was dead? Their retreat was eerie.

Pier cursed when he saw Colstadt listing to his side. "Allel save us."

"What?" He felt woozy, enough that he did not realize he had stopped walking. Marek was pulling him. Pier examined his shoulder by touch in the dark.

"You've a nasty gash in your back. Barely missed your spine. You should be dead."

And well he knew it. Blood pumped madly from the jagged skin. Colstadt tried to reach around to feel it, knowing he could diagnose it himself. Pier slipped two fingers into the severed flesh instead.

"Went deep. I'll have to look at it when we stop."

"I cannot climb," Colstadt mumbled.

"You'll have to." Pier secured a rope of substantial thickness and length to a rock and then slung it over the side, pausing to gape at Marek. "By the Derm, you've a wound as well?"

"Nothing I haven't hurt before. Where did you get the rope?" Marek started to lower himself with his right arm, his left cradled against his chest.

"You know I have my ways of procuring things. It should be easy enough to climb down one-handed. Colstadt, between us."

Unlike Marek, Colstadt's left arm was just as strong as his right, but his balance was off and the trek down was tedious for him. His only worry was that he might pass out and have to be carried by the one-armed Marek below him. Or worse, that both of them might. He knew Pier's loyalty. He would haul Marek back on his shoulders before he dreamed of carrying Colstadt, in spite of the difference in weight.

The beach was a relief, but the cold water of the surf presented another obstacle. It was easy to drift out with a wave, but fighting to *stay* out was not. The salt water stung Colstadt's wound and he couldn't focus on the movement of his body.

"Give me your weapons and armor. It will make it easier to move."

Colstadt was surprised when Marek unquestioningly did Pier's bidding. "Take Colstadt. I can swim."

Pier frowned openly at his leader's refusal, but slipped an arm under

Colstadt's wounded side, leaving his left to swim. He dropped Colstadt on the beach, waited until Marek was there, and went in search of horses.

"Do you think we will see him back here?" Colstadt asked. He stared off in the direction Pier had gone.

"Why shouldn't we?"

"I'm sure there's far more money on the head of a royal than there is on that boy."

Marek only shrugged. "It makes no difference now to anyone but Otreya."

"I learned two things I don't need to know today. First, that you are Mikel Orion as we knew him, Captain of the Guard, that you owed your sword to Serengard, to the preservation of the treaties and the Books. And second, that even that was a farce—that you weren't of the bloodline at all. As a renegade, I shouldn't care, but Pier? As loyal as he is to the Dreibourge of old, to the treaties with the Eight Generals and to the Knights of Rilch... Intrigue such as that ought to incense him greatly."

Marek was quiet for a long minute, waiting for Colstadt to say more. But he did not want to say more. He wanted Marek to explain.

At last Marek whispered, "Pier was bound to hear of my bloodline someday, but his loyalty is certain. He hates The Council of Four enough that he would rather keep me alive than aid their regime."

Colstadt let out a tiny sigh, his chest weighing heavily on his breath. He had thought at first that this had all been Otreya's fantasy, but Marek confirmed it without a moment's repeal. "He knew you only as one of the Knights of Rilch?"

"No. Pier was my lieutenant in Ashlin."

To the Drei, a man answered to his leader, whether he agreed with him or not. It was all about loyalty. What Marek said made sense if they were in Dreibourge. But he knew that Serens were different—how different was obvious every time Gernan sought an argument with Lord Marek.

"Then he helped you lie to the rest of us, when in truth you fought because you were hunted. Not because your lands needed a savior."

Marek shifted, his gaze focused on the churning sea beyond them. "Pier could have trusted all of you with the knowledge if he wished. He didn't. There were enough betrayals in those days." He turned, and his eyes bored heavily into Colstadt's. "None of us fought because we were hunted. We'd have been fools if we had."

He was fierce, protective. Of someone besides himself. Of...

A memory flashed in Colstadt's mind. A night when Marek was injured. Before the cliffs. Before he was Marek. Tev, dragging him to safety, hovering over his body, searching for a Drei to treat the wound... "She lived, too, then. Your sister. Kierstaz."

"You would do well to forget everything you've heard this night. I'll see harm come to you if you speak that name ever again."

"Is she in such danger?"

"Far more than I. The dogs that have nipped at our heels these ten years have wanted nothing with me and everything with her. She is the heir, albeit a false one. I'm just a knight. No matter if I tried, I couldn't lead as she would."

"I never thought... She is never afraid...of anything."

"She never was. I was always the one who was afraid for her."

"What does this mean for her? Not being Orion blood? She should be free from her throne, shouldn't she?"

"The Treacher if I know. Hodran hunted her—back when the Knights held the border—but I've no knowledge of Otreya's schemes. I thought the cliffs were far enough to hide from the intrigues of the Cities. I was wrong."

And then they were silent, their words exhausted, each of them listening to the mad pumping of their own heart, trying to keep up with the blood that pulsed out between layers of skin, each in its own time.

Pier returned an hour later, four fresh horses in tow.

"Gernan?"

"No sign of him."

"We should move. Deal with these wounds later."

THE HORSE THREW HER TO the ground half way down the canyon. Trzl managed to keep from landing on her back or her face, instead skinning her hands so badly that they started to ooze. She stared at the ground for a few minutes before she stood. Her legs wobbled beneath her. It was too dark to see the stars anymore, let alone the other canyons that connected to this one. She could get lost.

Was that what the horse was trying to tell her? She wanted to stop and make a fire, but she was too close to the castle.

Then she heard what it was that startled her horse. Hoofbeats, right behind her.

She reached for the reins and tried to mount again, but horse and rider were bearing down hard. Her mount jerked away, stamping its feet in a circle.

And then the other rider reined in, angry eyes the first thing Trzl could see clearly all night. Tev's feet landed on the stone floor, took two strides straight for her, and Trzl saw the flash of steel.

"Do you know what you've done?"

Trzl gathered that she must not know, else Tev would not be dangling that short, blunt blade around in intimidating circles.

"You would try the limits of your fate by attempting to escape when it is only by his infinite mercy that Lord Marek has allowed you to be here? Or perhaps it's sense of guilt." There was personal anger in the voice. A deep attachment to Marek. "Do not take us all for desperate nomads, girl. Marek has been here many years, but as soon as you arrive, now everyone wants to challenge and disrespect him?"

Trzl wondered if Tev was going to use that blade or if this was all some sort of show. To scare her? That was what Marek had tried to do. It hadn't worked. But this—this *was* scaring her.

"You are fortunate that you were not run through at first convenience. These mountain folk can be very clear-sighted when it comes down to their lives or yours. That your fate was a mere beating should make you grateful to Pier. *Grateful.* And Lord Marek? He keeps you only because he feels he has a debt to repay you. Only Allel and I know why. You assume he has protected you on some virtue of your own, but the debt is not yours. He owes it to his love, who is dead, and his son, who is dead as well."

Marek had a son? All of this made Trzl feel suddenly very foolish for thinking that she knew Marek at all. Even that she had known Mikel well.

"I could hate you for manipulating him so, for convincing him to offer you safety. But I feel only pity for you. His friendship is a matter of honor, not something you have earned. And if you have not earned it, it will never be anything but an obligation, a thorn in his side. I only pray he is not killed for it."

Trzl tried to look up into Tev's eyes but found that she could not. There was one thing, at least, that Trzl knew about Marek—something she believed no one living knew better. Something she could use. "You know that when Marek holds something as a matter of honor, there is no forcing or coercing him into or out of it. It was he who would not let Malcom and I leave. He could have traded us himself."

Tev at last let vehemence creep in. "You owe him now. You owe him your son's life and your own. If you have any sense, which I doubt, you will stay where he put you and trust him to return your boy. My hope is that he will consider enough done and send you away where you belong."

"You don't understand. You don't have a child, do you? I will try to escape again and again and again. Because he is my son and I must have him back."

Tev caught her by the collar of her dress and tossed her at her horse.

"That animal knows its way back. Don't tempt me to add to your stripes once we get there."

{27}
Lies

THE CHAMBERLAIN OF THE SECOND City entered the council chambers with as much pomp as he could muster at this time of night. The empty sky was dark to his eyes. He was accustomed to fire and light and dance. Parties with color and style. Endless wine and plenty of young faces.

All this he was being taken from by some strange nefarious scheme of Kovim's. The more he thought about it, the worse it sounded. A feeling of foreboding encroached slowly on his temples, made his ride here unpleasant and deserving of some heavy liquor to calm him.

But the Emperor's chamber held no one but Otreya—an Otreya who looked slightly more ruffled than usual. Hodran did not fail to notice the wrap of silk about his bloody hand.

"You've opened it without me, I see." He would not have been so bold without his thirty best soldiers behind him in the great hall.

"Ah, yes, Hodran. How good to have you here."

"Don't use false pleasantries with me." Hodran strode in, seated himself in the high-backed chair with gold filigree. It felt nice, sitting in the chair of the Emperor.

"Nothing false about it," Otreya said. "Some strange men from the hill country disrupted our peace here in the First City this night. From what we could determine, there were only a few. And one of them carried a sword of Seren steel."

"I beg your pardon?"

"They passed through your jurisdiction, and it is known you owned an armory full of Seren steel at one time. Perhaps you've saved some for yourself? Equipped some men of your own to meddle in the affairs of the Council? Some of my men think they were trained in the Seren arts of the sword. Much like yourself."

Hodran squirmed slightly in his chair. "I cannot be responsible for everyone who passes through my territory."

Otreya came forward. His beard nearly brushed against Hodran's nose. "No? That amazes me because I've seen this type of cooperation between you and your sort before. Old Corsai families, calling themselves by fresh names, thinking they have a place in our Cities... When, in truth, it is nothing more than the putrid stench of Orion trying to slip through our fingers with the aid of their nymph-like dark arts."

Hodran's face blanched a fair white. His stomach sank into his feet. "What are you saying?"

Otreya's soft tenor became a loud roar, red hot with a fury he must have saved for this day. "ORION! *Orion* was *here*! You let him live, Hodran. You who were supposed to kill him ages ago, who proclaimed him dead and his body scattered and crushed in a million pieces in the streets of Ashlin. Do you think I have any patience left for you?"

Hodran laughed, though the precariousness of his situation was beginning to dawn upon him. "And so it is my fault he is alive? That we received false information from a turncoat? It was more important for us to focus on finding the princess. Hearing not a word of either of them, what else could I assume but that they were dead? Even if he was hiding in Dreibourge—"

"Yes, yes! There were Drei with him. And it does not stop there. They killed Kovim, and they took your son."

Hodran's mouth dropped. "Malcom?"

"Did you hear me? Kovim is *dead.*"

"May our Emperor rest peacefully," Hodran choked out.

He understood the play now. Otreya was not a vindictive man. He was a thinker, a precise mover and a passionate believer. But to say that Hodran had hired the Knights of Rilch to retrieve Malcom and thus procure the upper hand, to preempt the opening of the crypt by Otreya and Kovim?

"I will leave first thing in the morning to catch these men."

"Good. Good." Otreya calmed instantly, sinking into a seat himself and stroking his beard. "I cannot understand how this could have happened. How could any of the Knights of Rilch still exist? Let alone slink into our city. We killed nearly all of them. Or so you have informed me."

"We killed hundreds of them, and those we did not, Dreibourge slaughtered when they tried to storm the border." Hodran waited a moment before turning the conversation back around. "You opened the crypt last night. I understand why Malcom must be here, but why would you do all of this without inviting *me?*"

Otreya waved a hand as if to say it was a minor detail. "Yes, yes, the key to the crypt was turned last night. I left it open with a heavy guard until morning. The contents are safe—no need to fear."

"But..." Hodran found himself confused and off-guard. Especially with Kovim's calm, scholarly brain missing from the mix. "Why open it, if not to threaten me?"

"It is a small matter, especially now that our brother is dead."

That was an obvious deflection. "If it is a small matter, why would you drag Malcom into it?"

"Kovim's idea. You know how much he feared you."

Still, it did not sound right. "How many were they? How could they get close enough to—"

"We are not sure of the actual number of them. Seven, maybe eight, my men are telling me."

"Have all of the men been questioned?"

"They have."

"We should take them to the securest section of the prisons. They must speak to no one. The less the population knows about Orion or Rilch or any of this, the better."

"Already done." Otreya offered a shallow grin. "I am still trying to decide if the former Prince of Serengard was attempting to destroy or retrieve something in the crypt or if he was after Kovim alone."

"But surely if they meant to destroy Kovim, they would find more people to help them. Desert People must be hopping mad at us by this point." Hodran cursed Kovim for dying so easily. Kovim, who was the one moving part in the whole Empire. Perhaps now Otreya would be ready to appoint two new Council members, and stop hoping for their fourth member to rejoin them. And who would be Emperor? Neither Hodran nor Otreya envied the position.

Or did they?

Hodran stood and walked across the room, finding a window to gaze from. The First City lay stretched below them, perfect and unspoiled. Thousands of people content in their dwellings. A calm and a control they all fought hard for, that Hodran paid for with his own money. Now, even greater power than what he desired was staring him in the face. Not divided power, but *real* power.

"You believe that Mikel Orion knew about the crypt and its contents and wished to steal the documents of his family lineage? Prove his right to rule?" It sounded doubtful to Hodran, but he needed to hear Otreya confess his own hunches.

"Who knows?" was the non-committal reply.

"You said they took Malcom. To what purpose?" He dared Otreya to lie to him. After what he had heard from the Drei at his palace yesterday, these explanations were sounding far too contrived. "What was Malcom even doing here? I've not seen the boy or his mother for years. Did someone think they could blackmail me with my only documented son? I know Kovim is not above it, but what could he possibly—"

"It is simpler than that, I dare say. Far simpler."

"What? Kovim needed his blood to open the crypt—because he wanted to do something I wouldn't approve of or because he wanted to cut me off altogether? But now that he is dead and we are staring at each other face to face, you deny all, claiming a mummer's show of some strange Drei arriving, led by Mikel Orion who is supposed to be dead. Why would you admit to Malcom being here? It makes you guilty for sure."

"Because I am telling the truth, Hodran." Otreya blinked at him calmly. "The answer to this riddle is beneath your very nose. How did *you* know to come here?"

"I...heard of Malcom myself. Through another channel." That, too, was beginning to disquiet him. Anyone could have hired some Drei to frighten him. Anyone.

"Do you wish to speak to the soldiers who were with us at the crypt? I've not killed them yet. Better, see the crypt for yourself, lying open on its hinges. You know that only Malcom's blood could have done this."

Yes, he knew because they tried many a time to break the lock, to fool the science of the tumblers, the same as they had the gates of the Cities, always failing. The Desert Man hired to design them was worth his weight in precious stones, for certain. So much that the Council had hunted him down and killed him to keep his gift from being turned against them.

"So they took Malcom with them."

"Yes."

"You are sure this is not the work of the Desert People? Seems likely they would be angry."

"Think closer to home."

This annoyed him, Otreya playing this game, always seeking to confuse, to muddy the water. At last, Hodran blurted out what he knew the man wanted to hear.

"Trzl."

"Ah. It has her fingerprints all over it."

Hodran gave a hearty laugh. "She might wish to destroy me, but why you? Besides, you said nothing was taken from the crypt. If the warriors were sent by her, they came for the boy."

"I was disappointed not to have seen her at all in this mess." Otreya looked away, his eyebrows drawing together. "I was counting on her being dragged in with Malcom. You see, I put out a bounty on Malcom's head. I am getting old, and I was desperate to see my offspring reunited with their country as it should be. I miss her. Her passion. What a lovely girl."

Hodran thought that a little sentimental for Otreya. "A horrid girl."

"You liked her well enough in your bed," Otreya snapped.

"You don't know her like I know her. She was leary of Kovim, yes. She may have wanted him dead and grown tired of hiding, but do you think she would hire someone to do her deeds? No. She would worm her way into *his* bed and stab him with her own hand."

"I would have believed in a motive this pure—excepting that I saw Orion with my own two eyes. I saw him take Malcom and vanish again. Now, how else could she have the former prince in her pocket if she had not known where he was throughout the war?"

Hodran shrugged. "She has a way of getting what she wants."

"At my age, it is sometimes hard to remember. Many times I have these gaps in thought, moments of blankness. But when I looked at that man, without his armor and helmet and banner of turquoise, I remembered that I saw him once in my own front parlor. That Trzl called him by name, Mikel, and that she was some attached to him for weeks."

So she was as power-hungry as her kin. But what was Otreya saying? Years ago, could she have been making a play on Prince Orion? Had they been friends? Lovers? She was not above it, for sure.

Otreya had him breathless, leaning forward, hanging on his every word. "Surely no playing card could be as valuable..."

"As what?"

"Hodran, are you sure Malcom is your son?"

"He must... He must be! Else how could his blood have...?"

Otreya let his breath out slowly. "Oh. Yes, well, my mistake. Like I said, my mind... Oh, I have not known relief like this in a long time. At least there was no child made between them. Not yet." He turned his eyes back to Hodran with a question, a challenge.

He stood immediately, his cheeks growing hot at the idea of Trzl entertaining even the slightest friendship with his enemy while making love to him. It didn't matter that it was years ago. He did not like to see himself as gullible.

Otreya spoke again. "Unless...it is all some scheme of yours. Bring back the reign of the Orion monarchy, and with it the families of the Corsai. You wouldn't do that to any of us, would you, Hodran?"

Hodran walked stiffly to the door, having had quite enough of Otreya tonight. "I will bring back his head for you, and then you can give me the title of Emperor yourself. Hold onto our dirt for a while. Keep it warm."

MALCOM HADN'T BEEN ABLE TO control the strange tingling, the flashes of cold that ran through him. He wondered if he was sick—if the powder that had been sprinkled on his skin would make lesions and give him a fever.

He didn't much mind that Gernan took the long way around everything. It was nice to be with someone familiar, although Gernan was, at first, sour with him. Then he started to talk, on and on, like the sound of the stream when it was swollen in spring.

They needed to stop at a village to reclaim a horse from some girl. Gernan told Malcom to stay put whilst he knocked on the door of the stable. It was answered by a short girl with freckles and a large nose.

"You want your horse back?" She looked up at Gernan with a mournful stare. "She is a beauty. I have taken the best of care of her in your absence. And she likes me." She added the last part with a quick, winning smile.

Malcom liked her instantly. She reminded him of the girls in his village. A village he suddenly missed greatly.

"You are nice, but my lady is nicer. And truth, I want her back." Gernan pulled out another handful of coins and placed them in her hands. "I wish you would take the horses you see behind me as well."

The girl nodded, counting the pieces. "Yes. Of course." She opened the barn door and led him in. "Ande," she called into the third stall.

Gernan looked shocked. "No one calls my pretty by a name," he mumbled to Malcom. "It is unnatural for such a beauty to be called a name as if she were a man. And look—she is too thin."

Malcom didn't think she looked thin. "That's a healthy horse."

"You did not feed her well," Gernan accused the girl.

She secreted the money in her dress. "I fed her as much hay as the other horses. And there was grass, every day."

"You did not feed her grain? A scoopful three times a day. And some molasses."

The girl shook her head. "We cannot afford grain. You can afford grain?" She reached at his clothing absentmindedly and kept up her running commentary. "You look like a raider. Do you steal your grain? Did you steal this money?"

Gernan almost laughed at her. "You needn't be ridiculous. I trade for that, fair as any man. And you can keep it. I'll take my horse now, and the saddle that was on her."

Oh, he expected the saddle to still be here? Malcom let his eyes go wide. Saddles were stolen all the time in the hill country. They were more valuable than the horses they rode upon. But the girl heaved Gernan's out from under a pile of other saddles as easily as a man would.

"Here."

"I am obliged. I know you do not usually keep horses that are not for sale." He smiled at her then, and she gave him a sweet, giddy grin in return.

"Happy to have done it for you." She paused, acting as if she would say more. "Don't you think it odd that a horse you care for has no name?"

"No."

The girl shrugged. "I've work to do." And she left.

Gernan watched her. He said to Malcom, "She is a strange girl, don't you think?"

Malcom just shrugged. No, he did not think she was strange.

"Well, I won't complain. After all, she kept my pretty alive and out of the hands of soldiers or other tools of the Emperor. That matters more'n anything to me."

Malcom stared as Gernan led his horse out into the night. Her proportions were perfect, her coat shining.

"You have a good horse," he said simply but with such awe that Gernan pushed out his chest.

"She is. Finest horse you'll ever lay eyes on."

"Are we going to ride her back to the cliffs? To my mem?"

"We are."

{28}
Recompense

COLSTADT'S WOUND BLED AT SUCH a rate that he could count the drips that escaped the linen bandage and reached the ground. No matter how fast they rode, there would be a scent for the dogs to pick up.

Pier was able to slow the flow of blood from Marek's arm with a simple tourniquet, but Colstadt's wound was another matter. It would not be slowed. Fabric kept it contained for the most part, but it did not stifle it. Not while he was moving and jostling atop a horse.

"We need to ride slower," Pier complained, "or that cut will leak too much and he will lose all of his blood."

Marek replied through his teeth. "We need to ride faster, or we will all be dead men anyway."

Colstadt hadn't much to say on the matter. He kept quiet. It hurt like the Derm, but he would rather have this than death, especially as the sun rose, making it necessary to stay in the trees as much as possible. It was to their advantage that most of the farmers had abandoned their fields years ago. The grass was tall and wild, sometimes even high enough to ride through without being visible.

"Horses," Colstadt said once, quietly, and both men stood-stock still, waiting to identify the sound.

Pier walked toward it, disappearing into the grass. When he returned he said only, "Hodran."

Marek started in his saddle. "Him? Or some of his men?"

"Special Guard from the Second City, near as I could tell. He'll have them spreading out, covering the territory."

"Curse it all."

Colstadt started to lose his concentration, slumped over on his horse, dealing quietly with the pounding headache from loss of blood. He overheard snippets of conversation. Most of it did not make sense.

"We cannot keep up this speed. Not if you intend to get Colstadt back alive."

"I've seen worse, haven't you?"

"I am telling you, if you want to—"

"We've escaped the depths of the Derm many a time before with far worse odds."

"Marek, we should swing south where they will not expect us."

"And let them tighten a noose around us? They'll not stop searching, Pier."

"Likely as not, it will be only a token search toward avenging the Emperor. There are three of us. They will assume there are more. Besides, Gernan will have already split their forces..."

"No. No, likely as anything, they are closing the gap ahead of us as we speak, planning to catch us between the rivers. We can cut north, above Ashlin. I know that country. We can make the meadow lands and lie low."

Colstadt came to suddenly, enough to say, "You haven't the materials to sew this up anyway, have you, Pier?"

"I could find what I need in this place."

"You couldn't," Colstadt insisted stubbornly. He knew about sewing wounds.

"I've known my medicine twice as long as you."

"Pier," Marek interrupted. "Pier!"

"What?"

"Otreya was there. He recognized me. Did you not hear…?"

Pier stared, his jaw hanging like a dog that had consumed too much of his master's mead. "Damn."

"Yes."

"What are you going to do?"

"I can't risk leading him back to the cliffs."

"You don't know they would find us." The gulp in Pier's voice didn't sound good.

"We're near Ashlin," Marek said. "I can meet him on my own ground. You should take Colstadt and get to the hill country. Have his shoulder seen to. Once they have me, they'll not follow you. I'll make sure of that."

"I am staying with you," Pier said.

Marek shook his head. "You are not."

Colstadt knew what Marek wasn't saying. Pier's wife, with child, and his two small children—something Marek did not have.

"I've waited long for a chance to kill Hodran. You know that as well as anyone." Marek methodically tightened the tourniquet on his arm.

Colstadt pulled himself up in his saddle, looked at him through fuzzy vision. "I will stay. Pier has a family. I have no one."

Marek actually grinned. "You think dying with me will earn you my sister? But then you would be dead."

Colstadt squirmed. "I am not that selfish."

"In your condition, you would likely die before you killed a single soldier," said Pier. "Leave Marek to fight alone."

"But…"

Marek sunk his heels into his horse. "He'll pass out soon enough, Pier. Then you can take him where you like."

ASHLIN WAS AS BLACK AS the day it burned.

The Third City was constructed a year later, five miles south of the ruin. No one presided over it at present, and no one needed to. It was the smallest City of all of them, the least involved in trade, and the last place Hodran would visit if he were to choose. But there was no way to avoid it today.

It had been a long time since he'd been out riding beyond his own lands and still longer since he chased any fugitive himself. Goblins, he was feeling old, even if he really wasn't. He'd become rather lazy. As expert a swordsman as he used to be, he had stopped training these past few years. He looked down at his waist, at the little roll of fat.

Yes. A few too many pastries.

To be completely honest with himself, he was frightened down to the tips of his boots. He did not want to scrap with Orion, however small his company may be. The Prince kept Drei with him and somehow managed to kill Kovim. No matter how many soldiers Hodran brought along, they could not comfort him.

He pulled off his thick, leather glove and looked at his hand. The fingers were shaking. Damn that Trzl. She got him into this, vile little snipe that she was.

He chuckled to himself about Kovim's death. All things considered, Hodran was glad the Emperor got his comeuppance before his regime had managed to humiliate or exile the Chamberlain of the Second City, second member of the Council of Four. Now, at least, Otreya had to have it on his old man conscience. That brought another nervous chuckle. Maybe Mikel Orion would finish him off first and Otreya would be spared the pleasure.

"Chamberlain!" one of his captains yelled, waving his hand from the edge of the ruins of the old city. Puzzled, Hodran urged his horse forward and joined his men at what used to be the main gate.

"What have you found?"

One of them looked as if he just saw a ghost. "We were on the trail of our quarry, four horses, three men."

"Well?"

"They turned into the old city. It is haunted, they say…"

"Nonsense." What kind of stories had Kovim been telling these days? Clever man. "How many men have you?"

"Thirty."

"Gather them. Thirty will do." But his palms were sweating. He waited until his men were assembled. "Ten of you, fan out and cover the tops of the walls. Some of these men are Drei, skilled with a bow. They may have lookouts posted."

Hodran could sense the tension of his men as they crept through the gate. The wide walk was familiar, but the houses that surrounded it were nothing but foundations of rubble and moss. The gate of the Castle of Orion was shattered, making a walk into the inner courtyard an easy thing, but Hodran was surprised by how much of the castle was still standing. He would like to walk through it, see if there was anything of value that the looters had not taken. After all, he knew the truth of what had happened inside those walls better than anyone.

"It would seem they rode straight through," his captain told him.

"How many?"

"Can't tell how many, sir. Wind sweeps the cobblestones too clean for a trail."

Still, a wave of relief hit him. If there were only four of them in this detachment, they surely would not split up again. He had no wish to search the entire city of Ashlin, let alone engage an enemy here.

He continued to eye the castle, a fresh lust returning to him. Suppose he did succeed in vanquishing Mikel Orion. No one could know, of course, because they had all assumed him dead long ago, over the drawbridge, in that very courtyard. But if he could do this, who was to say he could not conquer any other who stood in his way?

"Wait. There's someone coming."

The sound of one horse on the broken cobbles. One could always mean more. "Spread out."

The rider entered the square and followed the edge of the rubble. He kept out of sight until he reached the bridge; then he stepped out and picked his way into the middle. He sat a horse the way a man of the Castle Guard would. The horse stopped at a quiet word from its rider.

"He's wounded," one of his men whispered. "We can take him easily."

Hodran raised a hand. "Wait. Not this one." He didn't want to lose his whole force. There must be a way to play this.

The man dismounted. His horse trailed behind him, breathing gently. He walked straight for Hodran with a stride that was purposeful, but Hodran saw how drawn his face was. That arm had bled considerably. Good.

Hodran nudged his horse into a walk and moved to meet him, his head tipped to the side, trying hard to see the eyes, the jawline, the Orion build. He had the height—that was certain.

"Hodran," Mikel said clearly. It was his voice. Clean Ashlin accent.

Hodran swung down from his horse and pushed her away, squinting at the former prince in the sunlight. "You. You are dead."

"I was, Lord Chamberlain. I often wish I'd chosen to stay dead."

"That arm is bleeding."

"I've been wounded before."

"I can see that." Hodran shifted his weight. He heard his men behind him, shuffling. He brought his hand around to the hilt of his sword. "What an unsightly beard. Have you been starving in the catacombs of Ashlin all these years until you were ready for a backhanded attack on your Emperor?"

"I never cared that much what Kovim did."

Hodran's eyes narrowed. He was certain that was a lie. Castle Guard always cared very much.

"The rest of you can go to the Derm. I came after the boy. Your boy, Hodran."

Hodran pulled his soft, velvet cloak out of the way so that his sword came out cleanly. "Doesn't seem you'll have much to say about us going to the Derm. Where did the rest of your men go?"

"You mean the two bodies I tossed into the river just now?"

Hodran did not see him draw his sword, but he must have for it was in his hand. "Who did you steal that from?"

"Who did the Knights of Rilch steal from?"

So he had been one of the Knights. That brought the anger up fresh. Was there ever a time Mikel Orion was not right under his nose, destroying his life? A fitting fate that at last they faced each other in the city of duels. A man he should have killed long ago—before he reached adulthood. Before he had gained the skill to survive in a world that hated him. Before he learned how to cheat death.

Hodran trembled as he asked, "Are you going to defend yourself, mercenary?"

Mikel laughed. A deep, bitter laugh. His eyes turned soft for one moment as he stared up at the crumbling edifice of the Castle of Orion. "I hope to."

Hodran cursed to himself. He slashed first, a blunt, wild blow. Mikel stepped out of his way, waited for him to turn. Hodran felt the humiliation of being spared a blow creep up to his temples immediately. He would not be played with.

He tried to calm himself, to breathe. He was better than this. He knew how to fight this man and win. He had watched him countless times, had even practiced for just such an occasion. He began to move his sword in slow, lilting motions, a style the Corsai took the trouble to learn because it looked beautiful, but also because it tended to baffle more practical folk.

Hodran wasn't sure it would baffle Mikel, but he knew the youth had a temper back in the Ashlin days. "I do not claim Malcom as my child. Sure, I was with his mother for a time. But how am I to know she was not with many men? How do I know she was not with you?"

That brought an instant reaction, but not the one he expected. Mikel carried one of Hodran's blows with his own, turned it back on him. It forced his shoulder to twist. Good goblins, how strong *was* he? Up this close, he could see bulging muscle beneath the tourniquet on his arm, thicker than it had ever been in Ashlin. Hodran trembled, shook it off.

"I should have killed the boy long ago. I would rather be the sole possessor of my blood."

"I plan to sample it today," Mikel said.

"Oh, no. You'll have none of it. I'm a part of something too valuable. You, on the other hand, will find no one in sympathy with you in the whole of Serengard. They've had enough of you and your whole rotten lot." Hodran parried a high slash that would have severed something near his neck. "One of the reasons I never desired a duel with you, Orion. I did not want to make you into a god for the people to worship. Too much to gain from your villainy."

"A lie. You were afraid of me." Mikel grinned. "I have been waiting for an excuse for fourteen years."

Hodran brought him toward a wall with a series of fast, darting blows that Mikel parried with a little too much ease. But then Hodran had him against the wall. His wounded arm hung limp. He was truly thrown off-balance.

"Trzl stole from me, the little devil, but it was a pittance to what I got out of her. You would use her as an excuse to persecute me when you yourself were with her?"

Mikel's brow grew dark. He took the offensive from Hodran, beat him out into the courtyard until he stood again before his own men. Hodran panted as he fought to keep up with the perfectly timed slashes of the Seren sword.

"I didn't treat her the way you did," Mikel hissed through tight lips. "I know what kind of bastard you are. How you followed Kierstaz, waited until she was alone in the dark, forced your body against her like some—"

"You know, I could never resist your sister. She was more of a bewitchment than any I've laid eyes on since. A pity she had to die."

Mikel showed a bit of his own temper. He brought the tip of his sword around with a yell and slashed open Hodran's left thigh. Hodran recoiled, pulling himself away, trying to cradle his leg. It hurt damnably. He lurched around and faced his own men.

"A hand?" he finally asked, having enjoyed his picturesque duel enough already.

Two of them came forward, but Mikel slashed out, left them each cradling an arm. Hodran seized the moment to come at Mikel from behind. He managed to draw blood from his right shoulder, but his target moved again before he was close enough. Why did no more of his men come forward? Were they transfixed by their friends bleeding in the street?

Cravens.

Hodran at last employed a style that he always laughed at other men for using. The driving offensive—trying to beat back his opponent until he ran out of maneuvers. It made Mikel laugh, and the laugh caused Hodran to burst toward him with fresh rage, swinging in a quick shot to the stomach that Mikel deflected.

Then, wonders, Mikel began to back up, to defend himself. Bland, slow. He was tired.

"You know that if I don't kill you now, you will still be running for the rest of your life. That girl is the real albatross of men such as you and I." Hodran was puffing now. Showing his age.

But Orion grew pale as well. "In my younger days, I would have felt guilt for killing a man whose skill was not equal to mine. I would have injured him and let him live."

Hodran narrowed his eyes. "You think you—"

"Goodbye, Hodran."

Mikel let him get in a few more blows and then changed his attack, brought his sword around in quick, decisive movements. Hodran stepped back many times—too many times—moving about in a full circle. He watched the moment arrive, made a last effort to feint a stomach jab and slash at Mikel's right arm... Unsuccessfully.

And then he was stabbed quickly through the throat. His vision went black. He clutched his front, his coat. Hit the ground on his back. Tried to talk. Wondered why his men did not stop the bastard.

He heard Mikel's steps on the broken cobblestones. His voice asked, "Any last words?"

Hodran shook his head, spit some blood out of his mouth. "Not for you," he rasped out.

He wanted to know that his men were going to kill Orion, but he didn't know it. He was going to die, right now, without the knowledge that his enemy died with him. As his mind turned purple and black and distinct orange, the last sound to hit his ears was a defiant yell.

The voice of Petrolai's second child.

"Do you know who I am? I am one of the Knights of Rilch. I have been on the Emperor's charcoal scroll for a long time. Who wishes to go first?"

{29}
Redemption

TEV LOOKED TWICE WHEN GERNAN entered with the boy. She was sitting cradle-wise across the wooden throne, her feet dangling over the arm. Gernan hid a smirk.

"Where is Marek?" she snapped at him and jumped up. Her slim little legs had to skip a step to walk as fast as a man.

"Don't know." He flung Malcom at her good-naturedly. "I brought the boy. Lord Marek told me not to wait for him. Not certain who is dead. Thought I saw Colstadt go down."

Tev just stared at him. He stared back. The light fell through the window at just the right angle for him to see into her eyes. They were grayish in color, almost the same gray as the stones of this hall. She was already dressed in battle garb, a small helmet on her shorn head and her sheaths tied on.

"Feed the boy, will you?" Gernan wiped some cold, frozen sweat from the back of his neck and flung himself on the nearest bench. "We've been riding heavy since the First City. Had to stay off the roads and go out of our way to keep my horse watered. Both are tired."

Malcom's cheeks were flushed. His eyes darted about happily. "I'm not tired. But I am hungry."

Tev called for someone to take the boy. "His mother is in Lord Marek's chamber. He can see her but do not let her out."

The brightly dressed cliffwoman took him with her, and Tev and Gernan were alone. He could see that she was a hair's breadth away from interrogating him at the end of her sword. The thought made him giddy.

"You left Marek there to die?"

"I did as I was ordered."

"Your brand of loyalty is precious and touching."

Gernan grinned at her. "As soon as you see to my horse and heat me a hot bath, I'll be happy to set out in search of him and my fellow warriors who stayed behind to protect their lord."

She was disgusted. She glared from where she stood, a few steps above him. Still not all that fearsome. "I will set out myself. No time to wait for you."

Gernan followed her into Marek's map room, down a little hall, up some steps to her chamber door. She swung around to face him.

"Get away from me. I am going myself since everyone around me is as helpless as a stuffed gremlin with his eyes poked out."

"Who will see to the castle?" He knew he was almost leering, but he could hardly help it. She'd not been separated from Marek in years. The whole situation was making her stormy and bothered.

"The castle can see to itself for a few days," she said.

"What of those who conspire to replace Marek? Skommek, for instance. Or me."

That stopped her. She glared at him, as if to say, *You wouldn't dare.*

He fidgeted. "After all, Skommek will hear the stories that Marek is possibly dead."

"Only if you tell them, you bastard."

"You can be crosswise with me about it, if you wish, but I'm thinking it'd do to wait for the better part of an hour whilst I rinse off this filth and accompany you."

Tev frowned at him. "Rinse it off and stay here like a spoiled fine lady, or come with me now. Your whole grimy self."

His grimy self spoke again. "May I make a suggestion?"

"What."

"Seems more than likely that we will end up outnumbered and in need a few negotiating tools…if not human shields. I would bring the boy along. His mother as well."

"A fine suggestion. It worked so well when Skommek tried it."

"You risk Marek's life on a matter of pride? I was right even then, too. You knew it. I saw it in your face." He leaned slowly toward her, and she took a step back. "The woman is a curse."

"Pack some food and bring them."

"Bring them myself?" He didn't really want to. She-devil that she may be, tying her up and dragging her out did not sound pleasant. And he certainly did not want to see what the boy would do.

"Lie to them, Gernan."

Of course he could do that. He sprinted down the steps, through the rooms and passageways to Trzl's locked door. The cliffman who guarded it was sound asleep. Malcom hadn't been brought here yet.

Gernan reached down and took the key from him, unlocked the door. Trzl was crumpled in the corner, her face resting on a hand. She must have been asleep because she started when he entered, glanced about guiltily. She looked haggard. Terrible.

"Is Malcom—"

"I brought him."

"Is he…alive?"

"Not a scratch on him, woman." *Except for a cut across his palm*, he thought.

Then the worst thing happened. She wrapped her arms around his neck, pulled herself close to him, her face nestling in his hard leather armor.

"Thank you," she mumbled. "I owe you my life."

Gernan just stood there, waiting for her to disentangle herself, but she didn't. He gripped her arms and tried to pull her off, but she drew them in close to her sides, pushed her face harder against him. Finally he had to lift her head away by her hair.

He felt a wave of guilt. Did she know he'd been the one to sell her son in the first place? He had a strange wish to tell her. "We need you and Malcom to come with us to find the others."

"What?"

"Marek and the rest didn't make it back...yet. Tev wants to meet them, and you, uh, know the Cities better than we."

"Why didn't Marek return? Did someone recognize him? Is he—" She slammed her own hand over her mouth. "I mean—I didn't mean—"

That puzzled him. Was Marek recognizable? "I don't believe Tev will find him unless it's at the end of a gallows, but we need your help, just the same."

"Malcom. Where is he?"

"Should be—" Perfect. Here came Malcom now. "Did you feed him?" Gernan asked the woman who escorted him.

"I did."

"Good. We must leave. Now."

NIGHT WAS NEAR WHEN THEY finally made the canyon. Colstadt could feel the familiar smoothness beneath his mount. He wondered how many hours had passed. He didn't remember a single one of them. Only this long, drawn-out throbbing.

Then the nicker of horses meeting theirs, of voices he knew. Tev.

"Pier? Where is Marek?"

"Dead," Pier said.

"No. He can't be."

"If he lives, it is at the mercy of Hodran."

"I'll steal him back."

"You shouldn't. He stayed to preserve you."

Tev was quiet. Colstadt could see her, just barely. She nodded her head at him. "Need that seen to?"

Colstadt rolled his head in reply. His face reflected his fever. Sweat ran along the edges of his chin, down his neck, and into his shirt.

"Gernan, you will take Colstadt back. You need to rest anyway."

Gernan said flatly. "I will not."

Tev drew her bow and nocked an arrow in one quick motion, pointed it at the drowsy Gernan. "Move. Now. Pier, you are with me."

Pier never argued with Tev the way he argued with Marek. He respected her more, and now Colstadt knew the reason. Pier leaned in close to her. Colstadt could hear him talking about Trzl and Malcom. "…Gernan's idea, no doubt."

"I'll thank you not to question my judgment, Pier. I saw no reason to question yours, leaving him to die alone. Now take me to him. Fast."

Then Gernan yanked on Colstadt's horse, and they headed into the canyon.

TRZL BREATHED EASIER WHEN GERNAN caught up to them again. She saw Tev toss him an angry glare, so Trzl gave him a smile. Marek kept his word—Malcom was alive and safely back to her. He rode behind her, hugging her waist. Every time he moved up and down, it hurt her skin inside the heavy woolen layers she wore, but she didn't mind.

Malcom was not scared a whit this night. She could hear him speaking to her, though the wind was often too loud for her to hear full sentences. He had found another man to worship besides Marek—it was Gernan this and Gernan that and some horse he kept calling Sweet Zel.

She wondered, as she stared at Gernan, if he would stick up for her. Tev and Pier scared her terribly—but then, so had Gernan when they first met. She wanted to trust him. Yet Marek himself had not trusted his own men with her secrets. There was a dark, rumbling feeling in the pit of her stomach that was not hunger. It was the slowly encroaching knowledge that chances of survival were not getting better for her and Malcom. They were getting worse.

If Marek were alive, he would find a way to let them live, gate sequences and bounties notwithstanding. If he was not alive…

A moon rose, a big, impressive moon with a glow around the edges. It looked teal to Trzl—the color of Ashlin's banners from before the war.

Tev led them on, a breakneck speed that allowed for no words, speed that no one ever attempted over this terrain. Trzl was scared one of the horses would trip and fall. Toss Malcom to the ground and roll over him. No one had asked her yet for any directions. No one asked her anything at all. Would they even notice if she turned around, disappeared into the meadow lands?

Malcom's head nodded against her back, and she was glad he slept. She wished she could. Wished she could find a safe place somewhere in Serengard, barricade herself in a little hut and never leave again.

The night was near over when Tev held up an arm to slow them. "We are near Ashlin. Ride quietly."

Pier rode up beside Tev. "You know that he is surely dead by now. He was determined to die. There is no way he escaped. Not from that many men."

Tev did not respond.

"He wanted them to think there was no one else so they would not come to the cliffs."

"You'll say nothing more to me except to tell me where to find him," Tev shot back.

More silence. Pier brought his horse to the front of the party, led the way through some trees to a hill that overlooked the ruined city. A mile beyond it, the lights of the lookouts of the Third City winked at them. Trzl suppressed a shudder.

They saw the torches, gathered in a circle in the ruins of Ashlin. Was that the Castle of Orion? The towers of Tame and Miraz? She had assumed it was all razed long ago.

"That's him," Pier told Tev quietly.

From here, there was nothing to see but the smudge of light. What they were doing could only be guessed.

"Seen enough?"

Tev's shoulders squared. "I want his body."

Pier nodded. He put a finger to his lips and led them down a slope, across a drawbridge. Was he mad? They all were mad. They stopped outside a crumpled gate, heaped with rubble, just as the gray of dawn started to come.

"Gernan, you stay here with the boy and the woman." Tev drew a sword and held it in front of him for a second—more of a warning than a threat. "Come a few minutes behind. We may need you."

Gernan rolled his eyes. "I will."

Tev and Pier hissed to their horses. They took off into the ruined city with as much speed as they employed in the open grassland, navigated the streets and corners in the dark. The echo of their hooves grew louder and louder, multiplied, until they sounded like many horses. Then they stopped, and the air filled with shouts and whinnies instead.

Malcom stirred. She realized he had been awake, just long enough to hear. He said, "Marek is not dead, is he?"

Trzl shook her head. "I don't know."

"I hope not. He is my favorite."

Trzl felt the hard heaviness pushing at her throat, then a terrible panic. Something cold and slippery and tangible. She had thought him dead before when he had still been a person, flesh and blood. He had not yet grown to be the epitome of strength in her mind. That came later. Now, he was dying again, but this time what he meant in her world was dying also.

"Mine too." she whispered. She wanted to talk louder. To drown out the sound of swords against each other, of horses' screams and the thumps made when their riders hit the ground. And yet she did not want to drown it out. She wanted Marek. She wanted him to be alive.

"I could fight too, Mem. I know how. Marek said I would make a fine warrior. He was going to train me. Even Gernan said I could defend myself well."

"He did?"

"I did," Gernan added, but he sounded absent.

"Malcom, what is this?" She finally noticed that he wore a sword strapped to his back. He'd been carrying it since they left.

"Gernan gave it to me. I told you."

"Oh." She looked at it. It was heavy. "You are a strong boy."

"I am not a boy. Stop calling me that. I'm braver than a boy."

She swallowed hard. "Yes, you are braver than a boy."

Then silence again.

"Mem, we should—"

Trzl urged her horse forward, as desperate as Malcom. They broke into the courtyard, a huge cavern. The torches were already out, the area growing dark. Tev had just killed someone, and Pier was finishing off a wounded man. Gernan ran toward another, an immobile body that sprang up and dealt a blow to his hand. Trzl's instinct was to take Malcom away from this madness. Instead, she swung off her horse into the mess. She tried not to look at the dead bodies, to ignore the stench and smell of death.

There was a finely dressed corpse half-loaded onto a cart. The soldiers who must have carried it lay dead beside it, blood still gushing. She would've tripped over them and moved on if she hadn't recognized his hair.

Even with blood dried across his face, Hodran was impossible for her to mistake. Well, she had probably been closer to his body than any man. Trzl looked at him for a second, just long enough to be sure he was dead. Then she swooped down to where Tev was. Her knees skidded on the cobblestones.

"Mikel," she gasped out, catching at his bloody arm—his bloody everything. Tev held his other side in the same grasp. Trzl cupped his jaw between her flat palms, tried to make him look at her. "Is he alive?"

The eyes rolled. Just enough.

Tev swallowed, eyes smarting with wetness. "Help me with him."

Trzl picked up his legs. Her eyes met Tev's above his body, and the look between them was the same. Protective, scared, sick with fright for him. They got him onto Tev's horse. Tev mounted behind his limp, heavy body and urged the horse to a gallop.

{30}
Sacrifice

WHERE THEY WERE GOING, GERNAN was not sure. They were following Tev. They headed away from the sun, through a wood, amid trees old enough that the brush had not grown in a long time. The ground beneath them was covered with leaves and moss and peat. No travelers lately. Not in years.

Still, Gernan thought it dangerous. The canyons and cliffs were their only safety. Always had been. Tev's horse was exausted already, and she was tiring all of them further.

"Tev," he called out once. She did not respond. He called again. "Tev!"

She pulled her horse up in the shelter of a knoll. "Help me."

Gernan pulled Marek's body from the horse's back, laid it on the ground. He was breathing. The man was *breathing*.

"By the Derm," Gernan swore like a city Seren. "He cannot be killed, can he."

"Do you think I would be heading west if he were dead?"

Pier checked for a pulse. He peeled off some of the shredded fabric from his torso and began the tedious business of examining each cut. "His side. Check the saddlebags, get something to staunch this wound—anything."

"Here," Trzl called.

Tev took the strawflower oil as quickly as Trzl could grasp it and hold it up. The girl knew a little about medicine? Obviously more than Gernan did.

Malcom stared at Marek, his brow furrowed deeply. Gernan walked to the boy. He put a hand on his shoulder and turned so that he stood between him and the sight. "Men fight sometimes. He'll be fine." It was inadequate and probably a lie, but he felt better after saying it.

Trzl caught Malcom in her arms and cradled him against her, looking at Gernan with a blank expression. Malcom struggled to get his face out of her dress. Gernan stood awkwardly beside her, sensing at last that she actually thought she had some stake in whether Marek lived or died. Funny, how women could be.

Tev and Pier worked over his body, tearing off the light linen—what was left of it—dousing the skin with liquor and oils. Gernan watched until Tev spoke his name.

"A fire, Gernan. Build a fire."

He felt stupid for not thinking of it, but these kinds of wounds were not common among his people. They didn't fight like this. He threw together a hurried pile of wood.

Trzl snapped out of herself for a moment and helped him, sweeping leaves into a pile for him to light. Once the blaze was going, she knelt behind Pier, as close to Marek as she could get. Her teeth bit down on her lip.

Gernan knew that look, and he knew what it meant. He nodded toward the boy. "Help me with this fire, Malcom."

Tev sprang to her feet, pulled out every weapon on her person, and shoved them at Gernan. "Heat these. As hot as you can get them."

Trzl's eyes remained riveted, even as they pressed the hot metal into Marek's flesh to burn the wounds clean. She stared straight at his body as she said, "Did you see? He killed Hodran. Killed him cleanly, with one cut. And they did that to him in return. Why would they do that?"

Gernan just shook his head, not sure if she was speaking to him or if she wanted a reply. He pulled away once the fire had done its job, stationed himself at the edge of their hollow, one arm stroking his horse and the other cradling his own wounded hand. What did he expect—Tev to come and coo at it when she was done with her little lord?

He almost thought of putting his spare arm around Trzl's shoulders, as she seemed to relish closeness. Then he talked himself out of it.

It was a while—maybe an hour, maybe more—before Pier finally bound Marek up with bandages. Bandages that would have to be changed in a few hours. Wounds that would have to be washed again.

Marek groaned once, his eyes rolling open. Not conscious eyes.

Tev quickly closed them. "Rest."

Then he sat up. Pier tried to slam him back down, swearing under his breath. "The Derm if he isn't delirious."

Marek thrashed wildly; then his hand clamped on a wrist. Trzl's wrist. "Did you get your boy?"

"Yes," Trzl said.

And then she saw that he couldn't see her, that he was staring into the sky at nothing. She started to sob violently. Pier pushed her away, and she ran back to the tree where Gernan stood.

"Will he live?" Trzl asked.

Tev answered, tense but confident. "I have seen him take this before. This and worse. Most of the damage is to his limbs. I do not think this side wound stabbed anything too deep in his gut. If I can keep it from turning bad..."

"Someone may still be following us," Gernan interrupted. "We must lose the trail. Get back to the cliffs."

"I know how to lose a trail," Tev said. "And I am taking him west. Not to the cliffs. You—the rest of you—may all go. I can care for him now."

Gernan crossed his arms and looked at her in disbelief. "You can't lift him onto that horse without help. Your skinny little arms."

"I can do it. Once he can sit up."

Gernan still did not like this. "You're heading west. What is west?"

"Dreibourge," Pier said quietly, longingly. "Tev, there is nothing for us there."

"At least there are no emperors, and no wizards." She spat the last words at Trzl. "No, Pier, now that they know his body was stolen, they will search for him and not stop. The rumors will be rekindled, and the bounties will resume. There is nothing for me to do but move far faster than they anticipate."

"I will come with you," Pier said.

Tev looked up, listened to the wind. She turned to Pier. "Don't be foolish. Your wife will drop her child within a fortnight."

She finally glanced at Gernan's hand. It was a nasty gash. She tore off one strip of fabric and grasped some leftover pasty substance she'd worked up.

Gernan looked at her with the face of a hopeful puppy, but she threw it at his chest and said, "Put it on."

TRZL STUMBLED BACK A FEW steps when Tev walked up to her, staring her straight in the face, yet still speaking to Pier.

"Marek wanted these two kept alive, but they have done their damage. You'll not want them in the cliffs. Leave them to fend for themselves in the meadow lands. If they end up in the hands of Otreya, it is not our concern. He's her kin." Tev's eyes bored into Trzl's. "You had an enemy, and Marek killed him for you. He owes you nothing now."

Trzl felt a horrible ripple run through her. Mikel hadn't owed her anything to begin with.

"Understand the strain it takes for me to not run you through, to not blame you for what was done to him this night." Tev finished her piece in a soft hiss. "I don't want to see your face ever again."

Gernan scrunched up his nose. "I'm not leaving you to haul that hunk of timber on and off of a horse. Besides, your horse will need to be paced, carrying a double load. Marek is heavy."

"And I am light. Also quite obviously the only one he can trust. I am taking these medicines, Pier." Tev stuffed them back into the saddlebags, tossing them over a horse.

"At least take the extra horse," Pier insisted.

Tev reached for the reins of the horse Trzl rode. There was no more said as to where Trzl and Malcom were going. With Pier and Gernan, to be sold to the highest bidder? Or were they to be left in this glade without horses?

Trzl bit down hard on her own lip. She wished she could break it open. Break herself open. Bleed as Mikel bled—for her, for Malcom.

"Take Malcom with you."

Three sets of eyes stared at her as if she had called on a cold dragon. Malcom fidgeted beneath her hand, and pain seeped into her chest at the thought of being parted from him.

"He has done nothing but follow orders. I am your trouble. I am the one who caused all of this. Malcom is small and light and easy to disguise. And he is good with a sword—Marek said so himself. He will be useful to you."

Tev was not speaking. "You know what you ask, woman?" Pier said.

"I know. I want you to take my child."

"You may never see him again."

"I know this."

"If he dies, you will not hear of it, and if you die, he will never know either."

Trzl didn't need to be told. She already felt dead and broken at her own plea. Malcom did not move a muscle. She ran her fingers through his hair even as she whispered, "You can protect him better where you are going. If you'll give me your word."

Tev's eyes narrowed. "I didn't think you had it in you, selfish rebel."

"I don't want my grandfather to have him. Please, you must understand, Otreya would not hurt him. He would...harm his mind. Destroy him that way."

"And you trust me?"

"I trust Marek."

Tev looked at Malcom. "Help me lift Marek onto this horse."

Malcom thrust his chest out and grunted a few times. His face turned red with the effort but he managed.

Tev didn't frown, at least. "If I do bring him back, it will be at the first winter melee of the year. Not this year. Maybe the next, maybe four years from now. See that you're there."

"I thank you," Trzl said.

"Do not thank me. He will earn his keep. And when we have no food, neither will he."

Malcom looked at Trzl now, not crying, not speaking. It was almost as if he didn't know what was happening. She hoped he didn't. She held her arms out to him, and he hugged her quickly, but she saw puzzlement in his eyes.

"Mem?"

"Go with them," she whispered. "I'll come back for you."

Tev took Malcom's arm and swung him onto the spare horse. His dark hair fell into his eyes from where Trzl had rumpled it. Their horses turned, and she saw only his back, shoulders square. She felt the urge to call him back, to tell him not to go, but stifled it.

She jumped when Gernan put a hand on her arm.

"Mustn't watch them leave."

He was right. She let him turn her away, give her a hand up, settle her on his horse. A chill breeze picked up as they turned east. Already Tev had made the first rise and was about to disappear.

Trzl swung back around, her arm breaking free of Gernan's waist for one last glimpse of Malcom.

He was gone.

The wind pulled at her hair, taking her fear with it. The sun rose where it always did, spilling bronze out over the cliffs. She knew he would not come back to her as a child. If Malcom returned, he would be as indomitable and raw as those faces of rock.

Acknowledgments

To everyone who bought the first rough little version of this story, thank you. I learned so much from the impressions you shared, and I treasured every bit of criticism and praise alike. Even before I knew where I was going with Serengard, you were willing to take my words at face value. I hope you enjoy what it has become (and I hope you shred the original!).

My sweet and brilliant editor, Becca Weston. This manuscript needed brutal work and you delivered above and beyond. I owe you so much more than words, but words are what I have. Thank you, forever and ever!

My friend, critique partner, and line editor, Darci Cole. So many times I wanted to throw this novel out the window. You saved it, and you saved my sanity. I love you!

The first readers of this manuscript, Amanda Aszman, M. Andrew Patterson, Michelle Roberts, H.E. Griffin and Steve Knapp. You all are amazing. Getting through the mud of early drafts would've been impossible without you. Muah!

E.M. Castellan. For loving my stories, for all the friendship and support.

My street team! Joshua David Bellin, Lauren Garafalo, Lucy Hershbine, Serena Lawless, Kathi L. Schwengel, and Mara Valderran. I wish there was a real way to write a hug because that's what this would be. The fact that you love me and my writing enough to want to shout about it has me humbled, awed, inspired, jump-up-and-down crazy.

Beau Barnett and Jenny Moyer, I couldn't have asked for better proofreaders. You totally saved my butt. THANK YOU!!!

Nazarea Andrews, for helping me with my blog tour; and Amanda Olivieri, for the blurb crit. You're both awesome.

Bill Murphy. For bugging me until I read *Timeline*. It changed my life.

Fellow writers who shared their inspiration, experience, triumphs and tears, Christopher Prickitt, Steve Chiasson, Uwe Kruger, Jens Kruger, Andrea Hannah, Leigh Ann Kopans, and Dahlia Adler. xoxoxoxo

Shauna, Gracie, Nicole, Crystal, Katie, Elisabeth, and Erin. You were always willing to listen to another revision idea, to forgo hangout time and movie nights because I had to make a deadline. I promise to make it up to you somehow.

My family, who never stopped asking about what I was writing, and was willing to hear the unsolicited update every 2.5 days. You guys rock.

My little men. This novel is more yours than anyone's. Every time you napped longer than usual so I could pound out a few more words, you made it possible. Every time you snuggled up to me and gave me a kiss, you made it worth it.

My husband. All of the sweat and tears that I pour into this is upheld by your endless patience and your willing shoulder. You give more than I would ever expect. You make my life beautiful, and without that I would be nowhere. You are my hero.

Lastly, to anyone who ever tweeted, pinned, shared, posted, or talked about my books, you made this a reality for me. Thank you, thank you, thank you.

About the Author

Obsessed with all things history, Rachel O'Laughlin grew up writing adventure stories and only recently fell in love with fantasy as a genre. She lives in New England with her husband and children, grows roses and tweets often. She adores lattes, The Fray, long drives in the country, and any dark story with a good twist. *Coldness of Marek* is her first novel.

Pronunciation Guide

Altrun (al-**tru**n)

Ashlin (**aj**-lin)

Berekst (ba-**rek**-st)

Calum (**cal**-um)

Colstadt (k**ohl**-stat)

Corsai (core-**sye**)

Derev (d**air**-ev)

Derm, the (d**ur**m)

Dermed (d**ur**-med)

Drei (dr**ay**)

Dreibourge (d**rye**-borg)

Elna (ell-**nah**)

Gernan (gur-**non**)

Hodran (**hoe**-drin)

Izannah (iz-**ahn**-na)

Karamov (kar-a-mov)

Klevt (kl**ev**-t)

Kovim (koe-**veem**)

Kymsai (kim-**sye**)

Lomius (**lo**-mee-uss)

Marek (m**air**-ik)

Mikel (mi-k**ell**)

Neroi (ni-**roy**)

Nersai (ner-**sye**)

Orion (oh-**rye**-an)

Otreya (**oh**-tree-yah)

Petrolai (**pet**-ro-lye)

Pier (pee-**air**)

Rilch (r**ill**k)

Seren (s**air**-in)

Serengard (s**air**-in-gard)

Sherp, port of (sh**urp**)

Sunn (**su**n)

Tame (t**ay**-may)

Treacher, the (**tre**-cher)

Trzl (t**urr**-zull)

An Excerpt from the Sequel to *Coldness of Marek,*

Knights of Rilch

Coming February 2014

Ashlin announced itself with billows of smoke and swarms of people, most of them leaving the city, a few of them massing and drinking and sharpening weapons. A militia that had been but a few fools in the shadows this summer had turned itself into multitude—a violent one.

She sunk her heels into the flanks of her third stolen horse and rode up and around the city to the east. She knew every trail and hollow and murky pool up here. She could hear the shouts and hoof-beats of men near the Gate of the Guard. This was the only way out of the castle, and it was blocked. Beyond the gate was a black funnel of smoke as wide as three wind storms. One could scarce turn west to look at it without the air stinging the lungs.

Kierstaz dismounted, leaned against a large tree, hidden in shadow, and let her breath out slowly.

Pem would be glad, she thought. He had ordered her out of the city. Taken her down below, into the crypts beneath the castle, told her the last few details of all those tales he had held back from her. She had seen the dread in his eyes that night. Seen the fear for her, for her mother and little brother— the same fear she felt now. They had lived and ate and drank and slept within these walls only days ago. Now, depending on the mood of the mob, they would be tortured, beheaded, or burned alive.

Perhaps the people of Ashlin would turn human and hang them.

Kierstaz closed her mouth tightly and ground her teeth with frustration. She knew where Pem was—or had been a few hours ago. Out in front of the Castle, sword held in front of him, fearless. Mikel would be somewhere nearby, quiet and martyr-like. He had never wanted anything to do with Serengard or the name of Orion. He wanted to be a farmer, left to his own devices.

She had told Pem to let her stay, that she was the better fighter, but he had gotten all stubborn and told her Serengard did not need Mikel the way they needed her. That it was their only course and Mikel had made his peace—and she knew Pem meant to die here. It made her angry. She had wanted to die beside him. Die fighting.

She heard a yell go up from the city. The people on the hillside began to cluster as a flag was raised on a staff high above them. Twelve hands by twenty, dyed with the teal poppy of Serengard, it used to wave above the tallest tower of the castle, the Tower of Miraz.

The fabric was already afire. It crumpled and fell amid euphoric cheers.